GRAVE CONCERNS, TRICKSTER TURNS

American Indian Literature and Critical Studies Series
Gerald Vizenor, General Editor

Grave Concerns, Trickster Turns

THE NOVELS OF LOUIS OWENS

CHRIS LALONDE

UNIVERSITY OF OKLAHOMA PRESS : NORMAN

✓

Grave Concerns, Trickster Turns: The Novels of Louis Owens is Volume 43 in the American Indian Literature and Critical Studies Series.

Library of Congress Cataloging-in-Publication Data

LaLonde, Christopher A.
   Grave concerns, trickster turns : the novels of Louis Owens / Chris LaLonde
      p. cm. — (American Indian literature and critical studies series ; v. 43)
   Includes bibliographical references and index.
   ISBN 0-8061-3408-9 (alk. paper)
      1. Owens, Louis—Criticism and interpretation. 2. Tricksters in literature. 3. Indians in literature I. Title. II. Series.

PS3565.W567 Z76 2002
813'.54—dc21

2001052224

The paper in this book meets the guidelines for permanence and durability of the Committee on Production Guidelines for Book Longevity of the Council on Library Resources, Inc. ∞

1 2 3 4 5 6 7 8 9 10

For this generation and for those that follow;
And for Stephen Alexander, with love

CONTENTS

ILLUSTRATIONS

Acknowledgments

This book is the product of much kindness and generosity from first to last, and it is with pleasure and humility that I give my deepest thanks to the individuals and institutions that have given me so much while I have been reading, talking, thinking, and writing about the work of Louis Owens. First and always, my family, especially my parents and my brother Steve, have given me safe haven to work, but more than that they have given me their love.

Anne Wilgus, Edna Farmer, and Diane Taylor of the Elizabeth Pearsall Library at North Carolina Wesleyan College satisfied all my interlibrary loan requests with speed and good cheer. The college gave its support in the form of funds enabling me to present early versions of portions of the manuscript at various national and international conferences. It also granted me a leave of absence in order that I might accept an appointment as Fulbright lecturer at the University of Turku and Åbo Akademi University in Turku, Finland. I was able to complete a draft of much of the manuscript during my year in Finland; my thanks to the Fulbright Commissions both in the United States and in Helsinki. I also want to thank my chairs in Finland, Professor Risto Hiltunen and Professor Håkan Ringbom, for supporting my work on Owens while I was a guest of their departments. In addition to their willingness to have me teach Native American literatures, Professors Hiltunen and Ringbom and the members of both departments showed a genuine interest in my research and writing. That interest, coupled with and supported by kindnesses too numerous to mention here, made my year in Finland rewarding and enriching to the extreme. The Scholarly and Creative Activity Committee of the State University of New York, College at Oswego, provided money to help defray the costs incurred in taking the photographs that serve as illustrations for the book. Thanks too to my brother Steve, who lent eye, ear, and creative talents to the effort to get the best possible images for the book. I would be remiss if I did not also thank Wendi Ackerman and Jeff and Deb Schwiebert for their help. I want to thank my colleagues in the English Department at Oswego, particularly Maureen Curtin, Bennet Schaber, and Robert Moore, for creating and fostering an environment conducive to scholarship in general and my work in particular.

The staffs of the libraries in Park Rapids and Detroit Lakes, Minnesota, particularly Mary Haney and Dotz Johnson at Detroit Lakes, were extremely helpful as I worked with the copyedited manuscript. I take pleasure thanking both Charles Martin and Gerald McMaster for granting me permission to use their works to help illustrate the book. Kimberly Wiar, Karen Wieder, Marian Stewart, and Daniel Simon at the University of Oklahoma Press deserve much praise; they tolerated any number of questions and concerns, and their answers and support made my work easier. Thanks, too, to Jonathan Lawrence for his fine work copyediting the manuscript. I want to thank Susan Bernardin, Linda Lizut Helstern, and Barry O'Connell for their sensitive and insightful readings of my work. I have benefited from their questions and comments and am certain that the completed manuscript is stronger for their words. Still, all faults herein are mine and mine alone. I owe much to Terry Smith, Mac Davis, and Stephen Lacey, each of whom has modeled a caring for and commitment to students and to scholarship that I have tried to emulate. Given Stephen Lacey's presence in my life, it is fitting that the letter that helped start me down the path to the completion of this book, from Hertha Dawn Wong accepting my paper on trickster and *Wolfsong* for her MLA panel, arrived while

I was sitting in his office. I owe no little debt to my students, too, for their interest, questions, and comments have kept me thinking and helped me in my struggles for comprehension and clarity; in particular, I want to thank the students I have had the pleasure and good fortune to teach and learn from at the Associated Colleges of the Midwest wilderness field station in northern Minnesota.

I have tried to listen, hear, and keep in mind a number of voices as I have thought and talked and written about Native American literatures in general and the works of Louis Owens in particular. The intelligent, caring, and careful voices of Arnold Krupat, James Ruppert, and John Purdy as they approach Native literatures have served me in good stead as models for my own writings on Native texts. Having Kimberly Blaeser's kind and smart voice, always encouraging and sensible, has aided me greatly as I labored to position Owens's voice and texts within the various contexts, cultural and theoretical, from which they spring. Gerald Vizenor's wise and playful voice, always decentering and enabling, has been extremely helpful as I have tried to articulate the importance of Trickster and trickster discourse to and in Owens's novels. Finally, Louis Owens's rich and nuanced voice, the voice that draws us to his fiction and criticism, has helped me keep in mind what is at issue, what is at stake, and what is important for us all as readers of and writers on Native American literatures.

An earlier version of portions of chapter 1 appeared as "Trickster, Trickster Discourse, and Identity in Louis Owens' *Wolfsong*" in *Studies in American Indian Literature* 7.1 (1995): 27–42.

An earlier version of portions of chapter 2 appeared as "Discerning Connections: Revising the Master Narrative and Interrogating Identity in Louis Owens' *The Sharpest Sight*" in *American Indian Quarterly* 22.3 (1998): 305–25.

I am grateful to the editors for their support of my work and for their permission to reprint this material.

All photos herein were taken by the author unless otherwise noted.

GRAVE CONCERNS, TRICKSTER TURNS

SEEING (FROM) THE TREELINE

Alison began walking, with the others following in a single
line. Behind the surviving twin, Sam Baca said, "Does some-
body want to explain what the hell's gone on here?"
"Well," Shorty Luke glanced over his shoulder at Sam. "It
is said . . ." He looked back toward the treeline above them
and was silent for a moment as he kept walking.
"It is said that Jacob Nashoba went home."

OWENS, *Dark River* 286

To begin our examination of identity, place, culture, and critique in the novels of mixedblood Choctaw-Cherokee-Irish-Cajun writer Louis Owens, we will do well to hear what Shorty Luke says at the close of *Dark River* (1999). By saying and repeating "It is said," a phrase akin to the conventional Western Apache story opening *natk'ide la djindi*, or "long ago they say" (Goodwin 2), Shorty signals to his fellow Black Mountain band member Sam Baca that his explanation will take the form of a story. We recognize the formulaic opening as well, remembering that not much earlier in the narrative, Shorty tells the mixedblood Choctaw Jake Nashoba that "It's best to begin a story with something like 'they say' or 'it is said'" (256). Shorty wants to explain with a story, moreover, because he knows that to do so is to honor it, on the one hand, and to position story, audience, and teller within a traditional oral context, on the other (207). Stories are to be honored because it is through them that identity and community are articulated, in the dual sense of giving voice to and joining together, and the proper relationship to others and the earth is maintained. For the Western Apache, such a relationship is marked by reciprocity (especially toward one's matrilineal kin and related clan), sharing, and working together (Basso, "Western Apache Witchcraft" 17–25 passim).

The traditional opening for the stories told by the White Mountain group of the Western Apache that Shorty Luke invokes emphasizes both orality and the storyteller's relationship to the story that he or she is about to tell. That is, "Long ago they say" situates the storyteller in relation to time, to ancestors, and to an earlier storytelling event. To be in a position to begin the story, the teller must first have been in the position of audience or addressee. As such, the White Mountain opening resonates nicely with what in *Just Gaming* Jean-François Lyotard recognizes as the decidedly non-Western perspective articulated with the conventional opening to the stories of the Cashinahua of the upper Amazon, which stresses the pole of reference and the pole of addressee, not the pole of the author. In Lyotard's words, the Cashinahuan narrator "situates himself in the two forgotten poles—actively forgotten, repressed— of Western thought and of the tradition of autonomy" (33). Thus a narrative opening that highlights the poles of reference and addressee is a telling indicator of more than orality and an oral tradition; it also signifies that the individual is subordinated to the story, the storytelling event, and the group.

Lyotard's understanding echoes and reinforces Owens's own sense of the traditional relationship between teller and story for Native Americans. In *Other Destinies: Understanding the American Indian Novel* (1992), for instance, Owens stresses that "the concept of a single author for any given text, or of an individual who might conceive of herself or himself as the creative center and originating source of a story, or of the individual autobiography, would have made as little sense to pre-Columbian Native Americans as the notion of selling real estate" (9). When Shorty Luke silences any note of the pole of the author and autonomy with "It is said," then, he is doing more than tacitly acknowledging that he is finishing the story that Jake had begun at Shorty's request after meeting his friend outside the underground home of Black Spider Old Woman, the powerful figure who aids Western Apache culture hero Slayer of Monsters when he is on his way to his father's home prior to killing all the bad monsters in order that the world might be safe for the People (*Dark River* 255–56). Shorty is situating himself, the story, and the audience in an oral tradition that, in honoring story and emphasizing the storytelling event, runs counter to both Western thought in general and the dominant discourse of Euroamericans and America in particular.

It is fitting that Shorty should have the last word in *Dark River*, fitting that he should speak from and to Western Apache tradition and culture, and especially fitting that his last word is "home." That word carries with it still more emphasis on stories for the Western Apache, stories as they are intricately intertwined with place. Jake's Black Mountain wife, Tali, tells him of the connections when she says, "There are stories, Jacob, stories about every place and everything you see" (50). Keith Basso notes that place-names enable the Western Apache to anchor themselves in space and time and "evoke prior texts, such as historical tales and sagas" ("Speaking with Names" 242) which help them know themselves and their place in the world. This is why Sam Baca phrases his question as he does at the conclusion of *Dark River*; it is imperative that he know what has "gone on *here*" both at the bottom of the canyon one hundred yards from where Elk Creek empties into the Dark River and in the hole, created when a downed tree's root wad comes out of the ground, where Jake's body comes to rest across the river from the camp. The story must be connected to place if Sam is to continue to know his home and his world.

Like the Black Mountain people with whom he has lived for twenty years, albeit for the most part as a stranger, Jake desires to know the place and to find a home. Displaced from his homeland first by the move west from Mississippi to California when he was five, and then, most significantly, by the trauma brought on by serving in Vietnam as a member of the Special Forces, Jake can shake neither the things he did and saw in the war nor the vision of the Choctaw elder Luther Cole that has invaded his dreams. Suffering from the ghost sickness connected with the former as the novel opens, Jake is unable to heed the latter and make his way home. The eddies, pools, riffles, water fast and slow, and banks of the Dark River deep inside the canyon it cuts through eastern Arizona have offered him some relief from the violence threatening to explode from inside him, but that river is not his river—the Yazoo in northern Mississippi. Mrs. Edwards, the Black Mountain matriarch respected and perhaps feared for her power, reinforces the connection between stories and home when she asks first, "Don't those Choctaw people you come from have stories?" and then, when Jake says they have plenty, "Then why have you never gone home?" (*Dark River* 42).[1] In answering evasively, saying that he is not an Indian and that "home is where the heart is," Jake replicates the tortured and tortuous route away from home that has brought him, finally, to this state. Denying his identity and capitulating to the emptiness of cliché, Jake can only live "with a vague yearning to go home" (50) that he is unable to satisfy.

Jake Nashoba is not the only Owens character to be haunted by place and home; nor is *Dark River* the only Owens novel to concern itself with the necessity of searching for and finding or making one's home. Home is central to Owens's fiction and to his autobiographical pieces. It is what Tom Joseph returns to and attempts to come to terms with in *Wolfsong* (1991); it is the last word in *The Sharpest Sight* (1992) as Hoey McCurtain and his teenage son Cole drive east from California to Mississippi to the waiting Luther Cole and Onatima; it is what an older Cole McCurtain needs to see and understand twenty years later in *Bone Game* (1994); and it is what Will Striker recovers, finally, at the end of *Nightland* (1996). As such, Owens's fictions share with other Native texts an emphasis on

what William Bevis terms "homing in": the efforts on the part of the
protagonists of a number of Native American novels to—contra
the efforts of the protagonists of many canonical American literary
texts—return or stay home. Home "is a primary knowledge and a
primary good" (Bevis 582) because it helps the individual connect
to community, tradition, and the past. Moreover, homing in can
help an individual recognize the relationship between the past (be
it individual or tribal), the present, and the future.

In a word, then, home is fundamental to identity. Owens is acutely
aware that Native identity has been made problematic by "centuries
of colonial and postcolonial displacement, often brutally enforced
peripherality, cultural denigration—including especially a harsh
privileging of English over tribal languages—and systematic oppression" (*Other Destines* 4). Nevertheless, he recognizes that despite the
difficulties and obstacles faced by Native writers, "the recovering
or rearticulation of an identity, a process dependent upon a redis-
covered sense of place as well as community . . . is at the center of
American Indian fiction" (5). We shall see that Owens joins his fellow
Native writers in working from and to that center. In the process he
explores the complex web of relationships fundamental to individual and cultural identity in twentieth-century America.

For Owens, place, home, and stories are vitally connected. Stories
help produce the sense of place that enables one to articulate and
realize one's home. Both are fundamental to identity. He makes
this clear in the first of four autobiographical pieces in *Mixedblood
Messages: Literature, Film, Family, Place* (1998), entitled "Blood Trails:
Missing Grandmothers and Making Worlds." In that essay Owens
continues his exploration of the problematics of the term *mixedblood*, of Native identity more generally, and of what it means to
be an "Indian writer" while focusing on his and his family's efforts
to make sense of place and absence. Owens recognizes that what
he knows of Oklahoma has "come to me almost entirely through
stories: my mother's, uncle's, aunt's, and grandmother's stories of
growing up in what they insisted on calling the 'Nation'" (150). He
also recognizes that the knowledge born of this "generational

storytelling is yet another sort of removal" (150) experienced by
most Native Americans. However, that sort of removal carries with
it the place from which the People have been displaced, the time
from which the People have been dislodged. In a word, as is true
of all stories, what is absent is brought into presence.

Native people are not the only ones with stories, of course. Nor
are they the only people for whom stories establish and reaffirm
identity. This point and its ramifications are made clear in *Wolfsong*
when Tom Joseph surveys the crowd gathered for the town meeting
to discuss the planned mine to be built in the heart of what is for
his people sacred land:

> He looked over the crowd. He knew stories about most of
> them, and they all knew more stories than he did. They met
> in the Red Dog or in homes during the long winters and slan-
> dered one another in rich detail, following ritualized patterns
> almost the way the Stehemish had once come together in the
> winters to tell the stories that told them who they were and
> where they came from, stories of Raven, Coyote, and Fox. For
> several generations now these intruders had gathered under
> the unvarying shadow of winter rain and snow to remind each
> other of their existences, and their signposts were the same
> mountains, rivers, and forests the Stehemish and Stillagua-
> mish and Skagit had known. The map was the same but the
> signs pointed in different directions, toward different destinies.
> (121–22)

Owens has stressed the relationship between maps, stories, and
erasure, noting that "mapping is, of course, an intensely political
enterprise, an essential step toward appropriation and possession.
Maps write the conquerors' stories over the stories of the con-
quered" (*Mixedblood Messages* 211). Tellingly, the stories told by the
Euroamericans are slanderous, and just as they wrong their subject,
so too do the maps drawn by the dominant culture wrong place.
Thus, while Jake Nashoba suffers from an inability to locate home
on any of the maps he has purchased in his effort to learn the

reservation, the Black Mountain land, and the Dark River, the map before Tom Joseph, his brother Jimmy, and what remains of their people locates home, ironically, as a place from which to leave in pursuit of different destinies. Those different destinies, created and perpetuated at least in part in stories, are seductive, as we shall see, but Owens's narratives make clear that they come at too dear a cost. For the destiny the dominant culture would have its subjects follow and achieve is threatening to Natives and non-Natives alike. The dream of home it offers threatens present and future generations, as well as the world, as *Wolfsong* makes clear with the whipsaw on the wall above the fireplace of the Brant home "menacing the girl in the [graduation] picture" (70) on the mantle. The home may appear comfortable, but the industry that built the house cuts down more than trees. While Tom and Karen had dreamed of a log house in a meadow on the edge of the old-growth forests where they would live and be self-sufficient (72), the narrative counters that dream both with Jake Tobin's nightmare of the log house he built coming apart after he is no longer able to work as a faller (218) and with the Josephs' home literally falling apart over the course of the novel. It is small wonder, then, that if Owens's fictions are informed by a desire for home and concerned with and about the relationship between stories, place, home, and identity, it is equally true that they are haunted by and concerned with the stories told by the dominant Euroamerican culture and its subjects.

In short, Owens's fictions are concerned with and concerned over the narrative of the nation, the home that is created in and with that narrative, and the figure of the Indian it employs as Other. Along with mixedblood writer and scholar Gerald Vizenor and other Native and non-Native artists and scholars, Owens understands that the Indian is vitally important to the construction of Euroamerican identity and America. The Indian is an *invention*, in Roy Wagner's use of that term to define an act of capture and mis-identification by anthropologists and others, a cliché, an "absolute fake" and "a bankable simulation," in Vizenor's words. Thus, Jake Nashoba thinks, "Maybe anthropologists were the real Indians, anyway. If the whole idea of Indian was just an invention, then it made sense that an actor hired to play Indians, even if he was a fullblood like Shorty, would have a lot in common with an anthropologist who studied what his own kind had invented" (*Dark River* 92).

Vizenor turns to the work of Jean Baudrillard on representation in the postmodern West to help illuminate the transformation of the Native American into the Indian in the service of the nation and its dominant ideology, capitalism:

> The interimage *indian* "masks the absence" of the real, the unnameable native, and in many narratives and motion pictures the *indian* "bears no relation to any reality." The *indian* named in treaties was a perversion of native transmotion; the federal agents were an "evil appearance." Commonly, notice of the *indian* is "pure simulation," the shelf life of a commodity. (*Fugitive Poses* 148)

The Indian, a simulation that masks the absence of the Native, denies the active presence, native motion, and sovereignty articulated with and in Native stories. Given this, it makes perfect sense that Owens would play on and play with representation, simulation, and what constitutes the real. In *Dark River*, Jessie dresses up in a wolf suit to simulate the spirit helper that comes during vision quests. The white anthropologist Avrum Goldberg dresses in traditional Western Apache attire and even pretends to be a Black Mountain band member to a *National Geographic* film crew. Rich middle-aged white men pay Steve Stroud thousands of dollars to play war games. Goldberg and Shorty Luke promote the idea of turning Black Mountain into a "theme tribe" in order to draw tourists and grant money. The word "real" is used again and again. The stress on real, for instance, comes up in a discussion between Jake and his comrades from Vietnam that brings together the nation, identity, and Native sovereignty. Jake asks the former South Vietnamese commando Phuong Nguyen what he is doing caught up in a "wacked-out American militia movement," and Steve Stroud, who was their commanding officer in Vietnam, replies, "Nguyen's an

American now, Jake. This isn't games in the woods. This is real. You know me and you know Nguyen. We don't play games" (*Dark River* 156). When Jake responds with "You're trespassing" and "This is sovereign tribal land" (156), Owens's narrative reveals that what constitutes or passes for the real is a trespass of Native places, and therefore, at least in this case, of Native identity. Stroud is more correct than he knows and says more than he means when he says and repeats that he is not playing a game, for such a declaration of the real, which is nothing less than a declaration of being, has the gravest of consequences for the People. In stressing that Stroud thinks he is not just gaming, then, the passage tells us that the gaming which produces what he holds to be the real is unjust.

In transforming the Native into the commodity Indian, the dominant culture "masks the absence" of the real, the presence of which would, for Derrida in *Specters of Marx*, signal the anxiety of and over displacement that lies at the heart of the modern nation (83). For if a native, indigenous population can be displaced, then so too can the displacers. Against this threat and the anxiety it produces, the dominant culture fashions its narrative and discourse. Much contemporary cultural criticism and literary theory stresses the importance of both well-established and new medias and mediums of communication to the transmission of the narrative. What Derrida calls the "techno-mediatic power" that both "conditions and endangers any democracy" necessitates that in order to understand and combat the hold the dominant ideology has on discourse and subjects, we must take "into account the new speed of *apparition* . . . of the simulacrum, the synthetic or prosthetic image, and the virtual event, cyberspace and surveillance, the control, appropriations, and speculations that today deploy unheard-of powers" (53, 54).

It is small wonder, then, that as we shall see, photographs, television, and movies play critical roles in Owens's fictions. In *Dark River*, for instance, Lee Jensen, the hyperviolent and maniacal man who was too young to have served in Vietnam and craves what he imagines to be the experience of war and death, turns to movies like *Chato's Land* and *Apocalypse Now* to explain himself and make

sense of what is happening. Shorty Luke was an extra in Hollywood in the heyday of the Western, and he is quick to tell stories
that make fun of the sham those films perpetuated. He tells Jake of
the time in Monument Valley when he and the other Native extras
"laughed ourselves about sick when the Mexican actor said 'Yatahey'
to the white guy who was supposed to be Comanche" (*Dark River*
255–56). Such an act of hailing only works if you are not interested
in communication. The Diné's greeting to address someone who
is (supposed to be) Comanche is indicative of the dominant culture's desire to objectify the Native as Indian and make certain he
or she cannot speak. The Black Mountain band member Jessie
doubly turns the stereotypic simulations against the dominant culture by selling vision quests to whites who want to find their spirit
helper, despite the fact that vision quests are not a part of traditional Apache culture, and using the profits to educate tribal youth.
His film series is an attempt "to make sure the kids know their
roles, develop their sense of irony so they'll know how to function,
how to adapt like Russell Means" (*Dark River* 31).

The problem, as Shorty Luke knows, is that "Hollywood never
stops" (*Dark River* 270). Of course, popular films are not the only
vehicle used to carry the Indian. Television, photography, print
journalism, fiction both high and low, and the academy churn out
copy after copy of the invention that is a misrepresentation at best.[2]
Given the proliferation of images of the Indian, it is understandable
that Jake Nashoba tells Mrs. Edwards, "Look, Grandmother, I'm
no Indian" (*Dark River* 42). Owens's character speaks beyond his
particular situation of displacement and crisis of identity to phrase
one response to the onslaught of Indian images. Those Othering
images, after all, "can inflict harm, can be a form of oppression, imprisoning someone in a false, distorted, and reduced mode of being"
(C. Taylor 25).

For identity to be articulated and the possibility of home to be
realized for Jake Nashoba, for many of Owens's other characters,
for Owens himself, and ultimately for Native people in general,
the invention of the Indian, the misreadings that produce it, and

the ideology that is at its heart must be revealed and surpassed. Until that time, the People have little option save what is explicitly and implicitly phrased when Lee Jensen stands over Jessie's body and says, "He's an Indian . . . [ellipsis added] Dead as hell, too. The only good one . . . [ellipsis in the original]" (*Dark River* 118). Identified as Indian and forever hearing echoes of the nineteenth-century refrain that transformed General Philip Sheridan's "the only good Indian I ever saw were [sic] dead" into what amounts to a rallying cry for genocide, the Native is offered only the silence of the ellipsis or, as we have seen with Jake Nashoba, the emptiness of cliché.

It is the particular sort of silencing that can be done by theory that Homi K. Bhabha addresses in his effort to indicate his own commitment to theory. Bhabha holds that theorizing the Other and its texts, no matter how ethically or morally right-minded, runs the risk of replicating the desire to contain it and them. In turning either spatially East, temporally to the pagan, or to both, theory produces an Other that is "cited, framed, illuminated, encased in the shot/ reverse shot strategy of a serial enlightenment" (*Location* 31). As soon as the Other loses the ability to be an "active agent of articulation" on and in its own terms, it and its texts lose their "power to signify, to negate, to initiate its historic desire, to establish its own institutional and oppositional discourse" (31). Bhabha wants theory to maintain its revolutionary force by focusing its efforts on cultural difference rather than on cultural diversity. The former is a "process of signification," the creation of a discourse that enunciates culture and in the process questions authority.

The task that Bhabha sets theorists and theory is commensurate with the task facing Owens and other Native storytellers as they turn to writing to articulate difference and question the ideas and ideology of the dominant culture. Indeed, theorists and critics of multiculturalism, diversity, and difference can benefit from the example of Owens, Vizenor, and other Native writers. The trick for them is using the "new technology" of writing in order that the Native might be an active agent of articulation. The task before Owens, as before all "minority" writers or authors of an other discourse, is to supplement the discourse of the dominant culture. By adding to in a fashion which reveals that things do not "add up," to invoke Rudolphe Gasché's provocative phrasing of the Derridean supplement, the other discourse "insinuat[es] itself into the terms of reference of the dominant discourse, [and] the supplementary antagonizes the implicit power to generalize, to produce the sociological stability" (Bhabha, *Location* 155) longed for by the dominant culture.

Our point of departure compels us to read in the light of the Western Apache and their conception of stories, of place, and of the relationship between them. This counters the power to generalize that has cerned Native peoples since contact. If we return to the concluding passage of *Dark River*, to what Shorty Luke says and how Owens presents it, we can begin to see how to combat the images of the Indian in and with writing. "'It is said . . .' He looked back toward the treeline above them and was silent for a moment as he kept walking. 'It is said that Jacob Nashoba went home.'" Here too Owens offers us an ellipsis, one that, ironically, speaks volumes. Whereas the ellipsis of Jensen's statement leads nowhere for the Native, whether we are speaking of Jessie, the Western Apache, or Native people as a whole, the ellipsis at the end of *Dark River* leads us to one place from which home can be found. The latter ellipsis, that is, should be read as the frontier, not from which Indians must be driven or exterminated, as the dominant culture would have it, but as a place of contact and possibility.

The treeline need not be seen as a line of demarcation between two zones—forest and mountain moor, for instance—but rather as the place where zones meet. As such, it is a metaphorization of the contact zone or seam that Owens labels the frontier. For Owens, the frontier as traditionally conceived by Euroamericans was dangerous precisely because it was a shifting site of contact with the Other where typical rules of engagement did not necessarily apply. Rather than embracing the possibility for change implicit in the frontier, Euroamericans chose to negate its transformative potential. Owens is well aware of the typical connotations and denotations of "frontier" when viewed from the Western perspective; he wants to rescue the dynamic possibilities of the term, though by gazing at it from the other side of the line, as it were. Following Mary Louis Pratt, James Clifton, and others, Owens sees the frontier, not as the "cutting edge of civilization" (*Mixedblood Messages* 44), but as a multifaceted, multivoiced, and shifting contact zone where identities and ideologies can meet, mingle, and transform. The frontier is understood as "always unstable, multidirectional, hybridized, characterized by heteroglossia, and indeterminate" (26). While for the dominant culture the frontier was a dangerous and unstable place because of its indeterminacy, for Owens it is a liberating one, and for precisely the same reason. What is more, to question and redefine the frontier, one of the foundational tropes of the country, is to question the very nature and idea of the nation.

Owens holds that the dominant culture and the nation attempted and attempt to counter what was and is for it the terrifying nature of the frontier with the idea of the territory. Territory was "a place of containment, invented to control and subdue the dangerous potentialities of imagined Indians" (*Mixedblood Messages* 26). Was and is, as Owens makes clear in *Dark River*. There Vietnam, the Gulf War, and Wounded Knee are yoked together to stress how in each case labeling a territory "Indian Country"—whether it be land controlled by the Vietcong, the Iraqis, or Native Americans— is a precursor to the massacre of "dark-skinned human beings" (107) in the name of occupation and control. What is more, the photos Jake Nashoba recalls seeing of "charred bodies" in Iraq and the "smooth sand where U.S. tanks had buried thousands of men alive during that phony war," on the one hand, and the frozen bodies of Bigfoot's band after the massacre at Wounded Knee, on the other, indicate that death is at the heart of the dominant culture's desire to fix and contain the Native.

Like Derrida's *revenant* and Freud's uncanny, however, the Native will not stay dead and buried. The *revenant*, then, is conjured by the West in a dual sense: both to call back and to exorcise or expel. The West runs from and chases the specter because mourning for the dead will not get rid of it (Derrida 101). Thus the act of conjuring evokes the ghost or specter only in order to conjure it away. In *Dark River*, Stroud's recollection of the Indian he thinks died in Vietnam reveals one reason why the mixedblood needs to be done away with. The Indian is Jake Nashoba, of course. Stroud recalls how an African American had taken issue with Jake's decision to be neither Indian nor white. Atkinson does not understand why Jake has the power to choose his "racial" identity and turns to Stroud to say, "This don't make no sense. How come this motherfucker ain't got to be nothing? He got to be something. You the man, so you tell the brother he got to be Injun or white, he got to choose. He can't be no in-between" (123). Owens's narrative playfulness cuts to the crux of the matter. Atkinson's first question to Stroud reveals that to be Indian is to be nothing. The double negative, the twice cancellation, is indicative of how, in and with language, the Native is canceled or erased first by an original act of misnaming and then by simulations that are based on the first. Two negatives do not make a positive here, since for Jake "to be something" he must be what is, finally, the nothing of the stereotypic simulations captured precisely in the word "Injun." Jake is "a motherfucker," on the one hand, because his position violates the rule of the dominant culture, and he is "a brother," on the other hand, because like Atkinson he is also seen by the dominant culture as Other. Stroud responds to Atkinson with a laugh, as do the other men, because this is serious and uncomfortable business. He recognizes the limits of his authority. If the mixedblood can choose to be in-between, then the efforts to fix the Native as Other come to nothing. The mixedblood comes back to the dominant culture unceasingly, to be sure, but it has traditionally been as the figure of the doomed half-breed, tragically caught between worlds. Not so here. Jake just grins and walks away. Stroud must think Jake dead, for to imagine him alive is to confront the disturbing possibility of uncontainable difference.

Owens recognizes the relationships among writing, textuality, and death that the dominant culture is keen to make and maintain, mind you. He reveals that recognition, for instance, in the opening chapter of *Dark River* when he uses the word "kerf" to describe the life into which cut elements of the Choctaw culture and worldview (4). Given Owens's interest in the Forest Service (for which he worked in the 1970s), in logging, and in their connection to the construction of the nation, kerf (the slit made by cutting with a saw and the cut end of a felled tree) is especially relevant. As both that produced by cutting and the remainder after cutting, kerf is at once a telling testimony of a life that issues from and is produced by the violence of the stereotype and indicative of the excess, remainder, and trace that can remain unmastered by it. We might think of the space created by violence and violation as analogous to the frontier: as defined by the dominant culture, that space is created by violence and the violation of its nature as a zone of contact; Owens's reimagining of it indicates that the frontier cannot necessarily be mastered by the dominant culture.

Ishkitini, harbinger of death for the Choctaw, is a messenger of what is to come for Jake Nashoba, to be sure, but insofar as Owens recognizes and wants to keep alive what is for him the liberating possibility of the in-between, *Ishkitini* is a harbinger of the death of the Indian. To ensure the unveiling and demise of the simulation, Owens must use writing against itself. To do so he turns to the particular writing of fiction. Indeed, if Shorty Luke's use of the phrase "It is said" signals to Sam Baca that he will answer the man's question with a story, then naming the White Mountain band of the Western Apache the Black Mountain band can be read as Owens's way of signaling to the reader that what he or she is reading is a fiction.[3]

Wolfgang Iser argues that literary fictions enable us to discover what is withheld from us because they are produced by crossing the boundaries of reality and the imaginary. The act of fictionalizing oversteps both, as the real is brought to the imaginary and vice versa, and the text that is created occupies a space between the real, the fictive, and the imaginary. Therefore, and this is the critical point that Iser does not make, the literary text is itself liminal. Its liminality, moreover, is what enables the literary text to produce change.[4]

Fictionalizing produces a space between from which to counter and supplement the violence and violation done to the Native. From the in-between, both/and space of the literary text metaphorized by the treeline, then, Owens is able to tell his other story and articulate an other destiny. The act of cutting the pages of the bound book, a Native American novel with an(other) discourse, produces and allows to be revealed the remainder and excess that the nation cannot master.

Owens's narratives do more than incorporate elements of his Choctaw and Cherokee cultures, of the Coast Salish, the Ohlone, the Diné, and the Western Apache: they are grounded in and determined by those cultures. As such, they speak to and from particular Native worldviews in order to tell their other stories and phrase an(other) destiny. A danger lurking in the act of telling, of the construction of an other discourse, is that the dominant culture and its discourse will be so essentialized that we are left with narratives that do to them precisely what they do to the Native. Owens's texts skirt that danger by incorporating historical and cultural particularity. In effect, the narratives are situated at sites of nationalism or colonialism, on the one hand, and protest, on the other. The "crease" of writing, again to invoke Vizenor (*Fugitive Poses* 4), brings together historical revolt with the revolutions in the sign, signification, and culture that Owens calls for and champions. At the same time, those historical protests and revolts—the Wobblie rebellion of 1916 in the Pacific Northwest, the Vietnam War student protests of 1968 in Santa Barbara, and the Santa Cruz Mission Indians' 1812 slaying of a cruel Catholic priest—enable Owens to interrogate the possibility and promise of various forms of insurrection.

The treeline that Shorty Luke looks toward at the close of *Dark River*, finally, reinforces an intertextual connection to Vizenor that is especially important for our understanding of Owens's fictions. The treeline is a trope for the liberating potential of the liminal throughout Vizenor's work. In general terms, the evocation of Vizenor and his work is representative of the invocation of Native writers and texts throughout Owens's fictions. Those references

and allusions function, in part, to establish a community and
connect Owens and his narratives to it. In so doing, Owens effectively avoids the trap of having his writing distance him from
community. More specifically, in evoking Vizenor and his work,
Owens evokes the figure of trickster and the creation of trickster
discourse. It is a trickster grin that flashes when Jake Nashoba
smiles at Steve Stroud in Vietnam. The figure of trickster introduces
chance and possibility, upsets binaries, counters terminal creeds,
and establishes the primacy of humor over tragedy. Thus, the trickster figure and trickster discourse are instrumental to Native survival.
Open-ended, dynamic, and playful to the extreme, trickster is first
and foremost "a 'doing,' not an essence, not a museum being, not
an aesthetic presence" (Vizenor, "Postmodern Introduction" 13).
Active and subversive, trickster shimmers at the treeline, cavorts
and beckons from the limen, and shocks, tricks, and teases us into
an(other) awareness of the Native. Like Vizenor and other Native
writers and artists, Owens turns to the figure of trickster and the
power of trickster discourse in order to liberate characters, narrative, self, and audience.

CHAPTER ONE

TRYING ON TRICKSTER
WITH *WOLFSONG*

In *Other Destinies: Understanding the American Indian Novel*, Louis Owens writes that "in spite of the fact that Indian authors write from very diverse tribal and cultural backgrounds, there is to a remarkable degree a shared consciousness and identifiable world-view reflected in novels by American Indian authors, a conscious-ness and worldview defined primarily by a quest for identity" (20). The quest that Owens says holds for Native novels from the work of John Rollin Ridge onward holds, too, for Owens's fictions. Indeed, it makes sense to think of the trajectory of Owens's novels as an attempt to write to and through his own sense of mixedblood identity. We can see this effort phrased succinctly with the opening of his autobiographical essay entitled "Blood Trails: Missing Grand-mothers and Making Worlds": "The word 'Oklahoma' resonates deeply through my childhood. This state with a Choctaw name meaning the land of red people was the 'Nation' in stories told by my mother, aunt, uncle, and grandmother, a place of great pain and beauty often remembered in the same utterance" (*Mixedblood Messages* 135). Owens and his family have to come to terms with their missing maternal grandmother, of whom there is neither written record nor picture. She is absent, vanished without written or photo-graphic trace. As such, she is emblematic of the gaps and voids that many Native people have to live with. She is also emblematic of missing Natives more generally, insofar as they have been replaced by the Euroamerican Indian. The Indian is a barrier that is surmounted by acts of construction that resurrect the Native in and with stories that are grounded in and speak to particular cultural traditions and worldviews. In doing so, identity is articulated and affirmed.

Wolfsong, Owens's first novel, reveals some of the potential difficulties contemporary Native Americans face as they work to articulate and maintain identity. Drafted in 1976, shortly after the landmark Boldt decision in *U.S. v. Washington* (which concerned Native fishing rights protected by various nineteenth-century treaties) had brought to the surface tensions between Washington State's Natives and its Euroamerican residents, and revised in 1990, Owens's 1991 novel is set against the backdrop of the contemporary land rights controversy in the Pacific Northwest. The small town of Forks has suffered economic declines due to shifts in the logging industry and diminishing timber resources. Mirroring that decline is the decline in the local Native population. Most of the townspeople have opted to embrace the construction of a copper mine deep in the heart of the nearby wilderness area because it promises jobs. Not so Stehemish native Jim Joseph (uncle of the text's protagonist, Tom Joseph), who dies of a heart attack while trying to protect the wilderness area in the mountains above the town from the scarring, pollution, and loss of water that the mine will bring. In telling the story of Tom's return home to the small town in the Cascade Range north of Arlington, and in juxtaposing Tom's relationship to home with that of his brother, Jimmy, his former girlfriend Karen Brant, and others from Forks, Owens's narrative illuminates how constructions of the Indian both complicate efforts to affirm Native identity and are fundamental to the dominant society's efforts to define itself and the nation.

Given the dominant culture's efforts to perpetuate its construction of the Indian, it is not surprising that Tom must find his Native identity before he can affirm it. Our understanding of his quest for a certainty of self is enriched by the figure of the trickster appearing throughout the narrative, for that figure helps us understand Tom and his actions. The trickster and trickster discourse, the figure and economy that both free us and compel us to reexamine the world, are also fundamental to the text's interrogation of the tropes of Indian and the vanishing Native. Interrogating both tropes is vitally important to resistance and an affirmation of Native identity. In order to rewrite the Euroamerican narrative of revolution and nation, in order to rewrite modernity, Owens must engage in a "working through" (Lyotard 26) of the figure of the Indian, for that figure—as projection, invention, spectacle, simulacrum, *revenant*—consigns the Native to the role of silent spectator and makes home unhomely.

Given Owens's interest in and emphasis on the importance of place, it is striking that the particular world we are compelled to reexamine both is and is not located between Puget Sound and the Cascade Range in Washington State. As Lee Schweninger points out, Owens takes great care to establish verity by using place-names of towns, rivers, valleys, and mountains (97). Incorporating such real places as Everett and Arlington, Eldorado Mountain and Glacier Peak, and the Sauk and the Stillaguamish Rivers serves to situate characters and actions concretely. The vivid and accurate rendering of these places, especially the river drainages and the mountainsides, grounds us in this world and reveals a knowledge of place that confirms Owens's authority to, as he has said, "write a novel about the wilderness area itself, Glacier Peak Wilderness, making the place the real protagonist" (qtd. in Purdy 6–7).

And yet, for all the richness of detail, for all the wonderful descriptions of hanging valleys along and underneath ridgelines where the trunks of old-growth cedars bend inward and their branches begin a dozen feet above the ground, where the forest bottom is a mix of humus and moss, fern and a half-dozen species of mushroom, salal and bunchberry, for all this accuracy, the world rendered is not quite locatable on any map between the Stillaguamish, Sauk, and Suiattle Rivers hard upon the Cascade Range and Glacier Peak Wilderness Area. Rather, Owens takes care to both give real places fictional names (the Snohomish River becomes the

Stehemish) and to transplant real names (the place-name of Forks is taken from the Olympic Peninsula and given to the town whose "real" name is Darrington). What is more, he locates in this place a fictionalized tribe, the Stehemish.

Susan Bernardin speculates that Owens places a fictionalized tribe in a specific, highly detailed area to "dovetail his concern for contemporary land struggles in a place he knows well with a broader interest in how questions of Indian identity get entangled with dominant cultural perceptions of the land" (80). This entanglement certainly figures in the narrative, as Ab Masingale, one of the valley's longtime Euroamerican residents, thinks that "what people like him and Sam and Floyd had come to the valley for was gone. Somehow the loss seemed connected to the dead Indian, Jim Joseph" (123–24). Owens has written that he created a fictionalized tribe based upon a Native American community in a northern Cascades valley with which he was familiar in order "to avoid embarrassing anyone" (*Mixedblood Messages* 21). While neither reason can be discounted, more can be made of the move. First, mixing real places, fictionalized places, and real places situated out of context calls into question the dominant culture's map of the world and thus, subtly, the ideology governing it. Second, the mixing of the real and the fictionalized makes explicit the power of the imagination to make a world that Owens implies with the title and opening of "Blood Trails." Thus, Owens shares with N. Scott Momaday a vision of the imagination and one's place in the world. Momaday holds that it is the "moral act of the imagination" that "constitutes [one's] understanding of the world" ("Native American Attitudes" 80) and oneself. Owens reads the vignette in *The Way to Rainy Mountain* concerning the medicine Momaday's grandfather Mammedaty received after watching a mole emerge from its burrow and "blow fine dark earth out of its mouth" (*Rainy Mountain* 73) as representative of what is necessary to understand the world: one must have "the greatest possible intimacy and communication with the world one inhabits" (*Mixedblood Messages* 227). With this intimacy and communication comes the power to heal oneself and the world through acts of the imagination. Owens returns to this point in the environmental essays included in *Mixedblood Messages*, going so far in "Burning the Shelter" as to conclude that unless all human beings recognize and act in accordance with this sense of intimacy, connection, and communication, "the earth simply will not survive" (217).

Third, because the northern Cascades valley that Owens renders in *Wolfsong* is distorted by the insertion of Forks, the Stehemish River, and the tribe that bears its name, Owens's decision should also be seen in the light of anamorphosis. The insertion that is an interruption draws our attention, as Lacan reminds us, and demands that we take it into account. In order to do so, we must either have a special instrument that resolves the distortion or change our position and perspective on the object. The transformation of the object or scene, then, necessitates transformation on our part if we are to see clearly. In Lacan's reading of Hans Holbein's *The Ambassadors*, the insertion that is itself distorted only swims into focus with a change of perspective that enables us to see, captured in the death's head, "our own nothingness" (92). The new perspective necessary to see this image is one which recognizes that our vision, like our speech, is a product of a network of discourses. This means that what we see when we see is "formed by paths or networks laid down in advance" (Bryson 93) of us and our seeing. Therefore, what we see exists independently of us in space and time.

Anamorphosis remarks a decentering and hence destabilizing of the subject. So too does the locale of *Wolfsong*, distorted as it is by Owens's insertions. These insertions, it is worth remarking, are of two kinds. In the case of Forks we have an undistorted referent that distorts the entire picture. We ask, "What is this place-name doing here? Why is this place out of place?" These questions throw both the real Forks and the fictional locale out of focus. In the case of the Stehemish tribe, we have a distorted referent that also causes the whole to be distorted. The latter is most akin to what Lacan sees in *The Ambassadors*, for at issue in both texts is a knowledge of death and our response to it. To make sense of both types of insertions, we must adopt a different perspective on the world and the Indian.

In the place of an unstinting realism ultimately complicitous with the ideology of the dominant culture, Owens imagines a world that blurs the line between the real and the fictive, and in so doing he asks his reader to reconsider the world and how he or she perceives it. The adoption of what will amount to a perspective diametrically opposed to that held by subjects of the dominant culture, past and present, is prefigured in the novel's first paragraph. We learn that the rain which has soaked through Jim Joseph's clothes and lies next to his skin is "familiar and comforting" (1). One may not typically associate being wet in the woods with comfort, but Jim Joseph finds comfort in the rain because, along with his people, he knows it to be, in Susan Bernardin's words, "a force of growth, regeneration, and cyclical return, which counters narratives of vanishing and loss" (87). It also counters those of mastery and control, the narratives that compose the dominant culture's discourse on the land.

One can also take comfort in the knowledge that rain calls to mind kinship and connections. Mad John, the Korean War veteran who haunts Tom Joseph and the text, asks a crucial question of the young man, and the reader: "Hath the rain a father, Tom Joseph?" (147). Tom cannot immediately answer Mad John. Nor can he shake the question. It is not until a sense of peace and understanding comes over him later, while praying during an intertribal and interethnic sweat lodge ceremony, that Tom is able to recognize and phrase an answer: "Uncle . . . Father of the rain" (192).

The connection with the rain that Tom articulates is part and parcel of the Salish worldview, which acknowledges the interrelatedness of all things and the fluid nature of boundaries. Numerous images in the narrative accentuate this fact, beginning with the way Jim Joseph's "elbows sank into the moss and rotten bark and the log seemed to grow up around them" (2) as he sighted his rifle in on the earthmoving equipment below him. The blurring of boundaries between human and plant, organic and inorganic, helps the reader to recognize a fourth reason why Owens blurs boundaries between the real and the fictive in his narrative: he is writing from and with a culturally centered knowledge of place. Swinomish Martin Sampson notes in his history of the Natives of Skagit County, Washington, that political and social boundaries were also flexible and mutable. For the Coast Salish, the blurring of boundaries includes those between worlds as well as within both the natural and social worlds. Owens emphasizes this fact with the image of a cedar nurselog, six feet in diameter, from which grows a line of two-foot-high firs. Seeing this, one recognizes with the narrator that "there was no demarcation, no place where he [Tom Joseph] could say 'This is alive, this is not'" (83).

Owens's narrative makes clear that it is this world that Jim Joseph tries to protect through his guerilla actions by revealing that the 30-40 Krag was sunk deep into the moss and decay when he fired rounds into the Caterpillars and trucks being used to cut a road into the heart of sacred tribal land. The land is sacred both because the Salish do not recognize a separation between the human and other-than-human worlds, or privilege the human over the other-than-human, as Schweninger points out, and because what the dominant culture terms the wilderness is essential to Salish identity, since it is there that one goes to receive one's guardian spirit. From the age of four through puberty, children could be sent by their parents into isolation in the forests and mountains around their villages in order that they might fast and obtain the vision revealing their guardian spirit or spirit helper. Attaining a state of purity is essential to the vision quest; this means that wilderness bodies of water where one could bathe play central roles. Thus, the threat the mine poses to Image Lake is tantamount to a threat to the heart of the Salish/Stehemish world. The wilderness is also connected to the spirit dance and spirit dance ceremonies, for there one receives the knowledge of one's particular dance and its relation to one's song. This is why the dancers from the spirit world appear to Jim Joseph when he is in the mountains above the Stehemish and Stillaguamish drainages. He moves with the music and the dancers because spirit dancing "provides a sense of relatedness to other people" (Amoss 160), to be sure, and his dancing in the wilderness indicates a sense of relatedness to place as well.

The narrative gives way to Tom Joseph, the person to whom Jim Joseph willed his guardian spirit, in order to focus on his quest for identity in the light of and in relation to his family, Forks, and the wilderness area. It also enables Owens to continue interrogating the possibilities of individual resistance begun with the rounds Jim Joseph squeezes off at the beginning of the text. Tom returns home near the end of his freshman year of college in California in order to attend his uncle's funeral. We learn that he also returns to reevaluate the decision he had made to leave his family, his girlfriend Karen Brant, and his home among the rivers and peaks of the Cascade mountains of Washington State. He tells Karen, "I didn't fit in down there" (73) at Santa Barbara because, he thinks, living in the valley had made him too dark inside. He also tells her that the campus is built on a sacred Native burial ground, that he felt the people buried there, and that he could tell that they did not want anyone there. Others do not seem to notice what Tom does, because they are too busy trying to cover the Native with—in this instance—the image of the Indian created and perpetuated by the academy. The Native refuses to rest in peace, however, as people take ill without understanding the cause. Tom knows, though, and he knows that he cannot return to the university.

Riding the bus north in the rain through Oregon and into Washington, Tom feels the dampness of the climate settle deep into his body and experiences "a great sense of going home" (13). That homecoming is tellingly marked by a lack of immediate recognition on the part of Amel Barstow, the truck driver who picks Tom up hitchhiking the last leg of his journey home. When Amel does place Tom's face, he laughs at his failure to immediately recognize someone he'd known for years and then says, "I'll be dammed. . . . Must've been the hair. You're starting to look like an old-time Indian, a whole lot like a picture I seen once of your uncle when he was a kid" (18). The comment is in keeping with the subject of transformation in *Wolfsong*, as are both Karen's later comment to Tom that his "hair's longer. You look like an Indian" (63) when she first sees him after his return and Bob McBride's remark to his college roommate late in the summer that he "sure look[s] like" a "timber beast"

(181) after working as a logger for a time. These transformations are external, however—changes of appearance that do not necessarily signify a fundamental transformation in Tom and the way he looks at the world and his relationship with it.

Amel's comment also effectively yokes together Tom with his uncle. That union or joining prefigures both Tom's connection with Jim Joseph's cause later in the text, as Tom eventually turns to militant action in order to at the very least disrupt the desecration of the wilderness in general and the Stehemish ancestral homeland in particular, and Tom's attempt to understand the connection between himself and his uncle. The difficulty of making and understanding the latter connection is signaled by Amel's statement that Tom is starting to look "like an old-time Indian," for the adjective "old-time" drives home that the image of an "Indian" which Tom mirrors and which his uncle personified is thought to be a part of the past.

The fact that the image is captured in a photograph reveals another aspect of the difficulty Tom faces, for photographs can offer what is at best only a romanticized and reified figure. Gerald Vizenor highlights this danger when he has Tune Browne stand between two photographs—one of himself sitting before a tepee in braids and feathers and the other Edward Curtis's "In a Piegan Lodge"—and announces, "We were caught in camera time, extinct in photographs, and now in search of our past and common memories we walk right back into these photographs" (*Crossbloods* 90). This means nothing short of walking back into what Vizenor calls "the simulation of the *indian* that is the absence of the native" (*Fugitive Poses* 152). With Barthes, Vizenor recognizes that photographs are about possession and death, that this is the truth of camera time. Moreover, if, as Barthes holds, "the photograph is the advent of myself as other" (12), then when the self as Other is the Native American transformed into the Indian, what is rendered in the photograph is necessarily apocalyptic.

This is the truth about photographs of the Native American taken by subjects of the dominant culture. They picture the end. In the process, they are born of and meant to invoke what Renato

Rosaldo calls "imperialist nostalgia": that which "uses a pose of 'innocent yearning' both to capture people's imaginations and to conceal its complicity with often brutal domination" (70). This nostalgia is "an attitude—a textual attitude, a colonization of the past—conditioned not merely by the passing of time but by the threat of shifting borders (geographic, social, political) that might redefine the meaning of home" (Green-Lewis 49). In the face of this threat, photographer and viewing subject become nostalgic and capture the object as an image, arresting it in and of the past, in order to render it powerless as a threat to the present. The photograph, then, like stories, attempts to bring absence into presence, but only to accentuate irrecoverable loss.

The moment of recognition in the logging truck does not sit well with Amel. He declares, not asks, "You're Sara Joseph's boy," after which we read that "the driver's eyes drew back a little, his voice grew cautious" (18). Amel draws back his eyes to get a fix on Tom. He lights upon the photo he has seen of Tom's uncle as a child because it gives him a frame of reference that enables him to think in terms of likeness and resemblance rather than of identity. The photographic capture allows him to deal with surfaces only because of "the indexical relationship" (Green-Lewis 50) of a photograph to its original subject. As such, the photograph helps him to assume a position of authority, even if he is not himself the photographer, for "to lay claim to the likeness, the surface, or skin of an object—palace or person, landscape or animal—is in a very real sense to assume rights over it" (Green-Lewis 50). Amel needs only to have seen the photo once to be in the position to allay any anxiety he is experiencing. He can now keep an eye on Tom.[1] The single shot of an "old-time Indian" helps him rest easy with the person sitting next to him in the Peterbilt cab. Imagination captured, Amel can see Tom from a nostalgic perspective.

This is not to say that Amel does not think highly of Tom. He tells fellow local and local thug Jake Tobin that Tom is "smart," "a good kid," and "the best damned fullback this town ever had" (100). This makes it all the more telling that it is Amel who knocks

Tom into a crevasse with a single bullet, although "he hadn't meant to shoot at all, not really, but in the excitement he'd just done it" (232). Amel fires without thinking: it is nothing less than a conditioned response. The narrative suggests a connection between that act and the earlier turn to a photograph in order to fix Tom when Dinker, one of the men pursuing Tom on the mountain, proclaims that the former was the "finest damn snapshot I ever saw" (232). It is clear that Amel is not conscious of what lurks behind his turn to each snapshot; it is equally clear, I think, that, notwithstanding his high regard for Tom, Amel is not in a position to see the young man. Indeed, he misses Tom crawling out of the bergschrund as he gives himself over to feelings of relief that he did not kill Tom; his mind wanders, and he thinks of the set of questions he is not prepared to answer: "What had caused the boy to do it? Why did it seem that for the Indians he'd known in his life something was always going wrong? What . . . was going on down inside that mountain?" (241).

It is important to note that when Amel first recognizes him and draws back in the Peterbilt cab, Tom "tried to smile" (18) as part of his response, for, as Eduardo Cadava's reading of Benjamin's understanding of the relationship between language, photography, and identity makes clear, a smile "registers our willingness to take on elements of the other and make them our own" (267). For Benjamin this constitutes nothing less than a willingness to lose oneself, to cease to be oneself, in order to become like that at whom we smile. This is especially damning for those whose culture is oral, for the smile silences speech. It puts a halt to utterance and the articulation of identity. Tom's attempt to smile signals, then, either the seductiveness of Amel's position, the degree to which he has been schooled to recognize it and respond in kind, or both. That Tom is unable to smile signals his difference from Amel and an unwillingness to close that gap.[2]

Tom enters the last leg of his journey home as an uncanny figure. While Amel masters him, fixes him, and puts him in his place, the fact that he has to do so indicates the threat to home that he and, by extension, all other Native Americans embody. This is true most forcefully at the level of the nation, for as Derrida indicates, the nation "is rooted first of all in the memory or the anxiety of a dis-placed—or displaceable—population" (83). Amel discloses the anxious root of the nation even as he attempts to tell Tom how sorry he is about Jim Joseph's death, and Tom's loss:

> "When I was a kid your uncle showed me how to make showshoes [sic] and how to use 'em." Amel glanced at Tom. "Couldn't nobody figure out what happened. Maybe he just stayed out there in the woods too long." He paused and then blurted out a final attempt. "I never thought he was nuts. I knew him since I came here with my family back in the thirties. *There was more of your people back then.*" (19, emphasis added)

Amel's effort to put into words how he feels reveals that he too has experienced a loss. That loss is tinged with nostalgia, however, inas-much as the memory he conjures up, for Tom and the reader, is one of Jim Joseph, the savvy, woods-wise Indian, showing a young white boy a bit of Stehemish material culture and lifeways. The comfort of nostalgia is fleeting, however, for Amel and for us, for the memory also brings to mind what Amel would rather repress— "There was more of your people back then"—in order to avoid the reminder that what has happened to the Stehemish could also happen to the Euroamericans.

Just such a reminder is what photographer and literary critic Charles Martin sees, potentially, being triggered by a photograph of a Native American headdress: "But as a memento of a people largely displaced from coveted territories of power, the image, for all who gaze upon it, could forecast and herald—like any image of ruins— eventual changes of peoples, of formations and ideas of nations and of the running out of eras" (258–59). Seen as an image of ruin, the headdress fits nicely with the dominant culture's creation of the Indian, of course. Phrased as such, it also resonates with and from the discourse of the dominant culture. The headdress is not neces-sarily an image of ruin, however, as Martin's photograph reveals.[3]

Martin's photograph counters any totalizing, romantic commentary: the headdress shot through a shop window doubles, triples, quadruples itself in the image (or does it?), and in the process will not give itself up as anything other than what it is (not): an image that is perpetuated endlessly in the gaze of the viewer. The addition of reflections cast in the window from outside the shop only adds to the (revealing) confusion. Indeed, the photograph is a peculiar example of anamorphosis. That is, in order for the photograph to be resolved, the viewer of the image would have to adopt a perspective on the object captured that the photograph itself does not offer. As such, it is like the image Tom sees in the window when riding home to Forks with Amel. While waiting to be recognized by a man he has known all his life, Tom tries "to look through the unlighted windows" (17) of the headquarters office of another tribe as they drive by. What he sees, however, is "only a blurred reflection of the truck" (17). Not only can Tom not see in, but when he tries to do so he is given back an image of the logging industry that defined Forks and helps define the nation. Owens constructs his narrative so that Tom and the reader resolve the blurred image, recognize it as the screen that distorts our vision, and remove it so that we may see the Native American, ourselves, and our world.

As readers of Owens's narrative, then, we need to be placed in the same position relative to the text that Tom is in relative to the one photo he has seen of his father. That photo and the stone that marks the grave of the elder Tom Joseph are twin poles of representation that attempt to capture his, and our, imagination. But the younger Tom Joseph's imagination cannot be captured, for try as he might, he cannot see the photo clearly. Although he stared at it again and again as a child, the image would not resolve. The same remains true for Tom now. The photo, which we, like Tom, never "see," gives up only "a dark figure in a long, gray overcoat and formless hat, more shadow than man"; consequently, this is a man who "didn't look like anything, or he looked like everything" (54). The hat shades the face, the overcoat conceals. The result is an image of someone "formless and a part of nothing around him" (54).

Twice we read that the figure in the image is disturbing (54, 55). Owens emphasizes this because the picture of Tom Joseph, Sr., is nothing less than an uncanny image for his son and the reader. From the perspective of the dominant culture, the image is, in Freud's words, "something which ought to have remained hidden but has come to light" (241). It is a figure without clear boundaries precisely because it has broken the bounds of the Indian fixed by those in power but has not yet resolved for Tom (or the reader) into an individual who can be identified as Stehemish. Owens's sentence structure accentuates the importance of the tribe as the necessary supplement of the construct created by the dominant culture: "He knew his father was Indian, Stehemish, but the man in the picture didn't look like anything" (54). The figure is disturbing both because it will not be captured by a discourse of mastery and loss and because it is a visual reminder that Tom does not at this point in the narrative have a discourse with which to identify, and identify with, his father as Stehemish. Charles Martin emphasizes both the personal level of apocalypse and the fact that the word suggests both climactic ending and revelations producing change and new beginnings (243–44). The photo disturbs Tom because it tends toward a nostalgic reading he is resisting—the figure seen as frozen in the past and therefore an artifact—and because it reminds him of what he does not yet have even as it does not have that which is necessary if he is to experience an apocalyptic revelation.

Many of those in Forks want to fix Tom with the image of the "metasavage" invented by the dominant culture. Karen Brant tacitly refers to this figure both when she tells Tom that he is "getting to be real serious. . . . Like the Indians they always show in those old movies" (104) and when she and others remark on his long hair. Like Tune Browne, who strips the invention bare and reveals it for what it is in both *Crossbloods* and *The Trickster of Liberty*, Tom must move beyond the invention and make the past a part of the present—and indeed, of the future—to make tradition live. This is what is at stake in *Wolfsong*, as it is in so many other contemporary Native American texts, for only through a living tradition can one understand what it means to be Native and attain a true sense of one's identity. Tom must move beyond the trap of resemblance, for "the experience of a resemblance, because it experiences a likeness and not an identity, encounters a distance at the heart of resemblance" (Cadava 280). This disturbing distance is why Tom does not respond to his mother when she remarks that he looks like his father after he has worked as a choker-setter for a time. He wants to negotiate the gap opened by resemblance. Until he can do so, until he can know himself as Stehemish, he is as haunted by the man he never knew as are those who would run into his father alone in the woods, "Not hunting and fishing or running a trapline the way guys do, but just *spooking* around out there" (152, emphasis added). In spooking around and not even getting objects of value from the natural world, of course, the elder Tom Joseph is the *revenant* that the men he meets in the woods wish to conjure away. Tom wishes to call him forth.

The sense of homecoming Tom experienced as he rode the bus north from California is quickly replaced by questions of identity and his relationship to the place he has called home. Seeing old-growth cedars hauled out of the valley as he rides toward Forks makes him realize that for nearly a year he had not thought about the copper company's plan to conduct open-pit mining in the heart of the wilderness area. As a boy, Tom had trekked throughout the northern Cascades with his uncle. Like him, he came to have an intimate knowledge of the place and, later, an understanding that the wilderness area is a fragile, delicate bit of what it had once been, a place "with everything connected so carefully like the strands of a spider's web" (82). Tom reminds his brother shortly after arriving home that that country was sacred to their uncle. And, he thinks, "if it was a sacred place, shouldn't it be sacred to him, too, and Jimmy?" (33). Tom knows the answer to that question, knows that the land *should be* sacred to him; that knowledge is the catalyst for his attempt to determine his identity so that the land *will be* sacred to him.

He begins by going to his uncle's room and carefully examining all that the man had with him when he died alone in the wilderness, opening himself up to his uncle's presence, and taking the room as his place to sleep. This represents no small risk for Tom, because the spirits of recently deceased Salish, lonesome for their near kin and in a liminal position between realms, can lead the living to join them in the spirit world. In such an instance, the survivor's soul "follows the beloved into the grave" (Amoss 75). That Tom will expose himself to such a danger not once but twice, and open himself the second time after his mother tells him that he has "come a long way and you must go a long way back to find out who you are" (78), indicates that he risks searching for and finding his uncle's spirit because he thinks it is crucial to his efforts to find out who he is. He does not feel his uncle's presence, however, and it does not take him long to realize that he is unable to see his identity and its relationship to the land so easily as his uncle had his.

Wolfsong drives home that Tom has difficulty finding out who he is because he did not listen closely enough to his uncle and the stories he told. Tom tells Karen, "My uncle knew a whole lot that he tried to teach me . . . but I never really listened. I mean, I never listened like it would really make a difference. And now I think of all the questions I should have asked" (105). Haunted by those questions, as well as by both an earlier vision quest that failed because of his inability to believe and his failure to have the language necessary to articulate his relationship to the sacred wilderness, Tom fears that while the "map" of his home is made up of the "same mountains, rivers, and forests the Stehemish, Stillaguamish, and Skagit" had always known, the signs now "pointed in different directions, toward different destinies" (121–22). Given such a map, and without his uncle to guide him, Tom comes to feel "alone, cut off, a distant speck in the whirling world" (163).

Raven, the trickster in the oral tradition of the Southern Coast Salish and numerous other Pacific Northwest tribes, is transformed into a figure in the written text that scolds, barks, watches, shouts, laughs, and mocks throughout *Wolfsong* in an attempt to help Tom negotiate the gaps before him and know himself. The figure is also part of Owens's effort to destabilize referents and readers in order

to compel the latter to see the world anew.[4] Raven's entrance into
the written world of *Wolfsong* in the text's opening chapter links
Jim Joseph, the trickster, and the theme of identity. Owens writes
that after Joseph fires at the bulldozers rending the wilderness,
Leroy Brant comes out from behind the cover he had taken to shout
up into the forest that "leaned in a black wall, wet and impenetra-
ble" (3). Unable to pinpoint Joseph's exact location, Brant can only cup
his hands around his mouth and yell, "We know you, old man. Now
come on down before somebody gets hurt. This ain't cowboys and
injuns." The narrative then discloses that "somewhere in the timber
above him a raven barked and he shifted irritably" (3). Brant shifts
to direct his gaze and voice to where the raven barked because, being
a good woodsman, he believes that the raven has revealed Joseph's
position. With that sentence Owens establishes a link between Jim
Joseph, who is described throughout the narrative as grinning, and
Raven. Brant shifts irritably because, like the trickster, Joseph is an
irritator. Most importantly, the passage also links the trickster and
identity because the raven barks immediately after Brant shouts the
hackneyed "cowboys and injuns," a phrase the dominant culture has
been all too quick to use to inscribe both the Native Americans and
their relationship to the vision of the white frontier hero.

Tom's actions, like his appearance, link him with his uncle, and
hence with the trickster as well. Indeed, the actions that lead to his
flight for freedom across the glacier are strikingly reminiscent of those
taken by the trickster. If we know trickster, it is through his actions:
sexually active, often violent, ravenous, impetuous, quick to play
tricks on others, quick to deceive, and at times the unwitting sufferer
of his own tricks. The Coast Salish trickster-transformer Raven is
just such a figure. By turns helpful and harmful, Raven, even more
than its fellow Coast Salish trickster-transformers Coyote and Mink,
can be greedy, hasty, playful, and quick to act without thinking.
Tom shares many of Raven's characteristics: throughout the narrative we learn that he is and has been sexually active, that he can be
quite violent, that he is willing to play a destructive trick, and that
he is an unwitting sufferer of the trick he plays.

Consider the subplot in *Wolfsong* concerning Tom's relationship
with Karen Brant, his former girlfriend, which might seem at best
tangential to the larger issues being explored in the text. What, after
all, does the story of Tom's return home to discover that Karen has
had intercourse with Buddy Hill, become pregnant, and gotten
engaged have to do with issues of identity, tradition, and what it
means to be Stehemish? The story of the failed relationship does,
of course, accentuate the degree to which Tom is separated from
others in the valley. One could also read Karen's physical transformation, which Owens highlights throughout the novel, as symbolic
of her psychological transformation: with the pregnancy and engagement, Karen loses both the dream of togetherness she had shared
with Tom and the dream bears, powerful figures that can connect
her with her Cherokee heritage, that had protected and nurtured her.
Either reading, however, fails to take into account the sexual intercourse between Tom and Karen after her engagement to Buddy.
The second time they make love is prefaced by a discussion about
Native identity and the mine:

> "Are you against the mine like your uncle was?"
> "I think I saw a wolf," he said. "The first night I was back.
> I'm almost sure it was a wolf." He reached to touch her neck and
> then he kissed each eyelid slowly and carefully, moving his hand
> to the softness of her neck beneath the long hair and then down
> over her breasts to the barely perceptible swell of her belly. (105)

Karen's question elicits both the invocation of the wolf spirit that
was Jim Joseph's helper and guardian and Tom's initiation of sexual
foreplay leading to intercourse. The invocation and initiation tacitly
form Tom's response to the question, for the combination of the wolf
spirit, which links Tom and his uncle, and the trickster, a character
whose sexual appetite leads to the transgression of social boundaries,
suggests precisely why and how Tom will deal with the mine befoul-
ing the sacred land.[5]

Like the trickster, Tom will turn to violence and destruction.
The opening of the chapter that introduces Tom into the narrative

begins to sound the connection between the young man and violence:

> The bus slid into sight on the coast highway, trailing a mist as the tires threw rain off the asphalt. Above the red bank where the road cut across the cliffs, tall black firs stabbed a layer of cloud. The rain slanted in on the wind, streaking across the window, and the ocean slashed at the base of the cliffs, throwing seaweed and polished logs and debris against the land. A hundred yards out, columns of black rock, pocked by the wind and water, guarded the empty coastline and mists of gulls lifted in uneven lines before settling again. The wind cut the tops off the waves and wove whitecaps around the broken stone. (13)

The paragraph is full of violent verbs: the road cuts, the wind cuts, the firs stab, the ocean slashes and throws debris against the land. The connection between Tom and violence is strengthened later in the chapter when Tom rides the bus and plays his own violent "game from childhood, sliding the razor-edged blade out from the bus and lopping off everything in its path, seeing the telephone poles fall in neat lines, the timber mowed like grain before the inexorable blade" (14). This image of seemingly indiscriminate destruction, as Tom imagines that both the telephone poles (symbolic of the artificial world of the white man) and the trees (symbolic of the natural world) are scythed off, is immediately tempered by the disclosure that he retracts the blade and spares a "dull farmhouse" that reminds him of all the Native homes he has seen. While willing to spare what is remindful of contemporary Native American existence, Tom is quick to slice in two the "shining, two-story brick house" (14) indicative of Euroamerican culture.

Later, Tom and his brother Jimmy are forced into a fight with Jake Tobin, Buddy Hill, and two other men. Tom uses violence so extreme that Tobin suffers a severely crippled arm. Tom feels "pity but no guilt" (171) for Jake and remarks that he is free of guilt because "some things just happen, I guess. Jake made it happen. Or he let somebody else make it happen" (171–72). Tom's lack of guilt is also suggestive of trickster, a figure frequently characterized as free from guilt.

Tom's most violent and destructive act, of course, is blowing up the water tank at the mining camp. Only after seeing the mine and being told of the damage it will do to the land does Tom understand why his uncle shot at the machines. With that understanding comes an awareness of what he must do, an awareness signaled by the fact that he "memorized the site" (169) while there with forest ranger Martin Grider. He does so in order that he will know what to look for and where to plant the dynamite when he returns. What he cannot anticipate, however, are the circumstances that lead to J. D. Hill's emerging from the relative cover of one of the camp cabins just as the dynamite is detonated and "ten thousand gallons of water exploded" from the ruptured tank. Caught by the wall of water, Hill is thrown against a bulldozer with such force that his back breaks and he dies (220).

Tom's decision to dynamite the water tank and cause a wave of water to wash away the camp is foreshadowed by the figure of the seal in the novel's first chapter. In the Salish oral tradition, a seal aids a young brave adrift on a raft with a young woman and the children of the tribe. They had been placed on the raft by the elders in order to survive the rains that caused water to cover the earth; the seal helps the brave because years earlier they had become friends while the man nursed the seal to health after it had been hurt. The fact that Tom only catches a glimpse of the seal as he rides by on the bus is an early narrative indication that he will be without friends as he attempts to save, not the tribe, but the sacred tribal lands. The fact that he remembers the seal as he walks down the lane to his home and imagines that its brown eyes watched him fleeing (24) is an equally early indication that his attempts to save the land his people call home will end in his flight.

As Tom races to avoid pursuit and capture after blowing up the water tank, the narrative reminds us that "Raven dreamed up death and then mourned bitterly for his lost daughter, the trickster tricked by death" (225)—a reference to a traditional Coast Salish Raven story that June McCormick Collins sees as one of many emphasizing Raven's "short-sightedness" (212)—in order to emphasize that the trickster is the sign for Tom's social antagonism. That is not, however, all that the trickster signifies in *Wolfsong*. Owens crafts his narrative so that the audience might see both the connection between Tom and the trickster and that Tom is neither conscious of the connection nor striving to forge it. Far from diminishing the importance of trickster in *Wolfsong*, this dual aspect of the figure is indicative of the complex nature of the trickster in the text. While, as we have seen, the sign of the trickster helps us to understand Tom's actions, the signifier of the trickster, particularly the signifier "raven," helps to accentuate Tom's isolation.

It is precisely Tom's isolation that prevents him from understanding the signifier for the trickster, the raven, and what it twice attempts to communicate to him. In the first instance, "a pair of ravens settled in the top of a tattered hemlock and began to mock and scold" (136) as Tom listened to Karen tell him she has chosen to go through with marrying Buddy even though she does not love him. As the ravens bark and laugh, Tom feels "in some strange way that the message was for him if only he knew the language" (137). But he cannot understand what the ravens are trying to communicate any more than he can understand the raven that later "ratcheted a question at him" (219) as he prepared to plant the dynamite at the base of the water tank. There, too, Tom can only glance at the "disappearing bird" while "wondering what it had tried to tell him" (219).

Vizenor takes Carl Jung to task for assuming "an inert trickster, an erroneous assertion because the narrator imagines the trickster and the characters are active in a narrative discourse" ("Trickster Discourse" 205). In *Wolfsong*, however, Tom is not active in a narrative discourse with the signifiers of the trickster—Raven and Coyote. His failure to participate in discourse with the trickster is the result of his increasing isolation. Even the articulation of community offered in the sweat lodge ceremony Tom participates in relatively late in the narrative is all too soon replaced by the "enormity of his solitude" (217) as he camps in the mountains the night before he blows up the water tank. By that time his mother has followed her brother to the grave, his brother has fallen further into the trap of alcohol, and Karen is all but out of his life.

Completely isolated from community, Tom cannot understand the trickster, "a sign, a communal signification that cannot be separated or understood in isolation" (Vizenor, "Trickster Discourse" 189), when a raven turns "a black eye bright with intelligence and skepticism" (219) upon him as he prepares to dynamite the water tank. The raven looks upon Tom's actions with skepticism in part because such trickster activity has in the past brought retribution. In raven stories of the deluge from the oral traditions of the Tlingit, the Haida, and the Tsimshian-Kwakiutl, the water comes to punish Raven for his trickster activities. Similarly, Tom's trickster activism will bring unforseen consequences and, at the very least, attempts at retribution on the part of the law and the men of Forks. Moreover, like the raven, we should be skeptical not of what trickster represents as the sign for social antagonism, but of Tom's ability to assume the identity of the trickster without the necessary communal base.

Owens's understanding of the meaning of the sign of the trickster is nowhere more brilliantly conceived and carefully articulated than in his description of the raven's "black eye bright with intelligence and skepticism," for the invocation of the philosophy that absolute knowledge is not possible and that we must therefore approach with doubt the world and what is offered to us as certain and true evokes a worldview that the sign of the trickster would have us see, understand, accept, and adopt. With that adoption comes freedom and the ability to interrogate the world that is given rather than merely accepting the world as given. Via trickster, we are in a position to recognize and adjudicate our anxiety within the postmodern world of pragmatics and language games articulated by Lyotard in *Just Gaming*. In that playfully serious world we recognize that we judge based not on matters of truth or ontology, but on matters of opinion. This necessitates that we "judge case by case" (27). Such an approach prohibits the adoption of terminal creeds.

The trickster in *Wolfsong*, the sign of freedom and chance, can liberate readers as well as characters and audience, then, if we are aware of and understand both the signifier and the signified that comprise the sign. Indeed, only then will the trickster be real for us. While Tom cannot understand the raven, we can. The trickster is also real and liberating for Owens, for it enables him to summon "agonistic imagination in a comic holotrope" and transform the narrative of *Wolfsong* into "a discourse on the revolution in [the] semiotic signs" (Vizenor, "Trickster Discourse" 193) or tropes of Indian and the vanishing Native. With the sign of the trickster and trickster discourse, the narrative of *Wolfsong* moves from the definition of identity inscribed by the "cowboys and injuns" of the first chapter, through the various invocations of "Indian" which are found wanting in the text, and to Tom's weak grin at a "cowboys-and-Indians joke" while he lies wounded on the glacier and "a raven made grave pronouncements somewhere in the rocks above" (243).

The connection between *Wolfsong* and trickster discourse is most clearly articulated in a passage that conflates the issue of identity with the land, economics, and traditional trickster tales:

> [Tom had] tried to imagine what it would've been like to have been a real Indian, before the whites came and began to cut the trees—and pay Indians to cut the trees—and everything changed. In the winter, when the valley was stiff and quiet with snow, his uncle and mother told the funny stories about coyote's tricks, about fox shrinking the animals so the Indians could hunt them, about the tall, bearded hemlock that stood near Concrete on the banks of the Skagit and stole the souls of foolish Indians who came too close, and threw the souls across the river to another tree which threw them back until the person died. (37)

Both Lee Schweninger and Susan Bernardin focus on the novel's illumination of the nation's perception of the land. In Schweninger's

words, "The novel recounts a confrontation in America's war
against the environment," a war that leads to the destruction both
of that environment and of "a fundamental spiritual connection to
it" (94). Bernardin stresses that *Wolfsong* juxtaposes "Euro-American
egocentric visions of the land" with "ecocentric visions of land long
held by Native American cultures" (79). The passage from *Wolfsong*
reveals that we need a trickster discourse in order to move to an
ecocentric vision and reestablish a spiritual connection with the
natural world. What might seem like a rupture in sense, then—
the jump from the all-encompassing change brought by the transformation of the natural world into a commodity to the invocation of the traditional time of year for telling trickster tales—is
in fact a narrative strategy designed to draw our attention to
the concatenation of identity, economics, tricksters, and trickster
discourse.

We see that transforming trees into commodities transforms the
world from real to unreal. Much earlier, according to the Coast
Salish, the culture hero *dukʷibəɬ*, in order to help the people, had
transformed the world from a place without mountains, where the
rivers ran in different courses and where some animals were the
same size as humans and acted the same way, into its present
shape and nature. The transformation of the world by the
Euroamericans, however, helps neither the people nor the world.
"Everything became crazy" (34), Jim Joseph announces, when we
stopped respecting the natural world and started destroying the
forest for profit. Owens makes clear the ramifications of hewing to
this perception of the environment with the other story he includes
in the brief passage. Those foolish enough to come too close to the
hemlock tree—those unable or unwilling to see the world correctly
and respect it accordingly—will die. Understanding this enables
us to resolve the blurred reflection of the Peterbilt tractor and
trailer and recognize how it and what it represents are killing the
natural world and us.

The trickster uncovers "distinctions and ironies" (Vizenor, "Trickster Discourse" 192), and the trickster discourse of *Wolfsong*, signaled

by Raven, early on discloses the irony in what Jimmy Joseph had told Tom to do about the heritage and tradition they share:

> He'd tried to tell his brother about *staka'yu* once when they'd sat on a windfall fishing for dolly varden trout, but Jimmy had laughed and said, "Forget that old crap. That stuff's for old men and crazy longhairs. You forget about wolf spirits and all those other things—Knife Man and Cedar Man and Old Man Raven and all that crap—and learn about chainsaws and carburetors. That ghost stuff is for movies." Jimmy had spit a wad of Redman chewing tobacco into the stream and grimaced. For a week he'd been trying to learn to chew, and he'd felt sick all week. (35)

Even as a boy, Jimmy has accepted the Euroamerican vision of progress and the future symbolized by chainsaws and carburetors, but Owens includes the sign of the trickster in Jimmy's admonition to his brother so that we might correctly read the passage as trickster discourse. The trickster frees us so we can see that what Jimmy champions both destroys the natural world and makes him sick: chainsaws and men perversely transform trees into timber by cutting them down for profit, carburetors pollute the air, and the juice of the chewing tobacco is poison. The irony of tobacco sickening Jimmy is deliciously complex, for the chewing tobacco making the Native American sick is at once symbolic of how what Uncle Jim called the now-crazy modern world sickens the Native and, subtly, of how acquiescing to the image of the Indian constructed by the whites, an image signified in the passage by "Redman," will make the Native American sick as well. Twice in the passage Jimmy calls their tradition, their heritage, their stories, crap; the irony is that he is unconsciously correct. The stories and the traditions are indeed crap: the remainder or excess that are Native American identities which the dominant culture cannot synthesize or handle and must therefore label excrement, and the "waste" material that is most valuable for anyone trying to make sense of the signs of Indian and the vanishing Native.

Both signs are fundamental to Tom's struggle to determine his identity. The struggle with what it means to be an Indian is bound up in his struggle to understand his connection with the father he never knew and with his Uncle Jim. Returning from the ancestral graveyard after burying his uncle, Tom recalls how when thinking of his father he sometimes felt as though "he were descended from some madman's dream." In that dream, "Indians rode spotted horses over golden plains after buffalo. They lived in the light of the sun, where nothing was hidden and earth rose up to sky, in tipis, not in cedar-slab houses crouched in the bowels of a rainforest. They sat horseback against the infinite horizon, barechested and challenging their disinheritors" (54–55). What Tom sees is the stereotypical image of the Indian as plains warrior that the dominant culture has been quick to hold up as representative of all Native Americans. Those warriors, Tom realizes, were after all "the Indians they studied in school" (55). How, he wonders, "could the remote, disturbing figure [of his father photographed] in hat and overcoat be part of that? He was unreal, as were all of them" (55).

A stereotype simplifies and violates, Bhabha points out, because it is a fixed and fixated image "denying the play of difference" (*Location* 75) from and within which identity and selfhood are constructed and emerge. Anxious over the possibility of such an emergence, those who create and perpetuate the stereotype transform the image into a fetish in order to foreclose difference and in the process allay their worries. Raven, the sign of the trickster, appears in the next paragraph to "scold" both characters and reader for falling into the trap of accepting the stylized, one-dimensional, monologic sign of Indian. The trickster and trickster discourse demand that we, like Tom, the narrator, and the author, free ourselves from that trap and interrogate the sign. Doing so, we come to share Tom's realization that "books and movies seldom showed Indians who looked like the Salish people of these mountains. Short, dark people dressed in woven cedar bark weren't as exciting as Sioux warriors in eagle-feather headdresses on horseback, the sun always setting behind them" (83).

As we have seen, the dominant culture makes clear with words and pictures that it wants nothing less than to have the sun set on the Native American once and for all. Failing that, it wants to define the light with and in which the Natives and their future are seen. Throughout the narrative, however, Owens transforms the trope or figure of Indian created by the dominant culture by disclosing the inaccuracies perpetuated by the stereotype. As a point of contact between peoples and cultures, between Euroamerica and Native America, the stereotype captured in the word "Indian" is dangerous because it enables one to hold to an image of the Native American that is at best an oversimplification and at worst a damning caricature. In either case, it denies anxiety, destinies, and destinations other than those fixed by the dominant culture. *Wolfsong* makes clear that understanding that "Indian" is a construct, a sign, created by whites to suit their own ends is only part of the struggle; one must also replace the stereotype with an articulation that is accurate.

The difficulty is knowing what articulates Native identity. Jimmy tells Tom: "Our uncle wasn't thinking straight. . . . He was too old and stuck in ways you and me can't even understand. . . . He didn't understand that Indian don't matter no more. What matters is that we're people and we have to live here, with other people like J.D. and all the rest. Hell, I don't even know what Indian means, and neither do you" (112). Unlike Jimmy, Tom is willing to run the risk of discovering what Indian means. Karen tells Tom that he is "getting to be real serious. . . . Like the Indians they always show in those old movies" (104), but Tom realizes that he cannot look to that source or others like it for help in discovering what it means to be Stehemish. Nor can he look to those who have romantic ideas of what it means to be an Indian, in no small measure because those romantic ideas are the product of that same appropriation and transformation of the Native Americans by the invading Europeans. Rather, Tom tells her, "You don't have to be a full-blood to be Indian. It just matters how you feel, what you think. Your dreams" (104). One's feelings, what one thinks, one's dreams—these

come from the traditions and stories that one's community keeps
alive in and through oral transmission.[6]

These questions that permeate the text—what the sign "Indian"
means and what it means to be Stehemish—take on increased
urgency because those people have all but vanished from the valleys
and mountains they call home. Early in the narrative we learn that
Bob McBride, the one-eighth Flathead from Montana with pale
skin and green eyes who is Tom's college roommate, liked to tell
him that "We're related, man. You Stehemish folks are Salish, too.
We're bros, man," but Tom had "trouble thinking of himself and
McBride as bros." Rather, Tom thinks, "The only bro he knew was
large and dark and waited for him upriver" (18). Jimmy waits
upriver to tell Tom that there is nothing for him in the dying valley
and that he is better off going "back to the land of opportunity"
(38). He also asks Tom, "You stop to think about how many of our
people are left around here? You ever look around? They're gone,
Tom. The whole goddamn tribe" (120). Jimmy only says aloud what
Tom had first begun to recognize when he went to the ancestral
graveyard for his uncle's rite of interment; there he thinks that "the
tribes and clans had melted like July snow, with people drifting
away to lumber camps and mills and the slums of Seattle, dying on
the skid road that became skidrow" (51). Tellingly, the movement
is from the natural world to the urban; the road used to help transform the felled trees into board lumber becomes literally and figuratively the thoroughfare on which far too many of the Natives of
the Pacific Northwest travel to their demise. Tom will put into words
the reality of his isolation when McBride comes to visit and, as he
leaves, asks him, "Where's all your people? Where's your tribe,
man, your family?" "Gone," Tom replies, "My aunt's in Rockport,
but that's about all. They're just gone" (195).

What Owens offers us in *Wolfsong*, in short, is the trope of the
vanishing Native tribe. The idea of the vanishing Native has been
stated with such frequency in North America that one cannot help
but begin to realize that it is the phrasing of an ideal created and
then clung to by the dominant culture. Consider, for instance, the

conclusion of Franz Boas's 1889 article on the tribes of the West
Coast of Canada:

> We find here very gifted people fighting against the penetra-
> tion by the Europeans under comparatively favorable condi-
> tions. Their ethnographic characteristics will in a very short
> time fall victim to the influence of the Europeans. The sooner
> these aborigines adapt themselves to the changed conditions
> the better it will be for them in their competition with the
> white man. One can already now predict that the Kwakiutl,
> who have so completely shut themselves off from the Euro-
> peans, are heading for their extinction. Certain Indian tribes
> have already become indispensable on the labor market, and
> without them the Province would suffer a great economic
> damage. If we can succeed in improving their hygienics and
> thus lower their ruinous child mortality, and if the endeavors
> of the Canadian government can be successful in making
> independent producers out of them, we can hope to avoid
> the sad spectacle of the complete destruction of those highly
> gifted tribes. (qtd. in Rohner 13)

Boas's conclusion focuses on both the romantic spectacle of the
vanishing Native and the potential economic identity of the Indian
that he sees as their salvation from destruction. In either case, Boas
contends that the future of the Natives of the Pacific Northwest
will be marked by transformation and, at the very least, a change
in identity.

Boas's conclusion is written in what Vizenor would term the tragic
or hypotragic mode; such modes are "inventions and impositions
that attend the 'discoverers' and translators of tribal narratives"
("Postmodern Introduction" 9). He continues: "The notion of the
'vanishing tribe' is a lonesome nuisance, to cite one hypotragic
intrusion that reveals racism and the contradictions in humanism
and historical determinism" (9–10). Trickster, however, "unties the
hypotragedies imposed on tribal narratives" (11) because the trickster is a chance which in *Wolfsong* articulates distinctions and

ironies and asks that we engage in a discourse on the nature and efficacy of signs that are fundamental to an articulation of identity.

Approximately one hundred years after Boas identified the Natives of the Pacific Northwest, the trickster discourse that is *Wolfsong* makes clear that the future of the Natives and their identity are all too easily bound up in economics. Tom tries to "imagine what it would've been like to have been a real Indian" (37), but he is unable to do so because the commodification of the wilderness fundamentally transformed both it and the Native Americans. That transformation, the narrative makes clear, occurred "when the first two-man crosscut took a wedge out of the first cedar to fall *for money* in the valley" (124, emphasis added). Jimmy, whose alcoholism serves to accentuate the hypotragic mode that the narrative is bent on undercutting with trickster discourse, has acquiesced to the change. He accepts the argument that the mine will not be so bad and looks forward to the prospect of working there even as he drinks himself into an alcoholic stupor that has nothing to do with the hypotragic genetic predisposition to alcoholism and everything to do with the harsh reality of life in the valley. J. D. Hill, the white man instrumental in selling the idea of the mine to the people of Forks, offers Tom what his brother hopes to get: a job, and with it a future in the valley. Hill's offer is presented in a fashion that highlights the text's concern with identity and what it means to be an Indian in contemporary America: "A guy like you that's Indian could be invaluable for an operation like this. You could symbolize the future for Indian people, progress" (67). Unwilling to have his identity determined by economics and to have that identity stand as symbolic of the dubious Euroamerican vision of linear "progress," Tom can only think, "A hundred years ago I would have known who I was" (197).

In a final effort to find out who he is, Tom attempts a vision quest that is bound up with his return trip to destroy the mine. He fasts on his way up the mountain and intends to rub his naked body with the branches of the hemlock tree after bathing in order that after three days, in the words he remembers from his uncle,

"When you are pure, maybe a spirit will find you and you will be a singer, a man with power" (217). He continues the ritual even as he is being pursued by the posse from Forks. The vision quest is successful, but Tom neither finds nor is found by the spirit of the trickster. Rather, the raven's final appearance in the text serves to show us that Tom is ready to assume his identity. Much earlier, Jim Joseph had responded with humor to Leroy Brant's effort to confer identity, repeating with a chuckle "It ain't cowboys and injuns" (4) as he disappeared into the forest above the Stehemish drainage. Similarly, while near the summit of Dakobed, Tom "grinned weakly at the cowboys-and-Indians joke" that he had only received a "flesh-wound" because he knows by that point in the narrative that the joke brings to light and makes light of the sign of Indian created and perpetuated by the dominant culture.[7] That identity cannot be his, and Tom "listened as a raven made grave pronouncements" (243) signifying that he is ready to complete his transformation. The use of "grave" is illuminating, for the word indicates the seriousness with which we should take both the sign of Indian and the trickster discourse that interrogates and makes light of it. Understood for its meanings as a noun and a verb as well as an adjective, "grave" also indicates that the bergschrund is the burial place of who Tom was before he completed his quest for identity, that the narrative is constructed to lay to rest the stereotypical sign of Indian, and that Owens appropriates written discourse to grave the importance of oral stories and tradition so that his audience might be transformed as well.

While the narrative of *Wolfsong* is crafted so that the audience might see the connection between Tom and the trickster, it is also crafted so that we see that Tom is neither conscious of the connection nor striving to forge it. Tom does not appropriate trickster; Owens does. Given that trickster "is real in those who imagine the narrative" (Vizenor, "Trickster Discourse" 190), the humorous figure is real for the reader imagining the narrative that is *Wolfsong* even if it is not "real" for Tom. In *Wolfsong*, trickster and trickster discourse help to untie a text that might otherwise be wrongly read as the hypotragedy of the vanishing Stehemish tribe and enable the reader to see the irony with which the narrative offers both the stereotype of Indian and the romanticized vanishing Native. Trickster is also the sign that articulates for the reader, the author, and the narrator the importance of the "social antagonism and aesthetic activism" (Vizenor, "Trickster Discourse" 192) in and of the text.

Owens contextualizes the activism in and of the text not with the contemporary conflict between the timber industry and those working to save the old-growth habitat of the spotted owl, but with that between the timber industry, workers, and organized labor in the mid- to late 1910s. That struggle pitted timber interests and mill owners in Everett, Washington, against workers organized by the Industrial Workers of the World (IWW). By 1916 Everett had recovered from the effects of depressed shingles and lumber markets and was booming thanks to the wartime demand for cedar being cut from the northern Cascades slopes and made, for the most part, into shingles in the town mills. The loggers and millworkers were not sharing in the prosperity, however, and management had little interest in changing the status quo. The shingle workers' efforts to make an eight-hour workday the norm had come to naught in 1914, and their wages had been cut in 1916 even as the demand for shingles increased and prices rose. While the American Federation of Labor, with whom the shingle weavers were affiliated, did not respond to the workers' call for help in 1916, the IWW did. The Wobblies recognized management's efforts to squelch opposition protest as an infringement on the workers' constitutional right to freedom of speech. According to at least some accounts, Wobblies and workers periodically resorted to subterfuge, sabotage, and violence during the summer and fall of 1916 and into 1917 in an effort to get management to agree to labor's demands. More importantly, they also attempted to rally and picket in Everett. Those efforts culminated on November 5, 1916, when the *Verona*, a ship carrying IWW organizers and workers in support of the shingle weavers' right to protest publicly, was fired upon by a militia deputized by Sheriff Donald McRae as it tied up at the Everett docks. The cross fire claimed the lives of five workers and two vigilantes. No one is certain how many other workers drowned when they took to the water to avoid the barrage.[8]

As the IWW recognized, the workers in and around Everett were being silenced and erased by those in power. To this extent, at least, they have something in common with Native Americans. Owens highlights the commonality by stressing the Scandinavian nationalities of the loggers Jim Joseph meets rather than any U.S. citizenry they might have had, referring to them as "the Swedes and Norwegians and Danes who looked upon Indians as strange creatures" (139), and by having his narrator remark upon their inability to speak English. Without the opportunity to raise a voice— indeed, frequently without a language with which to protest—the "men wear out and break down" (139) in the forests and mills, becoming, as Owens's description makes clear, nothing more than machines run by management until they run down and are replaced. However, Owens's rendering of the woodsmen's response to losing their voice indicates both a difference between their activism and his and the flawed thinking behind what they do.

Jim Joseph is told the story of the Everett massacre by Wobblies he meets at their campfires deep in the forest after he had "learned to spook through the woods" (140) and avoid the strike- and union breakers who had come to the valley to crush labor. After the massacre the woods are home to bitter and increasingly desperate men. Sabotage and subterfuge had not brought the desired results. IWW and socialist leaders had been arrested, tried, and jailed under the Espionage Act that winter. Federal officials had created the Loyal Legion of Loggers and Lumbermen and stipulated that all workers must swear to support the war effort "against our common enemies" (Clark 229). Organized protest and the airing of issues had been met with beatings, bullets, and death. In short, overt militancy and direct public confrontation had failed. If Everett was the test case for organized labor in the Pacific Northwest in 1916–17, then management's victory rang out with the volleys fired into the men topside on the *Verona* and the lack of criminal charges brought against the murderers of the workers killed in the massacre. The men around the campfires tell young Jim Joseph of their last-ditch plan to burn the valley. Just as the story of the Everett massacre had shown Joseph that whites were capable of killing anyone, not just Indians, the plan shows him that "these good, desperate men were the enemy, too . . . men who would destroy their mother earth" (140). Susan Bernardin points out that these "good, desperate men" are linked to the workers of Forks as well, for their contemporary counterparts are vulnerable to changing economic conditions and management, are aware of ever-diminishing possibilities for work, and are willing to destroy the land by allowing the mine to go in.[9] The former, though, act in an effort to bring about change.

Like the IWW, Owens wants to bring about change. However, he cannot follow the example set by the Wobblies and their supporters in 1916–17. It is wrongheaded and shortsighted; it will not work. Nor is Jim Joseph's activism, finally, a model to emulate. While it is born of an awareness of humankind's relation to and place in the natural world, the act itself is of at best limited effectiveness. And yet some sort of activism is necessary. Owens's narrative makes this clear from its opening when Joseph communicates with the spirit world. As a medium and conduit between worlds (Amoss 76), Joseph is attempting to defend both the spirit world and the physical world. Owens would do the same.

Like other Native Americans, Owens must first find his voice. Such an act is as much an exercise in recovery as it is discovery. Owens emphasizes the importance of finding or healing a voice in the preface to *Mixedblood Messages*. There he offers the story of how as a boy he and his friend Chuck would take crows for pets. Chuck cut the tongues of his crows in an effort to have them speak human words. Wanting to have a conversation with the crows in his language, Chuck ends up silencing his pets. Owens continued to think about those birds over the years, and he has come to realize that his friend's efforts parallel the dominant culture with respect to Native people. "Desperate to give his words to the 'other,' so that the whole world will ultimately give back the reflected self, the colonizer performs his surgery" (*Mixedblood Messages* xii) and the people lose their voice. Such was Jim Joseph's experience at the Indian government school where those in power had "cut out the tongues of Indians, sewing in different tongues while the children slept" (*Wolfsong* 5). This need not be the people's fate, however, nor Owens's, for "rather than merely reflecting back to him the master's own voice [and story] we can, in an oft-quoted phrase, learn to make it bear the burden of our own experience" (*Mixedblood Messages* xiii). In order to get his voice back, then, and bring absence into presence in the name of change, Owens turns to writing. This move is not without dangers, of course, and Owens must, to use his own phrasing in another context, "take apart" writing in order to "take a part" (*Other Destinies* 5) in the efforts to voice what has been silenced.

It makes sense, then, that Owens's novel is concerned with and over its own becoming. The latter, in particular, is what sets contemporary Native American fiction apart from its equally postmodern counterparts created by writers in the dominant culture. The dilemma for Owens, a dilemma shared by other Native American authors, is how to transform and transport into writing what is vital from and of the oral tradition, generally and particularly, without perverting it and losing its vitality. Native writers must be concerned about the potentially harmful transformation that results when they transport stories from the oral tradition into the written tradition of the white man; it is that tradition, after all, that has been used throughout the history of Native-white relations to identify the Native American as Other, as outsider, as inferior. It is that tradition which has gravened the sign of Indian that *Wolfsong* interrogates and transforms.

It is the narrative's articulation of the appropriation of written discourse that makes *Wolfsong*, finally, a metafictive text. Owens reveals the trickery at the heart of writing even as he appropriates written discourse. In reply to his nephew's question of why logging "boots were called 'corks' but spelled 'caulks,'" Jim Joseph "had just laughed and said, 'Either these white people are all the time tricking language or their language is always tricking them'"

(149). The passage discloses the difference between what is written and what is spoken and articulates Owens's relationship to written language. Refusing to be tricked by written language, refusing to be blind to the fundamental difference between what is dead on the page and what is alive in and through utterance and oral tradition, Owens nevertheless tricks written language by crafting a narrative that uses the sign of the trickster to revitalize words, transform the text into trickster discourse, and establish a community of interlocutors capable of seeing both the nature of written language and the ends to which Owens appropriates it.

Owens stands in tacit juxtaposition to both Dan Kellar, the copper company representative who uses words to convince the people of Forks that the mine will be good for them, and "the famous Indian poet" spoken of by Aaron Medicine "who's always writing about Raven" without knowing "the difference between a raven and a crow" (193). Owens knows Raven, knows what he is writing about and how best to write about it so that the essence of the trickster is unperverted and his text can resist the metamorphosis insisted upon by the dominant culture even as his narrative articulates Tom Joseph's resistance to the identity the dominant culture would confer upon him.

Trickster is a trope to action, and it is by taking action that Tom is able to achieve a transformation of self. One might be tempted to point to the fact that the coyotes are silenced by the wolf's howl at the close of the novel as evidence suggesting that the trickster is finally of limited usefulness. Such a reading, however, succumbs to the trap of trying to fully fix the figure of the trickster. Vizenor again sets us on the right track when he writes that the trickster is "a semiotic sign for 'social antagonism' and 'aesthetic activism' in postmodern criticism and the avant-garde, *but not 'presence' or the ideal cultural completion in narratives*" ("Trickster Discourse" 192, emphasis added). While Tom is trickster-like and while his militant, socially antagonistic actions are best understood in the light of the trickster, to have Tom become trickster—identifying himself finally and fully with the trickster rather than having the discourse of *Wolfsong* identify him with the trickster while he identifies himself with the wolf spirit willed to him by his uncle—would be to confer a damning presence upon the trickster and incorrectly offer it as the ideal cultural completion in the narrative.

Wolfsong, rather, offers us the trickster as "a semiotic sign in a third-person narrative, [which] is never tragic or hypotragic, never the whole truth or even part truth" (Vizenor, "Postmodern Introduction" 11), and in so doing Owens's text becomes a model of social antagonism and aesthetic activism as the trickster and trickster discourse enable us to interrogate what has come down to us as the truth. Trickster unfixes things, overturns terminal creeds, destabilizes referents, and "attempts to destroy hypocrisy and delusion and bring about self-knowledge" (Owens, *Other Destinies* 216). In the narrative of *Wolfsong*, the trickster "summons agonistic imagination (Vizenor, "Trickster Discourse" 193) and asks that the readers join with Tom, the narrator, and Owens in seeing the tropes of Indian and the vanishing Native not as the cultural givens determined by those in power but as figures to be interrogated so that we might understand both why they exist and how they are meaningful. It is for those reasons, finally, that the trickster, the trope to action, is most valuable, for the sign is what enables the text to become both a model of and an instrument for a necessary activism more insidious, even, than overt militancy.

Located "literally at the end of the road, and poised on the edge of the continent," in Susan Bernardin's words, "Forks . . . signifies the geographical terminus of America's westering pattern of settlement and ensuing resource depletion" (80). It shares this fact with its namesake. The real Forks, Washington, was a logging center on the Olympic Peninsula in the first half of the twentieth century. In redrawing the map in *Wolfsong* by making Forks his own, as we have seen, Owens appropriates the act of removal and displacement that the dominant culture has used to help determine the Indian. His act helps to loosen those determinations by transforming Forks into the fictional representation of the frontier as he reformulates that trope in his recently published criticism and theory. His Forks

is the place where civilization and the wilderness meet. It is a
"trickster-like, shimmering zone of multifaceted contact . . . always
unstable, multidirectional, hybridized, characterized by heteroglossia, and indeterminate" ("The Song Is Very Short" 59). As such,
it is also a metaphorization of Owens's literary text. The indeterminacy is liberating, affording Owens the freedom to interrogate
with and in *Wolfsong* the end point and "achievement" of America
and the costs to Euroamericans, the natural world, and—especially
—Native Americans. In Owens's eyes the landscape of the northern
Cascades is the protagonist of his novel, and I think this is so
because he recognizes that both civilization and wilderness are
constructs of the dominant culture and that a landscape incorporating the figure of the Indian is a metaphor for national identity
emphasizing "the question of social visibility [and] the power of
the eye to naturalize the rhetoric of national affiliation and its forms
of collective expression" (Bhabha, *Location* 143).

Bhabha holds that "national time becomes concrete and visible
in the chronotope of the local, particular, graphic, from beginning
to end" (*Location* 143). Such is the case with the Loggers Memorial
in the "real" Forks. The eleven-foot statue of a logger with his ax
atop a three-foot-high tree stump bears a plaque on the blade that
reads: "In tribute to those in the timber industry who perished
providing the materials for the backbone of America's greatness.
And in gratitude to those working there now." *Wolfsong* denies
such a totalizing move, just as it denies the apocalyptic rendering
of the Indian captured in the photos of Tom Joseph's father and
uncle, opting instead to reopen the narrative of the Nation and the
People in, but not on, the nation's own terms: civilization, wilderness, Indian. As such, "The nation's totality is confronted with, and
crossed by [emphasis added], a supplementary movement in *writing*"
(Bhabha, *Location* 154) that adds to the national narrative without
adding up to the image of the Nation and its People held by the
dominant culture. Thus, *Wolfsong* is one of those writings that are
"pluses that compensate for a minus in origin" (Gasché 211), and
in the process it counters the nation's tendency to "celebrate the

monumentality of historicist memory, the sociological solidity or totality of society, or the homogeneity of cultural experience" (Bhabha, *Location* 157).

Wolfsong participates in what Owens calls the Native Americans' "unending battle to affirm their own identities, to resist the metamorphoses insisted upon by European intruders" (*Other Destinies* 21), whether those transformations be to figures of Otherness, assimilation, or apocalypse. In denying the transformation of the many into one, indeed in revealing what such a transformation means for Native Americans, Owens opens a space in which to inscribe the quest for identity that he sees as fundamental in Native American novels (*Other Destinies* 20). That space is a liminal one in both textual and narrative terms. Just as the liminal is the other space and time within which individual Salish receive power, song, and identity; just as the liminality of Tom Joseph's final vision quest brings together activism and identity; so too does the liminality of the literary text and discourse enable Owens to articulate identity for himself and his characters while at the same time actively critiquing the dominant culture. Moreover, because Owens's own quest to articulate an identity is at issue in *Wolfsong*, we can imagine that he fictionalizes a tribe in order to create a minority or other discourse with and from which he then can explore mixedblood Choctaw and mixedblood Cherokee identity in his later novels. Intertwined with those explorations of individual identity in The *Sharpest Sight* and *Bone Game* are Owens's references to and interrogations of the addresses of the nation that work in support of the metamorphoses insisted on by the dominant culture: canonical American literature and history.

DISCERNING CONNECTIONS AND REVISING THE MASTER NARRATIVE IN *THE SHARPEST SIGHT*

The novels following *Wolfsong* look squarely at the difficulties of learning and articulating mixedblood identity within and against the ideologically driven constructs and definitions created and perpetuated by what Anishinaabe writer Jim Northrup has called the "manifest destiny dominant society" (105).[1] Consider *The Sharpest Sight* (1992), winner of the PEN Oakland Josephine Miles Award and named one of the top fifteen novels of the past fifteen years by the *Bloomsbury Review*. The work is an intricately crafted murder mystery that tells the stories of Vietnam veteran Attis McCurtain, the murder victim; Cole and Hoey McCurtain, Attis's brother and father; Luther and Onatima, Mississippi Choctaw to whom Cole goes for help; Dan and Helen Nemi, whose oldest daughter, Jenna, was killed by Attis after his return from Vietnam; Diana Nemi, who kills Attis to avenge her sister's death; Mundo Morales, a mestizo deputy sheriff and friend of the McCurtains'; various other inhabitants of Amarga, California; and Lee Scott, an FBI agent sent to Amarga to deal with Attis's disappearance from the state mental hospital. As several of these characters work to discover the location of Attis's body and who murdered him, the text explores issues of death and identity, bringing us, as it were, back into view of the distorted death's head of *The Ambassadors*. Owens's novel also reveals the negative and positive roles literature has played and can play in articulating a sense of self.

As is the case in *Wolfsong*, there are two telling photographs in *The Sharpest Sight*. The first, of Attis and Cole McCurtain's mother, serves to remind the reader early on of difference and loss. Cole looks at the photo of a beautiful young woman and contrasts it with the image he has of his mother. The two are incongruous, for the picture he carries in his mind is that of a woman always tired. Thus, while Cole recognizes the nostalgic trace of the photograph framed and displayed on the dining room wall, he is not seduced by it. Instead, he reflects on how it is that his mother could have grown to be so tired and wonders if it had had to do with his father's efforts to create himself from both an assortment of books on the Choctaw and manufactured memories, efforts that reveal "it was plain he was leaving the rest of them behind" (*Sharpest Sight* 15). Photo and reflection come together here to indicate a concern for characters, text, and reader: how the past might become part of a living present such that the former is not romanticized and the latter is not subject to reification. It is fitting that Cole's perspective shapes the matrix here, for it is through the articulation of his developing mixedblood identity, especially, that Owens addresses it.

The second photograph presents Mundo Morales and the reader with graphic evidence of the vehicle whereby questions of past and present, and the relation between the two, are phrased in the text. While scanning the river for signs of Attis's body, Mundo imagines what is happening to the corpse of his friend, treated as just another piece of flotsam by the Salinas, and recalls a photo he had seen of a body pulled from an Alaskan river, silt packed into mouth, ears, and eyes. The photo of a corpse emphasizes that it is how we see and deal with the dead—indeed, how we see and deal with death— that *The Sharpest Sight* is bent on interrogating. Photography depends on light, of course, whether naturally occurring or artificially created, and given that fact, the photo of the corpse is thus also part of the narrative's emphasis on the relationship between sources of illumination and what we see and do not see.

The *Sharpest Sight* opens on an illuminating scene:

The rain came toward the headlights in long, curving lines. Mundo flipped the switch on the spotlight to let the beam sweep across the edge of the road. Metal posts danced in and out of the light, the thick brush reaching between strands of wire toward the car and then leaping away. Rain caught the light in racing lines along the barbed wire.

He turned the spotlight off and let the car pick up speed down the side canyon. (3)

Boundaries and their transgression are revealed, to be sure, and this is of no small importance in the novel, as it is throughout Owens's fiction and criticism. Still, what the novel's first paragraph highlights is not so much what the different beams catch as the fact that objects are caught in them at all. Fence posts dance into and out of sight as the spotlight beam alternately catches and releases them. Underbrush comes alive thanks to the source of illumination, as the beam reveals branches reaching toward the car and then leaping away as the beam sweeps past them. It is fitting that Mundo turns the spotlight off in the first line of the novel's second paragraph, because we have seen all we need to in order to see what is at issue.

While the spotlight is in a prominent position at the opening and throughout the first chapter in order to emphasize the text's concern with sight and what one needs to see, it being the spotlight's beam that captures Attis's body in the river for Mundo after all (6), the penetrating beam of the patrol car's spot also brings into relief the relationship between sight, illumination, surveillance, and authority that Foucault sees operating in the modern Western world. The reader has no idea what Mundo is looking for when he turns the spotlight on and directs its beam past the road's edge. The reason he later gives to Deputy Sheriff Angel Turkus, that he was "looking for poachers" (34), does not wash, and Owens makes sure that we know it; Mundo tells Hoey McCurtain just prior to talking with Turkus that he "didn't think anybody poached deer in this kind of rain" (33). Nor does the reader know whether Mundo is satisfied with what he sees. However, what the reader does learn, and what is important, is that Mundo has the power to direct the beam of surveillance where and when he sees fit. This is nothing less than the power of the state, of course, one that attempts to captivate every subject with the knowledge that, without warning, anyone can be caught in the light of the authorities. With the opening scene, then, Owens throws into relief the impulse that works to drive the nation and determine its subjects.

Of equal importance in this opening scene, although the reader is not yet in a position to see it, is that the spotlight is controlled, not simply by a person of color, but by a mixedblood who is himself unsure of his mixedblood identity. As such the scene models the search for mixedblood identity Cole and, to a lesser extent, Hoey and Mundo conduct throughout the course of the narrative—a search complicated by the fact that the dominant culture's source of illumination, as we have seen in *Wolfsong*, keeps the Native, mixedblood or no, invisible. The narrative reiterates this when FBI agent Lee Scott tells Cole late in the text that he was sent to Amarga to make sure that Attis remained invisible (254). Moreover, the scene metaphorizes Owens's relationship to writing and the literary text as he uses the dominant culture's instrument of authority to illumi- nate and reveal that which has been concealed. Here, too, Bhabha is instructive, reminding us both of the relationship between the quality of light and social visibility (*Location* 143) and of the possi- bility of a minority or other discourse revealing that relationship and the ideology driving it. In order for such a discourse to come into presence, an alternative, interstitial time and space must be recognized or constructed. If for Owens the mixedblood embodies the liminal frontier, and if the literary text is itself liminal, then the first chapter of *The Sharpest Sight* accentuates the latter so that the liberating possibilities of the former might be plumbed.

The narrative highlights the other time and space of the literary text by repeating Mundo's act of acceleration after turning through an intersection: "He swung the car left and accelerated toward the bridge, watching the rain curve in more sudden threads now as if he had entered the luminous web of a spider. When he pushed the gas pedal, the tires spun and the car fishtailed onto the bridge, and he stared in amazement at the silver rain woven about the car" (4). Chronological sequence disappears with the repetition and is replaced by the other time of fiction. At the same time, the bridge stands as analogous to the other space of fiction and, more specifically, of a minority discourse. The narrative accentuates this with its next line: "And then he stabbed his boot down on the brake, and the tires locked, and the car slid toward the great cat that was there, in the middle of the bridge, crouched as if it would spring" (4). The clause "in the middle of the bridge" occupies an interstitial position in the sentence, mirroring the interstitial nature of both the bridge and the literary text. Situated in that space and time, literally and figuratively bringing both the vehicle of the state and the mixedblood to a skidding halt, is *nalusachito*, or soul-eater, the figure connected to (an)other way of seeing and knowing one's identity, death, and the world. The "new story" (7) Luther dreams and Owens articulates depends on this other way of seeing.

The importance of identity to Owens's new story is highlighted early in the text when we first meet Cole McCurtain and the combat fatigue jacket Attis had sent home to him from Vietnam is described:

"I shall fear no evil, for I am. . . ." That was on the back of the jacket, too. "I am a half-breed, like my father," he thought as he looked down the bank for signs of [their dog] Zeke. "Actually," he said aloud to the river, pronouncing his words precisely, "I am a three-eighths breed, since my mother is a quarter Cherokee like just about everybody who ever lived in Oklahoma." He gestured toward a cottonwood with the rifle. "Well, you see, the fact is she's really three-eighths Cherokee, since her mother was three-quarters and born in the Nation and had my mother when she was thirteen and not even five feet tall. So I guess that makes me a seven-sixteenths-breed— almost a half-breed like my father. Let's say I'm nearly a half-breed, whatever that means. Hoey McCurtain knows, but

what I know from books in school and those old TV movies
is that a half-breed can't be trusted, is a killer, a betrayer, a
breed." He smiled as he finished the speech; it had become a
litany, something he told himself frequently almost like a
ceremony, always the same words and rhythm. ". . . the
meanest motherfucker in the valley." He wore the jacket when
he hunted the river, and he recited his identity when he wore
the jacket. "I shall fear no evil," he thought, "for I am." (10–11)

The narrative accentuates identity with the repetition of "I am" as
it moves from Attis's revision of Psalm 23 to Cole's meditation on
blood and who he is. The subject of that meditation is also the
subject of the opening concern of Owens's *Other Destinies*. In that
text Owens begins by asking, "What is an Indian? Must one be
one-sixteenth Osage, one-eighth Cherokee, one-quarter Blackfoot,
or full-blood Sioux to be Indian?" (3). While Tom Joseph's weak
grin at the end of *Wolfsong* indicates that he is ready to complete his
vision quest and assume his identity, Cole's smile as he concludes
his speech early in *The Sharpest Sight* indicates that he is both well
aware of the dominant culture's use of blood quantum to fix Indian
identity and able to make light of it.

The "litany . . . he told himself frequently almost like a ceremony" (10) announces the primary concern of *The Sharpest Sight*—
for Cole, for Owens, and for us—even as it and the smile indicate
what Cole must turn away from and toward if he is to learn and
understand his identity. That is, by fracturing a part of one of the
foundational narratives of the dominant culture, a narrative itself
concerned with identity, the ritual response of the litany suggests
that Cole must turn from that and other narratives of the dominant
culture if he is to know himself. In addition, Attis's revision of
Psalm 23 suggests that Cole has to revise the dominant culture's
narrative of blood and its relationship to identity if he is to
succeed in moving from practicing something *like* a ceremony to
something that *is* a ceremony connected with and informing who
he is. That revision necessitates a return to the place of his birth,

the Yazoo River country of Mississippi, in order that he might then return to California, successfully hunt the river for Attis's body, and articulate his identity in the process of searching and finding it.

The path to that articulation is difficult both to see and to travel, as Owens makes clear with his description of the barely discernible trails Cole must use to get to Uncle Luther's cabin and, once there, to navigate the swamp. Indeed, the description of what Cole does not immediately recognize as a trail as he moves through the darkness to the bank of the Yazoo River is followed by his thinking "back along the route that had brought him at last into the middle of a river" (61) flowing through the heart of his ancestral homeland. He and the reader recognize by this time that that route traces a tortured path through the labyrinth of mixedblood identity. Cole remembers Attis once saying to him "It's hard to tell who you are in this family" (11) because of his lighter skin and green eyes, and early in the text he says to his father "I'm not an Indian. I'm mostly white" (21). Hoey responds with a telling corrective, "That don't matter. You're a mixed-blood and that's Indian. It's what you think you are that matters" (21), but Cole is not disposed to hear it because he thinks of his father as "a California Choctaw living in a made-up world who was busy creating himself out of books and made-up memories so that it was plain he was leaving the rest of them behind" (15). It is only later, when they are driving through the hills to the coast highway on their way to the airport to catch Cole's flight to Mississippi, that Hoey reveals how problematic that creation is, how difficult it is to make the past a part of a lived present and thus think yourself into an identity; he tells his son, "You know, I guess I don't understand how to be Indian anymore" (56). He says that, like Tom Joseph, "The damned trouble is I don't know very much. I didn't listen well enough back then" (59) when he was growing up and his mother and Luther would argue with each other in Choctaw over whether or not Hoey's hair should be cut. Consequently, Hoey cannot rest comfortably with the identity he has manufactured from books and memories.

Like his father, Cole "don't know very much" at the beginning
of the novel. The narrative makes clear that he is "left behind" in
a world where Indian identity is either the dominant culture's stereotype of the "half-breed" Cole repeats in his litany or the romanticism offered by wealthy landowner Dan Nemi, the unnamed mental
hospital orderly, and FBI agent Lee Scott. Nemi, in response to the
news that Attis is missing from the mental hospital, tells Mundo,
"Don't forget, McCurtain's sort of an Indian and you know how
they are; they just melt right into places and you never see them.
Stoic, don't talk, no broken twigs, that sort of thing" (51). The orderly,
paid by Diana Nemi to help Attis "escape," rationalizes what he will
do by thinking that "it would be a good thing to help the Indian
escape. Maybe he could return to the wilderness and live naturally.
Some of them, he knew, had forgotten how to live that way, but
probably not this one" (93–94). The fact that he identifies Attis as
"the Indian" stands as tacit evidence of his inability to see beyond
the sort of monologic, one-dimensional stereotype Owens lays bare
in *Wolfsong*. And most odiously of all, Lee Scott announces, without
a trace of irony or awareness, "I've always been fascinated by Indians.
Made a hobby of Indians when I was a boy. Collected arrowheads
and stuff. It was like I was trying to find out who I was, and those
things could tell me" (168). Hobby indeed. Scott also says that he
"made a study" of Native traditions, but his efforts lead only to the
romantic image of the vanishing noble savage: "They're raised not
to show pain, you know. It's a shame they're all vanishing. A noble
way of life goes with them, something valuable and essential in all
of us" (86–87). An agent of the federal government, Scott will fittingly
voice a completely different vision of Indians to Dan Nemi, one
that has its roots in early European and Euroamerican depictions
of the first peoples of the continent: "That's how our great nation
began. Protect the innocent and cut the fucking nuts right off the
guilty. . . . The servants of Satan in the howling desert. That's Indians
from the word go" (190). Like the predecessors he echoes, particularly the Puritans William Bradford and Mary Rowlandson, Scott
defines Natives as the evil Other. Such a definition is necessary, of

course, in order to rationalize the whites' actions in the names of the nation and nation building. Scott is more correct than he knows when he says "it was like I was trying to find out who I was" by collecting what one suspects he would call relics in order to keep the Indian firmly in the past, for his turn to the Indian, which is nothing less than an example of the dominant culture's desire to conjure the *revenant* that is the Indian in order to conjure it away, is born of the anxiety over displacement that he, his government, and the dominant culture are unwilling to face.

Prior to his stay with Uncle Luther, Cole had succumbed, at least in part, to the stereotypes, romantic and otherwise, created and perpetuated by subjects of the dominant culture. In fact, the morning after his arrival at Luther's, Cole "thought of his father, trying to imagine Hoey McCurtain as a boy in the cabin, standing by the same stove. Abruptly the distance his father had traveled was sad, tragic, and he knew all at once what his father must have known for many years. They'd all gone too far, and Attis had been right. None of them, not even Hoey McCurtain, could ever go back" (72). N. Scott Momaday, in particular, has stressed the importance of imagination to Native cultures and peoples. In *The Names*, for instance, Momaday says that his mother "imagined who she was. The act of the imagination was, I believe, among the most important events of my mother's early life, as later the same essential act was to be among the most important of my own" (25). Here, however, Cole's turn to imagination is compromised. "Tragic," set off in the sentence so we might catch and linger on it, reveals the extent to which Cole has been conscripted by the dominant culture.[2] This conscription is far more dangerous than the military draft Cole attempts to avoid by heading to the swamps, woods, and backwaters of his Choctaw homeland. It leads him both to see Hoey's life in a tragic light and to think that *nalusachito*, the soul-eater, "was only what Cole had already imagined it to be, a genetic accident that had come to this place only to be angered by a white man who, like Cole, knew what it really was" (72). Cole is blinded by the master narratives of tragedy and science, but fortunately for

him, as Hoey said, he has "a world" (60) in Uncle Luther. Thanks
to that world and the teachings of Luther and Onatima, by the time
he is ready to leave Mississippi and find his brother's bones Cole
can ignore the literal and figurative light being shined by the FBI
agents who have come to the swamp looking for his brother and
"see only the trail." As a consequence, "the trail began to be clear,
a thread somewhat lighter than the surrounding dark," and Cole can
travel it easily while "behind him he heard the white men stum-
bling and cursing in their haste to keep up" (123). Moreover, back
in California, as the story builds to its climax, Cole can, in Luther's
words, remain "on a straight path" (244) as he walks the river.

By concentrating only on the path, Cole is able to see. Figuratively, then, by roughly the midpoint of the novel he has received
from Luther and Onatima what he needs in order to have the
sharpest sight, a more than simply visual acuity that is necessary
if he is to return to California, find his brother's body, pick clean the
bones, and return them to Choctaw homeland in Mississippi. Such
sight stands in telling contradistinction to that which Jonathan
Edwards refers to in his 1741 sermon "Sinners in the Hands of an
Angry God," the text of which furnishes Owens with his novel's title
and epigraph. With his sermon Edwards attempted to coerce his
listeners into religious commitment and conversion by describing the
control God has over their life and death. Edwards's is a vengeful
God, as is clear from the passage he takes for his sermon's point of
reference and departure: sinners "shall slide in due time" (Deutero-
nomy 32:35), and the "arrows of death" that cause the wicked to
lose their footing and fall to hell "fly unseen at noonday; the
sharpest sight cannot discern them" (368). Cole's "sharpest sight,"
on the other hand, grounded in Choctaw ways of seeing, knowing,
and being in the world, enables him to discern his identity, death,
the world, and his place in it.

Such discerning sight, Owens makes clear, is associated with a
different worldview than that held by subjects of the dominant
culture. Part of the necessary education Cole receives from Luther
highlights the difference between Western organized religious

worship and the Choctaws' relationship to the creator. Cole asks his uncle how "Choctaws worship the Great Spirit," and Luther responds, "We don't. . . . Why would we do that? The creator ain't never told us to do that" (95). While Luther enjoys the ceremonies of the Holy Rollers who congregate nearby, with their ecstatic responses to the Lord, he "wouldn't want to live scared" (95) that God would get mad with something he had done and punish him. What Luther says gives Cole pause, for he had never thought "that people only worshipped God because God told them they'd better. Or else" (95). Such is not the creator of the Choctaw; rather, Luther tells Cole (and the reader) that, contra Edwards's God, "The great spirit don't want churches and hullabaloo, he just wants us to stay awake and look with more than our eyes" (112).

To "look with more than our eyes" means to see with dreams and stories. The dreams of the characters help the reader to see the narrative's emphasis on death and identity and the relationship between the two. For Attis, death, as it is manifested in his Vietnam experience, is what transforms dream into nightmare. The good dream of fishing in a stream coursing through a meadow in flower is ruptured by blackness rising up from a corner to overwhelm it and him. Just prior to that dream in the narrative, we learn that a cobra rose above fifteen-foot-high elephant grass to momentarily freeze Attis, mesmerized by "the beautiful form that death could take" (93), until another man in the patrol sees it, screams, and they all run. This is no ordinary snake, Attis knows, but rather a crystallization of all the fear, anger, and hatred associated with death that the men experience in Vietnam. Unable to come to terms with either the dream or the experience that had led to its creation, Attis is doomed. The narrative subtly yokes that doom with sight by indicating that Attis remembers the snake while he watches the eyes of the mental hospital orderly as he tries to convince Attis to escape. With those eyes the "short white boy" (93) can only see "the Indian."

Cole's dream of his brother standing at the edge of a clearing that symbolizes for us the contact zone of the frontier indicates both why the dominant culture sees only the Indian and what it will be necessary to grasp in order to see the Native. Attis wears his combat fatigue jacket, yoking him and his identity with his tour in Vietnam, and he tells Cole the first part of what is written on its back: "I shall fear no evil" (67). Thanks to Psalm 23 fractured and revised here and earlier in the narrative, the reader is granted the perspective to see that the Chumash artifacts Attis holds out to his brother are symbolic of the Native ancestry and heritage Cole must take if he is to see with more than his eyes. The arrowhead and stone doll are also medicine Cole will wear to help protect him from the evil that has taken his brother.[3]

Luther teaches Cole that dreams enable us to see both during the day and "in the dark, when we're most awake" (112). Hoey McCurtain knows something has happened to Attis because he "dreamed it" (33); it is this knowledge, coupled with his knowledge of the traditional ways of the Choctaw, that compels him to seek revenge. Cole stays "on a straight path" late in the text, while the story is rushing to its climax and Hoey and Mundo are still in danger, because "he is beginning to dream" (244); as a consequence, on the day he finds Attis's bones he first "felt something pulling him toward the heart of the river" and then "knew he was there" (251) when he comes to the location of his brother's remains.

If dreams help us see, then stories give us words for all those things we need to know of and watch carefully. As Luther says, "If we didn't have the stories we couldn't live in this world" because "it takes stories to keep the balance" (97). They remind us of how the world really is and needs to be, "with everything in balance, good spirits and bad ones and all" (91). Diana Nemi believes that by murdering Attis she has revenged her sister's murder and restored balance, but Mundo tells her that "things aren't balanced" (135) because Choctaw tradition necessitates that Hoey avenge his son's murder. Of equal import, things are not balanced because there is as yet no told story. Indeed, Diana never tells her story. It is not enough to have one's own story or even to know the stories of one's people; stories must be told in order that connections are made that will help us to live in balance.

One of the first stories Uncle Luther tells Cole highlights how it is that stories forge connections and establish identity in and with their telling. The day after Cole returns to Mississippi, Luther takes him to the place he was born. Standing together before the abandoned wood cabin, he asks Cole if he remembers his name and then tells him:

> "When your brother hit you that time you was bleeding bad. All over everything, like a stuck shoat. But you never cried, never made a sound. So I give you a Choctaw name then. Not the regular way to do it, but I done it anyway."
>
> Cole waited and the old man began to grin the jack-o-lantern grin once more. "*Taska mikushi humma*," he said . . . "Means something like Little-chief-warrior Red. Because you was bleeding all over but you was brave like a warrior." (75)

The brief story locates Luther and Cole in an oral tradition by emphasizing the pole of reference and the pole of addressee that Lyotard sees as indicative of oral cultures. Cole is at once the audience of the story and its named subject. He is, to use Lyotard's words, "spoken to as well as spoken of" (*Just Gaming* 35). As such, Cole is connected to Luther, and Luther to him, and he is identified. This is why Luther, who is "educated" enough to "know" better, speaks in the present tense when he tells Cole, "So I give you a Choctaw name then." Moreover, it is also why Cole next fingers the bag containing the medicine he and Attis had found together in the California hills, remembers being with Attis in their Mississippi home, and knows, already, "that he would have to go back for his brother" (76).

One should not be quick to judge Diana Nemi harshly for not telling her story, however, or to consider her necessarily evil because she is Attis's killer. Diana lacks the sort of family and tribal connections Cole has and Mundo discovers. Thus, while Hoey carries her from her house to the sweat lodge he has built, thereby duplicating Luther's act of carrying a young Cole McCurtain home and caring for his wound, he has neither a story for or of her nor a name to offer. Moreover, the relationship between the character and the mythological Diana of Nemi, explored by Margaret Dwyer in her essay on *The Sharpest Sight*, indicates that Owens's character is too complex for a reductive reading. As is the case with the Roman goddess of fertility, motherhood, and the forest, Diana Nemi's sexuality is emphasized. What is more, Diana both knows that she is an object of desire and uses this to her advantage. The difference between the two women is that while Diana of Nemi was used by her priests to attain power and maintain control (Dwyer 53–54), Diana Nemi is not so clearly a tool of men. Nor is she, like her namesake, associated with fertility. Not only is her sexual activity divorced from any notions of pregnancy, childbirth, and motherhood, but she hates the tiny oak trees that take root in her sister's grave. Given that Diana of Nemi is traditionally associated with oaks, it is small wonder the narrative shows us that Diana Nemi "smiled ironically at her reflection" in the mirror immediately prior to the passage describing her trip to "pluck the sprouted acorns from the grave, hating the little curling roots that split each shell and twisted into the earth like the tails of pigs" (190).

The object of Diana Nemi's hatred takes us directly to the complexity of her character and the root of the irony. That is, Diana hates the roots, not the sprouting stems, hates that which penetrates the earth and takes hold there, because it is a reminder of the male penetration of the female. For Diana, intercourse has marked either loss or abuse. At fourteen she had rushed home to be with her older sister, only to see Attis and Jenna in the act of making love. "Frozen" in the doorway before the sight of "Attis shoving himself into her sister, while Jenna made sounds midway between laughing and crying" (148), Diana is as mesmerized by intercourse as Attis was by the cobra. And like Attis, who is unable to come to terms with death as symbolized by the snake, Diana is unable to come to terms with what she sees and its relationship to life.

The narrative suggests that Diana's inability to make sense of this disturbing primal scene is due at least in part to the fact that she associates it with her father's infidelity. His affairs make it clear to

Diana that intercourse can have more to do with power, control, and abuse than with love and regeneration. She thinks that all men are like her father, and she has sex with Attis in an attempt to prove this to her sister. In turning the tables on men and using sex to get what she wants, however, Diana simply replicates the abusive pattern she has seen her father practice. The connection to Diana of Nemi, therefore, is ironic at least insofar as Diana has lost sight of the role sexual intercourse plays in the cycle of life. Attis comes to lie with her in her dream, not just because she killed him, but because she also feels guilt over having made love with him in an effort to destroy his relationship with her sister. It is this guilt that Luther tells her she must let go of if she is to be healed.

However, the deeper irony is that Diana is only able to have a relationship to Diana of Nemi that yokes sexuality and power. This too is a result of the dominant culture's way of seeing. The lake known as Diana's Mirror in the Roman myths becomes the "unnatural pool" (204) of the sandpit Diana peers into when last we see her. The product of man's rending of the earth and breaking the river for profit, the sandpit is a perverted image of the lake before Diana of Nemi's shrine, one that helps us to understand what the viejo Antonio Morales, who appears periodically after his death to help his grandson, means when he tells Mundo that Diana "is not entirely wrong" (223) in what she does. Objectified by men to satisfy their desires, Diana remains trapped in the doorway she was frozen in when she witnessed Jenna and Attis making love.

Moreover, a third photograph in *The Sharpest Sight*, the snapshot of Amarga resident Louise Vogler that is pinned on the wall above Jessard Deal's desk in the office of the bar he owns, suggests that Diana is not alone. Louise is dressed in "a miniskirt and tight sweater" (233), and her smile indicates a loss of self in the presence of another as she strikes the pose of a sex object for the camera, its operator, and the malicious Jessard. The fact that the photo is wallet-sized suggests that the pose and smile are created for and offered to more than one person. It is small wonder, then, that the only time Louise is physically present in the novel, "her straight hair, turned up at her shoulders, and the skirt that rode up past her thigh gave Cole a terrible feeling of loneliness" (17), as Owens's narrative discloses that the objectification weighs heavily on her.

Rather than attempting to forge connections with others, Diana Nemi has little choice save to hew to the model of the self-reliant, isolated individual following her rape by Jessard and the subsequent purification rite Hoey has her undergo. In her last appearance in the text she watches steelhead in the sandpit pool left after the Salinas has returned to its underground course. She is envious of the clean lines of their movements, and thinks that "to be surrounded by the isolate, invisible water was a dream." She longs to, like the fish, "find a holding place of such perfect clarity, and to hang, suspended on the facing current like a kite on a strong wind, effortless and alone. If one could live that way" (261). But one cannot, as the narrative makes clear, and Owens punctuates that truth, and punctures Diana's problematic ideal, with the brief chapter's final paragraph. A crow perched in a tree across the pool leans toward Diana as she admires the steelhead, cocks its head, and then takes off, "rocking the clear day with its laughter" (261) at her for longing for a life of splendid isolation.

As dangerously wrongheaded and shortsighted as a way of living that denies connection are ways that establish false connections to others and to the natural world. Jessard also recognizes isolation and separation, telling Diana that "loneliness is the essential human condition." Unlike Diana, he desires to bridge the gulfs that he sees, but thinks that "connection is made through pain. Only through pain is someone truly reached, touched" (234). For Jessard, arguably Owens most disturbing and reprehensible character to date, connection comes via the particular pain produced by violence, so he carefully orchestrates bar brawls in his tavern and rapes Diana at knifepoint. His recitation of lines from Edward Lear's nonsense song "The Owl and the Pussy-Cat" while ripping off Diana's clothes indicates how debased a union rape is.[4] The falseness of this sort of connection is forcefully revealed both by the physical and psychological brutality of the rape, vividly rendered by Owens so that we cannot avoid recognizing that it is the antithesis of a connection, and by Jessard's grabbing *and* breaking Mundo's wrist just prior to being shot and killed by Hoey (250). Lee Scott yokes connections and death even more explicitly, telling Cole late in the novel that the death he saw in Vietnam was "part of a very big pas de deux that's being danced out everywhere. We learned the steps more precisely over there, but we were dancing before we went and the ball goes on" (253–54).

This dance with death is done by more than U.S. soldiers in Vietnam and after their return. As Onatima notes, the whites have "a romance going with death" (216). Seeing this helps the reader make sense of the murder of a hobo whom Owens introduces early in the narrative, returns to on several occasions, but leaves unsolved. The murdered hobo is in perfect keeping with a society that prizes death and is predicated on senselessly "killing off everything" (113). Mundo is depressed by the image he conjures up of kids with a rifle taking potshots at hoboes on a passing train. He is also smart enough to know that the more than plausible scenario of the murder he spins out is not something he can tell the highest authorities in county and state law enforcement, because they will not want to hear "that a man had most likely been killed just for fun and that they'd never find out who did it" (34). Those in power do not want to hear what he and Sheriff Carl Carlton know: Carlton says, "that dead hobo just don't matter," and adds, "the same goes for your buddy. Wherever he is, he's saving the taxpayers a lot of money for room and board" (200). Such phrasing reveals a devaluing of life, a romance with death, and the importance of economics to actions and relationships. The latter, in particular, connects *The Sharpest Sight* with *Wolfsong*, for as we have seen, Owens's earlier novel is very much concerned with the importance of economics to identity that Carlton only hints at with his comment.

The romance with death extends to the natural world, as is made clear by the Salinas River that Luther says "the whites have broken" (26) by damming it. As a consequence, "it's all cockeyed" and "when the river can't stand it no more, it rears up and starts smashing everything. Then everthing's [*sic*] confused" (97). Remindful of Yellow Calf's statement to the narrator of *Winter in the Blood* that "the world is cockeyed" (Welch 68), Luther's phrasing is telling, for "cockeyed" accentuates the painful truth that the whites' inability to see clearly and correctly their relationship to the Salinas has caused the river and its ecosystem to be skewed and out of balance. Steelhead return to the river when it flows above ground, only to be trapped in ever-shrinking pools when the Salinas returns to its underground course. The fish are doing what is natural when they return, but such actions lead only to death because, as Luther tells Cole, "It's part of a circle, you see, and they broke the circle when they broke that river" (97). Owens and Luther know, moreover, and would have both Cole and the reader see, that the plight of the Salinas is only one instance of a larger pattern of abuse and destruction by the whites: "And they are doing that all over the world, breaking all the circles" (97–98).

Owens links the Salinas River with Native Americans when he writes of Cole thinking of the Chumash (the original inhabitants of the area of the coast and coast range from around present-day San Luis Obispo south to below Ventura) as "a people who seemed to have vanished into the pale hills the way the river disappeared into the sand" (53). The Chumash were "the first major group of California Indians to be discovered by Europeans" (Grant 505), the Spanish explorer Juan Rodríguez Cabrillo first contacting them in 1542, and the mission system into which they were indoctrinated beginning in the eighteenth century broke the circle by severing the people from their culture and exposing them to the diseases that annihilated them. In order to avoid suffering the fate of the Chumash, Cole must work to restore the world to balance by finding his brother's bones and returning them to Mississippi. This will repair the circle. The act is crucial so that Attis's *shilombish*, or what Onatima terms his inside shadow, can proceed to the place it is supposed to go. Until then, Attis's *shilup*, or what she calls his outside shadow, will, like the spirits of the recently deceased Salish, continue to threaten to take someone with it to appease its loneliness. The act is also crucial for the Choctaw, because the bones of their ancestors, brought east during the migration to what is today Mississippi, were and are vitally important to the people's sense of place and self. Patricia Galloway points this out in *Choctaw Genesis, 1500–1700*: "Places of burial were no accident. In numerous examples throughout the world, they are chosen to reflect the relationship of social groups to their land. . . . The bones of [Choctaw] ancestors, in other words, functioned to structure the world of the living by structuring the supernatural world of the dead; by placing the bones of ancestors one established a settlement charter" (303). Luther makes this clear when he tells Cole that "it took a long, long time to come here to where the pole stands straight, but we made *this country our home with our bones*, you see. A Choctaw's bones must not be lost" (98, emphasis added).

Here again Owens's narrative is revealing, for the seemingly superfluous "you see" serves to emphasize sight and remind us of the sharpest sight Cole needs if he is to see, succeed in his task, and hence realize his identity. Earlier in the chapter, Owens has Luther use the same phrase, "It's part of a circle, you see, and they broke the circle when they broke that river," to indicate that connections, circles, and cycles are what Cole will discern and understand with his sharpest sight. Like his friend, Mundo comes to see and understand who he is and the connectedness of all things. Fittingly, his path to seeing clearly begins on a bridge over the Salinas when *nalusachito* appears before him. Mundo tells his wife, Gloria, that "I keep feeling like there was something that brought me to the bridge right when he [Attis] was there [being carried downstream by the flood]" (100). That something is the story Luther is dreaming, of course, but the location is particularly relevant because it accentuates the act of making connections. It is also linked to seeing: Mundo will later use a bridge as a vantage point from which to scan the river for Attis's body (107).

Furthermore, the location accentuates Mundo's liminal, betwixt-and-between state as he searches. His efforts to find the body and solve the mystery lead him to think about water and the river in ways he had not before. In doing so, he comes to recognize connections and circles, and Owens encourages the reader to see this by omitting punctuation: "trickles making streams running into creeks that all aimed toward a river that sought the ocean that laid itself out before the sun so that it could be sucked up and spit back at the mountains again so that trickles would make streams" (128). Mundo is also forced to confront his ignorance, thinking about how "he'd lived next to this particular river all of his life and knew nothing about it" (130).

Mundo realizes that, just as the river is connected to other things and is an integral part of a cycle, Attis's death is connected to something larger. He tells Gloria, "It's beyond Attis, now. . . . I don't know how to explain it, but it just feels like it's huge, like it has to do with the whole damned world somehow" (154). Owens's punning use of "damned world" reminds the reader that the world is broken because connections have been severed and circles broken. It is fitting that after learning that Diana "fucked" Attis and figuring out that she killed him, Mundo stopped on the bridge, vomited, and then "began to cry, sobbing in loud, wrenching wails that came from his center, mourning for Attis and Diana and all of them. On and on it went until he became aware of tears pouring from his chin to the river below" (222–23). His tears trickle into the river to become part of the circle, suggesting that the proper sort of mourning is essential to establishing and maintaining connections.

Mundo also realizes that the "story" of Attis's life and death which he is attempting to read and understand is connected to identity. He reflects:

> Somehow it all seemed related, tangled up together like a ball of used baling wire. He and Attis and Jenna and all of them were caught up now in whatever this story happened to be. Indians, Mexicans, gringos, mixed-bloods. He, Mundo, was part Indian, though no one in the family had ever liked to admit it. Pure Castillian, they had always pretended, holding out their underarms to show the whiteness. And the McCurtains

were white and Indian both. Tangled, mixed, interrelated. He thought of the Mondragon sisters and vowed, again, to speak with them. The sisters might be able to sort something out of the mess. (196–97)

As the passage makes clear, with Ramon "Mundo" Morales, whose nickname fittingly means "world," Owens ups the ante to indicate how seeing and understanding identity and connections is vital to all of us, not just to Native Americans. Problems arise when one loses his or her identity or tries to hide it. One errs in attempting to deny connections. The Mondragon sisters, it turns out, work to ensure that the connections are traced and not lost, for those connections articulate identity. Alicia tells her sister, "Ramon has come to find out who he is" (227), and instructs Mundo to "trace your identity from your name" (228) at the bottom of a large sheet of old, yellowed paper upon which are written the family trees of the past and present inhabitants of Amarga and the surrounding area. The emphasis placed on the relationship between one's name and identity here reinforces the text's earlier yoking of Cole's name and his identity. The sister's record is far from linear; rather, it is "a spider's web of crossing and connecting lines" (229) that stands in contradistinction to the earlier image of a tangled ball of baling wire. Seeing that web helps Mundo to become, as Luther tells Onatima, "aware now that his own story is very, very old and complicated" (244). It also helps him to—in the words of his grandfather—"become more comfortable with the dead" because thanks to the complicated, interrelated story, "he knows at last who he is" (262).

Cole's and Mundo's eventual success stands in juxtaposition to the brief section of the novel concerning Bucky Travis's disinterment of his grandmother. In addition to bringing into the open the culture's romance with death and discomfort with the dead, the conclusion of the scene highlights the fundamental disrespect for one's ancestors, one's culture, and the world that plagues the dominant society:

Watching the boy's friendly face, Mundo said, "Why'd you do it, Bucky?"

Bucky's expression became incredulous. "Didn't you ever want to do that, Mundo?"

Shaking his head slowly, Mundo said, "No Bucky. The dead are special. Your grandmother deserves her rest."

"My grandmother," Bucky replied flatly, "was a cunt."

Mundo let out a deep breath. "What's wrong with kids today, Bucky? We never used to do things like this."

"You know what I say, Mundo? Fuck the world. That's what I say. Fuck the world." (146)

There is nothing approaching mourning here. Bucky's attitude is that of an extremely selfish, uncaring adolescent. Tellingly, his facial expressions and tone reveal a movement from openness and warmth, through shocked disbelief, and finally to a cold bluntness that prohibits the possibility of making a connection with Mundo— or anyone else. He is more correct than he knows when he says and repeats "Fuck the world," for his attitude toward others and his environment is a vulgar perversion of connection leading inexorably to disconnection, the breaking of circles, and destruction. It is small wonder, then, that Bucky transforms his act into a parody of ritual by writing "Just Buried" on the back window of his pickup. His perversion of "Just Married" accentuates how radically different his act is from the reaffirmation of community and connections that is a result of successfully completed rites of passage in general and the rite of marriage in particular.

In digging up his grandmother's bones, Bucky is establishing a perversion of the Choctaw settlement charter, a perversion that is predicated on movement, pollution, and a lack of respect. He is representative, finally, of whites as they are characterized by Uncle Luther: "You see, grandson, whites don't really want to grow up, so they tell these stories about kids that go around acting like they never heard of growing up. They don't have no homes, and they don't know about taking care of mother earth or any mother at all" (109).

Luther's criticism is especially damning given that the traditional Choctaw kinship and family structures are matrilineal and matrilocal. To not know about taking care of any mother is, in the Choctaw worldview, tantamount to being outside of and without culture and connection.

To be inside and with culture is, among other things, to engage in ceremony and ritual. Such engagement in turn assures home and identity. In Cole's case engagement means moving from the litany on identity that is "like a ceremony" (10) to the ceremony of picking clean his brother's bones and returning them to their Mississippi burial mound. Owens's narrative links the two by having Cole place Attis's bones in the field jacket upon which are written the words that are part of his initial recitation of identity (10–11). After finding his brother's body, Cole acts with "enormous care" (252) when retrieving the bones and refuses to let Lee Scott appropriate them as evidence. He tells the FBI agent that "I have some things to do, so you'd better leave" (254) in order that he might complete the ceremony begun by the natural world when water, current, and trees had joined to place "Attis's body . . . cupped in the branches" of four oak trees that had "grown up together" (251) to form the natural equivalent of the raised platform of traditional Choctaw mortuary practice. The force of the current has stripped the clothes from the body, and sun and water have decayed the flesh. Fittingly, by assuming the role of the bone picker in the ceremony, Cole makes a connection to his brother and Choctaw culture that celebrates circles (and cycles) even as it helps him realize his identity as a member of that culture and thus his sense of self. Traditionally, the bone picker would preside over a feast and serve food to the people of the village after having stripped the flesh from the bones of the deceased; therefore, "the bone picker's role in funeral rites and feasting thus reinforced the integral relationship between life and death" (Kidwell 7).

As we have seen, culture, stories, and identity also share an integral relationship. Having and sharing the right stories will establish true connections, articulate balance, and thereby bring an end to

the twisted, perverse dance of the dominant culture. This is difficult, however, because subjects of the dominant culture want to
write and perpetuate a nationalist narrative of mastery and control
and a particular reading of the nature of the world. When he comes
to get the bones, Lee Scott tells Cole that "they were afraid he was
loose and was going to dance the ghost dance some more and
remind people" (254). Scott's comment is telling because the Ghost
Dance, insofar as it celebrated life and cultural renewal, is the opposite of the dance with death. He also says, "They sent me to make
sure that your brother never surfaced again. They want him controlled and invisible" (254). They want, that is, precisely what they
have all too often wanted when it comes to Native Americans.

The desire for mastery and control is manifested not only in the
actions of subjects of the dominant culture, but also throughout the
dominant culture's stories. In what Owens terms the "Chief Doom
school of literature," the texts present the reader with "Indians who
are romantic, unthreatening, and self-destructive. Indians who are
enacting, in one guise or another, the process of vanishing" (*Mixedblood Messages* 82). Therefore, just as Cole has to interrogate and
revise the master narrative of the dominant culture if he is to know
and articulate himself, so Owens interrogates and revises the master
narrative as it is manifested in canonical American literature in
order to make a space in which to situate his work and the work of
other Native writers. Thus, throughout *The Sharpest Sight* numerous
allusions to canonical American and English literature appear in
order to show how those texts are part of that story. In doing so,
Owens reveals what is wanting and dangerous about the stories
making up the traditional canon of American literature.[5]

It makes perfect sense that Jessard Deal is the character in *The
Sharpest Sight* who champions literature and most frequently quotes
from canonical texts, for just as his way to connect with others is
fundamentally flawed, so too in Owens's reading are many of the
canonical texts flawed because they fail to establish and maintain
real connections between characters and between characters and
the natural world. This is most graphically apparent in Melville's

Moby Dick and Twain's *Adventures of Huckleberry Finn*, two of the many texts Onatima has brought to Uncle Luther's home over the years for him to read. Luther tells Cole that he likes "to read these books [Onatima brings] because they are always making up stories and that's how they make the world the way they want it" (91). Luther acknowledges that the stories Ishmael and Huck tell have a certain seductive attractiveness; both characters, after all, are excellent storytellers. Moreover, regarding *Moby Dick* and its narrator, Luther tells Cole that "the man that told the story thought kind of in a Indian way. He knew the world had to be balanced, and he knew a man's job was to keep awake and watch everything and know the witchery that was loose in the world" (90). Luther's reading of *Moby Dick* and its narrator resonates nicely with much traditional and contemporary Native American thought, as well as with contemporary Native American literatures. To cite just two instances, one can hear echoes of the Anishinaabe worldview, with its emphasis on balance and connection, and Leslie Marmon Silko's *Ceremony*, which reminds us both that witchery "works to scare people, to make them fear growth" (126) and that "there are balances and harmonies always shifting, always necessary to maintain" (130). Moreover, like Silko's text, and Owens's, *Moby Dick* indicates an awareness of the nature of evil: Luther says, "You see, that captain didn't know you can't kill evil, that you just got to see it and know it like the storyteller did" (90). Nevertheless, *Moby Dick* is ultimately "a white man's book" because Ishmael forgot his own story and "killed off his brother" (90, 91). As Luther says, "When that white storyteller came bouncing up on the Indian's coffin, he killed off half of himself and he lost his power but didn't know it" (91).

With the allusions to the *Adventures of Huckleberry Finn*, *The Sharpest Sight* connects Attis's story to the dominant culture's narrative of mastery and indicates its preoccupation with separation and death. The narrative links Attis's story with Huck's when Sheriff Carlton chides Mundo for searching the river because "We have reports he's been seen in Texas, Oklahoma, Mississippi. Official, typed reports. The story is he's hightailed it for injun country" (198). One must be wary of the official *written* story featuring Attis, the "typed report," and its connection to Huck's written story, however, because through Luther, Owens has already given us a reading of the latter text that reveals how problematic such a yoking is, especially given Huck's decision to "light out for the Territory ahead of the rest." Although Huck might well be "running away from all the witchery in the white world that made him think wrong," and while it is possible that once in "Indian Territory" some Native family will take him in, Luther thinks that the stories Huck makes up about families and death indicate that the "white boy knew he was part of something that wouldn't let him live with no Indians" (113). That something is the "romance" the whites have "going with death, they love it, and they want Indians to die for them" (216).

Luther tells Onatima what Owens would have us realize: "They do that, try to write us to death" (216). Fittingly, Luther has just used Faulkner's Chief Doom as an example of the whites' romance with death. Unable to face death the Choctaw way, Faulkner's creation is a "kind of devil." In Luther's reading, "It was like that white writer took all the death that ever happened to us Indian people and put it in one devil character" (216). Faulkner's mistakes are thinking change means death and caring more for the latter than he does for life (216). As is the case with other texts produced by the dominant culture, Faulkner's stories are dangerous because they are examples of the "bigger stories, the ones that they make up to change the world" (110). Jessard Deal's reading of Robert Frost's "Design" and "Stopping by Woods on a Snowy Evening," for instance, accords with the dominant culture's take on death. He tells Diana, "It really *is* design of darkness to appall" and the dark woods are full of "uncounted deaths" (235). In Luther's eyes, Faulkner, his contemporaries such as Frost, his literary ancestors, and the subjects of the dominant culture share the desire, the need, "to keep killing off everything so one day they'll be alone, no parents, no family, not even mother earth" (113). So it is that the narrative yokes "The Bear," "Rip Van Winkle," and madness, for instance, all captured in the figure of the last black bear to be shot in the Amarga area. The bear is memorialized in a photo showing it "staring down from the oak tree with an incredulous expression, like it had slept for a hundred years and awakened to madness all around" (37) prior to being shot. While the last bear must be shot first by a camera and then by a gun in order to be captured once and for all, Attis's bones must be lovingly brought down from their oak tree platform and brought home. The difference drives home the differences between the ways of seeing and being for the dominant culture and for the Choctaw.

More than canonical American literary texts are interrogated and brought to light over the course of the narrative that culminates with Hoey and Cole duplicating the Choctaws' migration east by traveling with Attis's bones to Mississippi and the Yazoo River bank, the reverse of Huck's planned course at the end of Twain's text, "where an old man and old woman were waiting to take them home" (263). Owens makes clear that even texts such as H. B. Cushman's *History of the Choctaw, Chickasaw, and Natchez Indians* (1899), a copy of which Luther owns and Cole looks at the second morning of his stay, must be read carefully and with an eye toward seeing their connection to the dominant culture's story. That Cushman admires the peoples whose history he writes is clear from his dedication onward. What is also clear from the passage Luther quotes to Cole as evidence that "This is a good book. Tells us all about ourselves" (88) is that Cushman is not immune to romanticism:

"The Choctaw warrior, as I knew him in his native Mississippi forest, was as fine a specimen of manly perfection as I have ever beheld." He looked up with a grin. "He seemed to be as perfect as the human form could be. Tall, beautiful in symmetry of form and face, graceful, active, straight, fleet, with lofty and independent bearing, he seemed worthy in saying, as he of Juan Fernandez fame: 'I am monarch of all I survey.' His black piercing eye seemed to penetrate and read the very

thoughts of the heart, while his firm step proclaimed a feeling
sense of his manly independence. Nor did their women fall
behind in all that pertains to female beauty." (88)

Luther's grin, erupting in the passage as it were, is telling, for it
reveals that he, Cole, and the reader cannot take Cushman's history
completely straight. Cushman claims near the end of his history
that he has "wandered far from the old and beaten tracks in which
former writers have walked in their accounts given of that people
known as the Red Race of North America" and as a result has
"escaped many of the ruts" (463) into which those writers have
fallen. However, the passage Luther reads Cole indicates otherwise.

Luther's is a trickster grin breaking into Cushman's description
of the Choctaw warrior as noble savage, casting it in a humorous
light, and thus standing as an appropriate response to the stereotype. Luther could also be grinning in necessary good humor at
the tense Cushman employs throughout the passage. While it is
true that in the section Luther reads Cushman is at least in part
referring to those Choctaw warriors he saw years ago, the *History*,
from its dedication to its close, makes clear that Cushman saw
these peoples as noble *and* vanishing. The dedication reads, in
part: "To the Choctaw and Chickasaw people, each the now feeble
remnant of a once numerous, independent, contented and happy
people" (n.p.). He uses the phrase "Noble race!" to begin two
of the last eleven comparatively brief paragraphs of his history,
including the final one, and just prior to the end makes the
announcement to which the text has been building since the
dedication:

> But, alas, as a falling star tumbling from its primitive place
> near the gates of heaven, bathed in primitive glory, so has
> been the falling of the North American Red Race, that noble,
> brave and wonderful people, into the dark clouds of misfor-
> tune and woe, tracking their lone and sorrowful course down
> through the deep midnight of despair to hopeless oblivion;
> and though their spring freshness and summer bloom have

forever faded away, leaving no hope of a returning morn, still
their silent, yet dignified despair, impresses an involuntary
respect and admiration. (461–62)

Such is precisely the track the dominant culture and its subjects
wish the Natives to follow, then and now, but Luther and Owens
work to make sure that neither Cole nor the reader goes down that
path.

The labor to reveal the dangers and limitations of Cushman's
History culminates in the chapter where Luther responds to Onatima's
questions regarding Cole's level of self-awareness ("Does he know
who he is, old man?") and readiness to begin the search for Attis's
bones ("Has he begun the hunt yet?") (162). Owens juxtaposes
Cole's identity, purpose, and sense of place against Cushman's
reading of the Choctaws' relationship to God and understanding
of sin:

> "What do you think about God, Old Lady Blue Wood?"
> Uncle Luther looked at her with one eye squinted.
> "What kind of foolishness is this?" she answered.
> "Well, listen. In this book you gave me they say some
> interesting things about these people called Choctaws." He
> took the glasses and green book from the shelf and set the
> glasses on his nose, carefully arranging the wire hooks behind
> his ears. Then he turned the pages slowly until he came to
> the place he wanted. (163–64)

Onatima's question and Luther's response could not be more apt,
for they reveal both that Cushman's depiction of aspects of Choctaw
identity (from which Luther's question springs) is foolish and that
what Cushman finally offers the reader is a "history" of the Choctaw
that does not give us an accurate sense of what makes them who
and what they are. Cushman's text is a part of the official story
"about these people called Choctaws."[6] Luther distances himself
from Cushman's depiction by using that phrasing rather than
saying "interesting things about us." In addition, the phrasing puts

the emphasis on the verb, thus enabling Owens to accentuate the difference between being called Choctaw by the dominant culture and being Choctaw, or Native American, or mixedblood.

Nevertheless, Cushman's *History* is of value. Beyond serving as a source for traditional Choctaw practices and worldview, and thereby helping readers see why Hoey and Cole do as they do, it offers us a point of reference for Owens the writer. Cushman notes that "the Choctaws were great imitators, and possessed a nice tact in adopting the manners of those with whom they associated" (109). So it is with Owens, who adopts writing, the novel, the murder mystery, and the traditional canon of American literature. Furthermore, Owens makes clear that like his character Luther Cole, he does so in the best trickster fashion. The traditional Cherokee trickster appears early in *The Sharpest Sight*, in the same scene in which Cole first meditates on who he is, in order to signal Owens's identity: "Watching the rabbit, he remembered his mother's Cherokee stories about rabbits. Cherokee rabbits were smart. They lived by tricks in a world of words and had a good time doing it" (12). Trickster-like, Owens lives in a world of words in order to give us stories so that we might live in the world. We have seen both how in *Wolfsong* Owens turns to trickster and trickster discourse to disclose the trap inherent in the Euroamerican's identification of Indians and how he continues his efforts to reveal the ideology governing representations of the Indian in *The Sharpest Sight*. His adoption of writing and the novel, then, is geared toward subversion, and here too Owens can be seen as acting in concert with his Choctaw ancestors. Cushman argues that the stratagems, surprise, and treachery practiced by Choctaw in times of war and decried by W. H. Venable in *A School History of the United States* are justified by the circumstances. The Choctaw were adept at deceiving their enemies, Cushman writes, and "to them, no less than to the whites, strategy was commendable, and to outwit an enemy and thus gain an advantage over him, was evidence of great and praiseworthy skill" (141). The example early in Cushman's *History* of the Choctaw using a fake council session and seemingly innocuous speech to lure a group of

Chickasaw to their deaths is especially telling because it highlights the role language and performance play in successfully outwitting one's enemies.

The invocation of John Rollin Ridge's *The Life and Adventures of Joaquin Murieta* (1854), the first published novel by a Native American, enables the reader to see what stratagem is necessary in order to outwit and defeat the enemy. Mundo Morales is sitting at home watching the evening news recount the sacking and burning of the Bank of America in Santa Barbara by students protesting the country's involvement in the Vietnam War. His thoughts turn to other student protests, to the war, and to his tour of duty, and he "imagined what it must have been like to burn the bank. It was an urge that went back to the beginning of time" (196). He also imagines how the "Indians must have felt . . . when the cabelleros came to raise cattle" and how his ancestors must have felt when the gringos came. Mundo thinks that the Mexican bandit "Joaquin Murieta had been like these students," at least according to "the cheap novel" written by Ridge. However, first the Natives and then the Mexicans had been, "like the students," outgunned. Therefore, Mundo thinks that "like the Indians and Mexicans" (196), the students will lose.

Owens has written that from Ridge's novel "would emerge a subgenre in American literature: the American Indian novel with its unceasing investigation of cultural dialectics, competing discourses, fractured identities, and historical genocide" (*Other Destinies* 40), and it is tempting to see his reference to *The Life and Adventures of Joaquin Murieta* in *The Sharpest Sight* as simply paying homage to it and acknowledging the concerns the two texts share. More is at stake, however. Owens invokes both Murieta's brief career as an outlaw and Ridge's novel. Acting like Murieta, pillaging and murdering up and down California (*Sharpest Sight* 196), gets you dead. You will lose. In Ridge's text, Murieta dies after his horse is shot out from under him, his mounted pursuers catch up with him as he attempts to flee on foot, and he is shot three times. Acting like Ridge, on the other hand, enables you to appropriate the novel in order to snare your reader and articulate another story, one that subjects of

the dominant culture do not want to read or hear. *In The Life and
Adventures of Joaquin Murieta* that story is of a decent man driven
by the encroaching whites to acts of revenge for the death of his half
brother. Ridge makes this clear throughout the novel. For instance,
Murieta tells a young Anglo he has captured: "I will spare you.
Your countrymen have injured me, they have made me what I am,
but I will scorn to take the advantage of so brave a man. I will risk
a look and a voice like yours, if it should lead to perdition" (79).

Owens reads Ridge's novel and career as representative of the
efforts necessary if Native authors are to reclaim and proclaim
identities and cultures:

> When he turned to face his more privileged audience, how-
> ever, Ridge was forced to veil his Indianness, to inscribe his
> identity within a context of sublimation and subterfuge. Fol-
> lowing in Ridge's wake, American Indian authors would face
> again and again the dilemma of audience and identity, being
> forced to discover ways to both mimic and appropriate the
> language of the center and make it express a different reality,
> bear a different burden. (*Other Destinies* 40)

The literary language of the center is powerful because it makes
worlds. This is what Luther and Onatima say and what Owens
would have us realize through his allusions to Wallace Stevens's
"The Snow Man" in *The Sharpest Sight*. The phenomenological nature
of literature, as Stevens highlights in that poem and elsewhere in
his oeuvre, is what enables the writer and the reader to, as Jessard
Deal tells Diana Nemi, "seek the nothing that is not there and the
nothing that is" (237). With a "mind of winter," the writer can create
and the reader re-create a world of winter. Like Ridge, Owens turns
to the power of imaginative writing and the novel in order to combat
the voices and texts so long held to be the center. Like the chief who
is at the center of Cushman's example of the Choctaws' ability to
deceive and outwit their enemies, Owens lures the reader into the
trap that is his novel in order to defeat his enemies. While the
spokesperson for the nation, Lee Scott, makes it clear that Attis

McCurtain is a burden because he threatens the master narrative by becoming visible, Owens would have us see that the burden of Attis's body is one that must be borne, for it reveals and celebrates connections and a reverence for person, place, and home. Unlike the chief, then, Owens is interested in educating his audience, and thus slaying his and our most dangerous enemy: ignorance, no matter the reader. For as Onatima tells Luther, "White people don't have a monopoly on ignorance, you old fool. Neither do red people or black people" (188).

The protest that serves as the backdrop to the allusion to *The Life and Adventures of Joaquin Murieta* links *Wolfsong* and *The Sharpest Sight*. It also reveals a difference between the protests of the 1910s and those of the 1960s and 1970s and reminds us that what is at stake is nothing less than political and cultural change. The workers who protested in Washington State wanted a redistribution of the income generated by their labors, better working conditions, and—especially—a voice. The students wished to "dispossess their elders of their right to dictate who would kill and be killed" (*Sharpest Sight* 196); they wished, that is, to put a stop to the nation's romance with death. Owens wants nothing less. *The Sharpest Sight* makes clear that it is all related: the plights of the Native Americans, of the Mexicans and their descendants, of the whites, of the earth. Mundo Morales gets it exactly right when he thinks that "he and Attis and Jenna and all of them were caught up now in whatever this story happened to be" (196–97). That story is the relatively new one created and perpetuated by the dominant culture, a story no less deadly for being comparatively recent. It has led to four murders in and around Amarga, to rape, and to destruction of fundamental circles and cycles throughout the world. It is supported by authorities like Sheriff Carlton, who says, "Let's just all stick to the official story and stop worrying about Attis McCurtain." He goes on to tell his deputy, "Just let it go, Mundo. They got their story all worked out. Don't try to read between the lines. There ain't nothing there" (200, 201). But there is something there. The official story is obvious and simple (262), but Owens's narrative leads us to see that it is based upon mis-seeing and misreading. The real story is complex and, as Hoey tells Mundo, "depends on how you put things together" (258). What holds true for Hoey and Mundo holds true for readers, because with the other discourse of *The Sharpest Sight* Owens offers us another story. Just as Mundo and Hoey must figure out how they will put together the story of Diana Nemi's rape, her father's murder, and Jessard Deal's death, so must we figure out what *The Sharpest Sight* is saying about identity and the dangers of the official story to us all, non-Natives and Natives. Once we see that, we, like Louis Owens, are in a position to act to produce change.

The original Atascadero town cemetery sits "deep in a wrinkle of the mountain" (*Mixedblood Messages* 188), a small plot overgrown by exotic vinca, its older markers either fallen and covered over or taken away.

Atop Pine Mountain today: some say the town's founder, Edward G. Lewis, did not want to have to look at any reminders of death. Pine Mountain cemetery, Atascadero, California.

"An image of a plains warrior padding silently through the forest came to him and he smiled. Books and movies seldom showed Indians who looked like the Salish people of these mountains. Short, dark people dressed in woven cedar bark weren't as exciting as Sioux warriors in eagle-feather headdresses on horseback, the sun always setting behind them" (*Wolfsong* 83). Photo © Charles Martin. Used by permission.

The Salinas River in late May; "the whites have broken it so that it runs only underground except when the big rains come . . . . It has the bones" (*The Sharpest Sight* 26).

"A vast mound of grey stones rising above the empty plains of eastern New Mexico" (*Bone Game* 74). Cueloze Pueblo ruins, south of Mountainair, New Mexico. Photo © Stephen E. LaLonde. Used by permission.

The owl, Cherokee harbinger of evil, stands "against a pale yellow moon, the bird's round, almost invisible eyes fixed on the street" (*Nightland* 172). Owl Cigar advertisement in Socorro, New Mexico. Photo © Stephen E. LaLonde. Used by permission.

Another painted owl, reminiscent of the image "Grampa Siquani won't go past" in Socorro, "its curving wings seeming ready to enfold everything into itself" (*Nightland* 172). Owl Café sign in San Antonio, New Mexico.

"Against the darkening plain, he could see the twenty-seven massive white dishes of the Very Large Array, and as he watched, the two-and-a-half ton antennas, with a single, painfully slow movement, began to turn their concave faces in his direction." (*Nightland* 2). The Very Large Array, plains of San Agustin, New Mexico.

"On one side the Pacific Ocean, on the other the great bowl of Monterey Bay where points of white dip and skate. First they sail the Atlantic with bloody teeth, he thinks, the deaths of ten million in their invader's imagination, and then they pile their loot on little boats and let the wind drive them in circles upon the bay" (*Bone Game* 72).

All Plains Indian tribes shared certain types of coup, yet each held its own views as to special ones.

"Time for a trick" (*The Sharpest Sight* 12). Gerald McMaster's "Counting Coup." © 1990 Gerald McMaster. Used by permission.

CHAPTER THREE

BONE GAME AND THE
TROPE OF DISCOVERY

In an interview with John Purdy, Louis Owens recognizes that *Bone Game* (1994), his third novel, is perhaps more difficult to read and follow than either of his first two. Imagined by Owens as "a non-linear novel, one that worked rather like a mosaic . . . in which all times and all actions coexisted simultaneously" (Purdy 9), the text is more formally innovative than either of Owens's earlier efforts. However, *Bone Game* nevertheless continues the interrogations of Native identity, the possibilities of finding and affirming one's home, and the nation's defining narratives and discourses begun with *Wolfsong* and *The Sharpest Sight*. In juxtaposing events occurring around Santa Cruz, California, in the nineteenth century with those occurring in the late twentieth century, the narrative helps to emphasize the text's concern and play with time, temporality, and the idea of history. At the same time, those juxtapositions put us in the same position as Cole McCurtain, now twenty years older than he was at the close of *The Sharpest Sight*, as readers and protagonist try to see and understand the connections between past and present, between the Ohlone and other Native peoples, and between an individual's story and a story of the People. In effect, then, Owens crafts a narrative that both turns on the idea of discovery and turns the idea of discovery around so that the reader might learn and profit from the narrative and finish the text with a heightened and more refined perspective on Native-white relations, past and present, time and temporality, and what it means to be a Native American, and Native American writer, in contemporary America.

There is much that needs to be discovered in *Bone Game*. Cole McCurtain is now a professor of literature and novelist on a one-year leave of absence from the University of New Mexico in order to teach at the University of California, Santa Cruz, and decide whether to take the permanent position he has been offered in the English Department there. He is recently divorced, the father of a college-age daughter named Abby, and haunted by dreams of the painted gambler Venancio Asisara. Over the course of the novel, Cole is compelled to discover the meaning and import of his dreams, the identity of the murderers terrorizing the people in and around Santa Cruz, and the relationship between the dreams and the crimes. He must also discover a profoundly different sense of time and place from that which he has at the opening of *Bone Game*. As they journey across the country to come to Cole's assistance, Uncle Luther and Cole's father, Hoey, discover the witchery that plagues contemporary America in general and Native Americans in particular and must then work to put a halt to the actions of some of the witches. Abby and Alex Yazzie, a fullblood Navajo and professor of anthropology who does not appear in *The Sharpest Sight*, discover each other and a deeper sense of the importance of place in their lives.

Just as the epigraph to *The Sharpest Sight* tacitly announces a central concern of that text, that being the relationship between canonical American literature and Native American literatures, so too do the epigraphs at the beginning of *Bone Game* serve to open that text by articulating its fundamental concerns:

> October 15, 1812. *Government Surgeon Manuel Quijano, accompanied by six armed men, is dispatched from the presidio in Monterey with orders to exhume the body of Padre Andrés Quintana at the mission of Santa Cruz, La Exaltación de la Santa Cruz. The priest is found to have been murdered, tortured* in pudendis, *and hanged.*

November 1, 1993. *The dismembered body of a young woman
begins washing ashore on the beaches of Santa Cruz, California.*

Children. *Neófitos. Bestes.* And still it is the same sky, the same
night arched like a reed house, the stars of their birth.

The first two epigraphs stand together on the same page and indicate what is at stake for characters, author, and reader. Calendrical
time, history, and violence are highlighted as the reader is given
two epigraphs that are historical moments, as it were, fixings in
and with the West's calendar that link the past and present of the
novel. Cole McCurtain, with the help of Alex Yazzie, Onatima, Uncle
Luther, and others, will need to understand and come to terms with
that connection in order to stop the murders and appease the painted
gambler.[1]

More is at stake, however, for the first epigraph indicates that
we are dealing with a particular past, that of history as inscribed by
those in power. That is, the first epigraph fixes in chronological
time not the murder of Padre Andrés Quintana by party or parties
unknown, but the government act of dispatch that leads to its discovery. This is what makes it into the historical record as it is presented here. Beyond accentuating the trope of discovery that will
be carried through the novel, the epigraph situates the Spanish
authorities as active agents and subjects. Indeed, the murder and
those who committed it are presented as being of lesser importance
than the authority of the colonialists, their ability to discover what
has been concealed, and their tendency to record the event with
the emphasis on their actions. It goes without saying that the reasons
behind the murder will be secreted from the record, if by some
chance those reasons, in all likelihood unsought by the Spanish
authorities, are uncovered. It is, after all, their discovery, their past,
their history.

Owens, then, like both his protagonist, Cole McCurtain, and like
other Native American writers, needs to confront and come to terms
with the history that has been handed down bearing the stamp of

authority and approval of the dominant culture, whether the agent of authority for that culture is the Catholic Church, the Spanish government in early-nineteenth-century America, the U.S. government, or the academy. That history captures and imprisons those whom the dominant culture defines as Other. This can occur at the level of the word and the unvoiced story behind it, as the third epigraph suggests with *"Neófitos."* In the Spanish mission system, those California Indians inside a mission were labeled *neófitos,* or neophytes. This seemingly harmless label suggesting either a recent convert to Catholicism or an individual just beginning on the path to conversion and salvation was anything but, however, for once inside the mission the Natives were not allowed to leave. They became prisoners. The California Natives in particular, and Native Americans in general, remain imprisoned by authorities, as the scene in which Alex Yazzie reads to Cole from the history books stresses. Alex is particularly irked by a history of the Franciscan missionaries published in the 1940s. On the first page the historian writes *"The entire history of human affairs relates no adventure of greater ambition and deals with no task more utterly hopeless than the noble effort of the Franciscan padres of California to raise a pagan Indian race to the white man's standards of living"* (Bone Game 178). Couched in language at once heroic and tragic, the colonial history uses the standard binary—white man/Indian, noble/pagan—to fix the Native in an untenable position. Moreover, the adverb "utterly" speaks volumes, as it suggests the overdetermined efforts of the dominant culture to define Indian.[2]

To free those imprisoned, one must do more than simply replace one history—that tacitly referred to with the first epigraph and forcefully represented by the quotations from the historian's text—with another. One must free them from history altogether, and in order to do this Owens and his characters must replace one concept of time with another. This is especially important for Cole McCurtain. He begins the novel acutely aware of what time it is: 4 A.M. For this and each of the previous five mornings "he had stumbled" out of bed in "exactly the same way at the same time" (8) after dreaming of Padre Andrés Quintana, Venancio Asisara, rape, and violent death. The seventh morning is no different, for "at four A.M. the owl called him from the seventh dream" (58). Only then does he write Uncle Luther, Onatima, and Hoey seeking advice.

The stress on the precise time of Cole's awakening for the past week accentuates the hold that chronological time has on him. Caught in a morass of alcohol and self-pity, Cole is all too happy to wake up into time, not because waking means the dream ends (it is with him in his waking moments, after all) but because of his need for a present moment that necessarily implies a past. Indeed, a part of an early conversation Cole has with Alex Yazzie highlights the importance of the past to Cole's identity. Alex invites him to a club, appropriately named the Catalyst, to hear Elvin Bishop, and Cole responds, "He's still alive?" (31). Shortly thereafter he asks Alex, "Who are you going to be?" His new friend replies, "Just me." Instead of replying to Alex, Cole lapses into reverie and talking to himself, and in so doing reveals a connection between the question of identity he posed and his own sense of self. Cole "thought of Elvin Bishop, one of the great bluesmen of the sixties and seventies. 'That was a long time ago,' he said aloud, more to his beer than to Yazzie" (31). Elvin Bishop, the blues, and death conspire to send Cole out of dialogue and into contemplation and monologue. The sixties and early seventies are a long time ago for Cole because they were when his brother, Attis, was alive. Earlier in the scene, he had "raised his bottle, remembering again the morning of hunting twenty years before" when "his brother had still been in Nam" (30) and was therefore still alive. Less than a year later, Cole would walk the riverbed searching for Attis's corpse. Cole has failed to come to terms with Attis's death, has relegated him to the past and thus conceived of him in terms of loss, so his brother haunts his dreams. He tells his lover, Rita, of the dream "he [has] had over and over, the one in which Attis reached out to him" (74). Rita recognizes that a sense of the past as past, as irretrievable, holds Cole firmly in its grasp, and she tells him as much when she ends their affair: "I can't see you anymore. I love my husband. But you're in love with the past. You're fucking the past, Cole, not me" (74). Now, twenty years after last field-dressing a buck, Cole addresses the bottle that he has been raising for months in an increasingly self-destructive attempt to avoid coming to terms with his brother's death.

Onatima reprimands Cole for feeling sorry for himself and tries to get him to see that his actions are connected to feelings of guilt. After acknowledging that she, like Cole, knows that the dream of the bear and the painted gambler merging into one figure "reaching toward him" (164) is what kept Cole from finding words of prayer in the sweat lodge ceremony, a paralyzing image for Cole in his present psychological state insofar as it is linked to the figure of Attis reaching to him in his dreams, Onatima carefully turns Cole to his brother:

> She lifted a thick strand of her hair and began toying with it. "He still troubles you, doesn't he?"
>
> "Who?"
>
> "It's very hard, I know. I've done it, too. But you brought your brother home. His bones are where they are supposed to be."
>
> He looked at his hands. "I don't know . . ."
>
> She cut him off gently. "It's not wrong to survive. I see Indians all the time who are ashamed of surviving, and they don't even know it. We have survived a five-hundred-year war in which millions of us were starved to death, burned in our homes, shot and killed with disease and alcohol. It's a miracle any Indian is alive today. Why us, we wonder. We read their books and find out we're supposed to die. That's the story they made up for us. Survivor's guilt is a terrible burden, and so we feel guilt if we have enough food, a good home, a man or woman who loves us. (165)

Onatima knows dreams, knows the relationship between Attis and the figure, and thus she goes right through Cole's "Who?" Refusing to allow him the false sanctuary of pretending ignorance, she gently cuts him off when he responds in the negative. The conclusion of

Cole's sentence is not important here; what is important is what the narrative stresses—that Cole *does not know* what Onatima is about to tell him. She recognizes that Cole, like other Indians she has known, acts as he does out of feelings of shame and guilt, shame being the preeminent social emotion and guilt that which is produced by an internalization of the *socius*. In doing so, he remains mastered by the dominant society and thus harms both himself and those close to him. It is as Rita told him when she left, "Those who are drowning don't mean to take others with them, but they do, don't they? They must hold to something" (74).

Cole's curious attempt to hold onto something meaningful after Rita leaves is connected to both the earlier scene in Alex's house and Cole's later attempts to obtain advice from Luther, Onatima, and Hoey by references to natural and chronological time. Cole went to Cueloze Pueblo after Rita left, and after departing the place that the Spanish called first Pueblo de los Jumanos and then Gran Quivira, he "drove northwest two hours before sunrise" (75) until, drunk and blinded by a snowstorm, he ran off the road, missed a tree only because of Luther's intervention, and took out a section of barbed-wire fence. At Alex's, Cole remembers the deer hunt with his father and that "the world that had been all before them was closing in as the sun rose" (30). After the owl calls him from the seventh night's dream at 4 A.M., Cole sits down at the kitchen table "two hours before daylight" (58) to write a letter to his relations in the Yazoo River country of Mississippi. The references to both chronological time and natural time are fitting given that Cole, at these points in the story, is psychologically and ontologically unwell.

In "An Introduction Aboard the *Fidèle*" for *The American Indian and the Problem of History*, Calvin Martin argues that the root of the problem addressed by the historians, anthropologists, and Native and non-Native writers who contributed essays to the book stems from historians' use of an intellectual tool, history, grounded in a worldview that is antithetical to the Natives' own. The West proceeds from and with a "speculative philosophy [that] . . . tends to be, at least from medieval times on, anthropological" (8). By the term "anthropological" Martin refers not to the discipline of anthropology, although it and its practitioners can be indicted for the same errors as history and historians, so much as to the word itself. Viewed in the light of its constituent parts, *logos* and *anthropos*, one sees that "'anthropological' is another way of saying 'the world according to, for, and about humanity'" (8). Given this frame of reference, traditional historians studying Native American history are bound to colonize their subject, for the core philosophy for Native Americans is biological rather than anthropological. As such, its articulation of time is fundamentally different from that of the West. Following Lévi-Strauss, who argues that "the characteristic feature of the savage mind is its timelessness" (qtd. in Martin 15), Martin holds that historians "have in truth largely missed the North American Indians' experience and meaning of it. We have missed their 'time' as they construed and sought to live it. . . . [W]e historians define them in and confine them to the terms of historic (i.e. anthropological) time" (15–16).

Such an act of imprisonment, Martin makes clear, begins with Columbus's act of "discovery" and the assigning of a date: "October 12, 1492: Columbus encountered the Bahamas and hailed America and its 'Indians' for European history" (210–11). From that moment, the Native conception of time as part of a biological rather than an anthropological worldview is threatened and begins to be taken apart, and with it "an American eternity . . . began unraveling" (210). Martin's distressing tendency toward pan-Indianism notwithstanding, a tendency I think he recognizes and combats in his epilogue by an accumulation and orchestration of Native and non-Native voices, the point he makes is of value to us in no small measure because it resonates nicely with *Bone Game*. Indeed, Owens's novel revises Martin's argument somewhat by indicating that in the case of the Costanoans of California it is inaccurate to speak of an unraveling of "eternity" and its related worldview. Immediate—indeed, nearly instantaneous—destruction was the case.

Venancio Asisara was Costanoan, or Ohlone, as the descendants of the Costanoans have come to be known. Talking over beer at the

Catalyst as Elvin Bishop takes the stage, Alex tells Cole that the Ohlone did more than merely avoid saying the names of the dead; the living "obliterated" everything connected with the dead, including memory. What this means, as Alex points out, is "there wasn't any history, Cole, no yesterday. There was only sacred time—the time of creation—and today, with nothing in between" (54). The Spanish brought more than death to the Ohlone: they brought history, chronological time, and Christendom's calendar, and in so doing destroyed a culture by annihilating the people's sense of time: "All of their care and precaution [regarding the dead] meant nothing. In one generation it was over. After ten thousand years, one morning they woke up and the world was unrecognizable" (54). Uncle Luther hears and sees what the Ohlone lived—the destruction of their world: "It happened so quick with these Indians here, not like with us where it took three hundred years. It's very sad. One minute these people was living like they always did, and the next minute everything was gone" (224). It is this change that the painted gambler Venancio Asisara recognizes and is vexed by. As a grizzly bear doctor, one of those individuals with great power who practiced what the West might think of as witchcraft, Venancio had worn the paws of the great bear with claws filled with poison and participated in the murder of Padre Quintana (57). Now, as the grizzly bear, he stands in a world that "was irrevocably strange and void" (224).

Martin returns to and amplifies his argument on this profound difference on the conception of time in the volume's epilogue, "Time and the American Indian." He weaves together elements of the traditional worldviews of Native Hawai'ians, the Diné, the Kiowa, the Cheyenne, the Beaver Indians of British Columbia, the Cree, and the Anishinaabeg; the Diné understanding of language, thought, and the universe as articulated by Gary Witherspoon; portions of the arguments made by some of the volume's contributors; and Mircea Eliade on myth and history. Martin argues that Native Americans turned to deliberate and conscious renewal ceremonies aimed at further repudiating time. It seems that the impetus for all this activity derives from the astounding (to us) conviction that humans can and must keep the cosmos intact, vibrant, and lucid through ceremony. Time is the focal issue in all this because it is the ultimate symbol of disconnection. A sense of time's passing produces a sense of distance from the grand unity which prevailed in the act of original creation and which indeed prevails still in the creation witnessed in one's lifetime. (207)

Here, then, Martin accentuates the essential role played by ceremonies and rituals in traditional societies, a role that is connected to and exists because of and for a concept of time that animates the peopled cosmos precisely because it is not chronological, not historical, not anthropological. Such is the case for the Ohlone, who, in addition to having a non-anthropological concept of time, relied upon ceremonies to attain and maintain the power necessary to keep the cosmos and the individual well.

Cole is profoundly unwell, and his sickness affects his imagination. While he knows that the Choctaw used their stories and bones to make home the world they found in their journey east, at the beginning of *Bone Game* he is unable "to imagine his own forerunners there, at that time. . . . In a world so different it was beyond imagining" (9). Such a world must not be beyond imagining, however, as Owens stresses throughout his fiction and as the close of *Bone Game* makes clear when Venancio Asisara looks down upon "a world so like his own" (243), but for Cole it is, at least early on. Indeed, when we first see Cole in *Bone Game* his inability to use imagination is reminiscent of the degree to which his imagination is compromised prior to the time he spends with Uncle Luther (*Sharpest Sight* 72). Together, then, a debilitating sense of time, a concomitant lack of place, and an inability to turn to the imagination have snared Cole. Alex immediately recognizes this and the nature of the trap, calling Cole "a poor mixedblood trapped between worlds and cultures if I can believe my eyes" (26). He reiterates the point at the Catalyst, saying to Cole, "You poor, homeless half-breed. . . . The real lost generation, trapped between worlds. Living your liminal life" (47). Cole has already recognized his own liminal state, however, imagining that his desk would one day be studied by an anthropologist charting his collapse; the anthropologist will conclude: "*As you can see, coincidental with this October level is a rather obvious decline in the mixedblood's socially acceptable behavioral characteristics. Notice the Mexican beer stains on the unopened envelopes, indicative of low survival quotient, intense liminality, possible homophobia*" (17). The anthropologist's language obfuscates rather than illuminates, and its incorporation here stands as a tacit critique by Owens of anthropology, or at least "bad" anthropology, and the social sciences in general. But while the concept of liminality can be abused by anthropologists, and others, operating with and within an anthropological concept of time, as is the case here, Owens's narrative also suggests that liminality can be both an accurate term to describe the position in which Cole finds himself and a necessary position for one seeking healing and the recovery and/or reaffirmation of identity.

Cole's liminal state is highlighted with his first appearance in the narrative. Awakened by the dream sent by Venancio Asisara, Cole "stands *in* the window" as he peers into the darkness "trying yet again to see" (6, emphasis added). Three times an owl calls, harbinger of death for both the Choctaw of Mississippi and the Ohlone who called and call the Santa Cruz area home, and then "it is there in the window, wings spread, white and covering the night" (6). Owl and Cole are together in the space of the open window, and that union suggests what has driven Cole into his present liminal state and what he must face and is facing. He stumbles backward away from the bird, but the message is clear. If Cole does not come to terms with death, the owl will enter the house (traditionally a bad omen for the Ohlone) instead of stopping short in the window frame, and with it will come death.

Although Cole is caught in a liminal, betwixt-and-between state, it is liminality as it functions in traditional ceremonies and passage rituals that can enable him to emerge from that state healed. Anthropologists from Arnold van Gennep (who first phrased the phenomenon in *The Rites of Passage*) onward have stressed the importance of the liminal stage of rituals and ceremonies both to the rituals and ceremonies themselves and to the participants, seeing liminality as the stage when participants are out of ordinary time and space. For instance, Victor Turner, who elaborated on van Gennep's idea to show how liminality helps communities and individuals confront and deal with crises, holds that the liminal stage of rites of passage, other rituals, and ceremonies allows participants the freedom "to contemplate for a while the mysteries that confront all men, the difficulties that peculiarly beset their own society, [and] their personal problems" *(Dramas* 242). Moreover, it is the vehicle or mechanism that enables the individual or group crisis to be staged, addressed, and interrogated in the first place, for the liminal stage is "a time and place lodged between all times and spaces defined and governed . . . by the rules of law, politics, and religion and economic necessity" (Turner, "Social Dramas" 161). Without liminality, then, there is no hope that the problem can be addressed, much less solved.

Given the importance of liminality to individual and cultural health and well-being, on the one hand, and Owens's protagonists' quest to realize and reaffirm their identities, on the other, it is fitting that three times Cole finds himself at traditional sites where ceremonies, with their inherent and necessary liminality, are conducted in order that healing might take place. The first occurs immediately prior to his departure from New Mexico for Santa Cruz. His trip to Cueloze Pueblo is a failed attempt at healing made after Rita tells him that he is drowning. The fact that he goes there "in the last light of the winter solstice" (74), a traditional time of ceremonies for various pueblos, stresses both his liminality and the liminality of the healing ceremonies traditionally practiced in kivas. And it is the kiva which is his destination at the pueblo the Spanish called de los Jumanos. He clambers drunkenly over the ruins of the abandoned pueblo, reaches the kiva over which the Spanish had once erected a Catholic church that has subsequently fallen in, and climbs down the six-foot walls to lie in the kiva's center and study the winter night sky. However, while Owens describes the kiva as "the sacred middle place" (75), and in so doing tacitly suggests the positive possibilities inherent in liminality, even before Cole reaches the site for societies to gather to pray for the world he is trying and failing to recall what brought him to Cueloze Pueblo; without that knowledge he cannot be healed. Nor can he if he persists in being alone. The kiva is a place for *communal* ceremonies, but as Cole looks skyward he feels only "the immensity of his *solitude*. Everything familiar had gone, and he had lost the path" (75, emphasis added). His attempt fails not because the kiva in which he lies is in ruins, but because he is. He does not at this point know what Onatima tells Abby: "Your father has always grieved for his brother and yet never lost him. To believe otherwise is to deceive ourselves and to never be whole" (176); he does not yet know, nor is he ready to hear, what Onatima will eventually say to him: "What Luther told you many years ago is true. You carry your brother inside you; he never left you. He wants you to be happy" (165).

What Cole does recognize, and what Owens wants to be sure the reader sees, is that "Los Jumanos had called him" (75). The narrative reveals that Cueloze Pueblo was the site of the massacre of nine hundred Natives and the enslaving of several hundred more in retaliation for the ambush and murder of a small group of Spaniards in the vicinity of the pueblo (75), and it has called Cole for several reasons. There is, of course, the connection between the atrocities committed at the pueblo and those committed at the mission in Santa Cruz. Cole is also called because of the connection between "the pueblo of the striped ones" (75), so called because some of its inhabitants painted their faces, and the painted gambler Cole must face. Finally, the pueblo has called Cole because it so graphically represents the imposition of the Western time and worldview upon the Natives, an imposition that affects Cole as well.

The Pueblo peoples use ceremonies to ensure that the world stays in a steady state. Many of those ceremonies take place in kivas. The disintegration of the world that was most visibly apparent in drought affecting the land and diseases affecting the people, a disintegration that led to the Pueblo Revolt of 1680, was held by the Natives to be a consequence of the Spanish mission system that prohibited the full and necessary practice of traditional dances, ceremonies, and rituals. As was the case with the Ohlone, the timeless existence of the Pueblo people was fractured by the Western concept of time and concomitant worldview, and with that fracture, powerfully symbolized by the mass of the huge church bearing down upon the kiva at Cueloze Pueblo and contributing to its ruin, comes harm to the world and its people.

Alex Yazzie recognizes Cole's isolation early on and speaks to him about it at the Catalyst. He is pleased to hear that Abby wants to come to Santa Cruz, knowing that Cole is alone too much. When Cole responds that Alex also lives alone, the young Navajo replies, "But not spiritually alone" (47). Alex reiterates the importance of human and spiritual connections after telling Cole about the Ohlone and their concept of time, saying that it will be good for Cole to have Abby with him and asking him if he can use Cole's house for a sweat ceremony. Although Cole refuses to entertain the former and resists the latter, Alex pushes him on the idea of a sweat ceremony until he relents. Alex knows the truth and is not afraid to say it to his new friend after he agrees to let them use the property he rents for the ceremony: "A sweat would be good for you. You need it. You ever take part in a Native American Church ceremony?" (55).

Nor is Alex shy about telling the appropriate people that Cole needs a ceremony of purification and healing, as is clear by the question Emil Redbull, the man who will run the ceremony, puts to him after meeting Cole: "Is this the one?" (160). Cole's inability to pray during the ceremony is not itself necessarily indicative of a failed ceremony, as Emil points out after the ceremony, but when coupled with the difficulty Cole has talking with Onatima about Attis immediately after the sweat's conclusion it suggests what Onatima makes clear later when she tells Abby, "I'd like to know more about this place. Your father is going to have to confront this thing eventually, but he isn't ready yet. So I want to know more"

(175). Emil too knows Cole has "something important to do here" (164–65) and tells him that it is good that he is not alone, that he is together with family and friends who, in effect, are the community necessary for the ceremonies Cole needs if he is to be healed.

The sweat ceremony is linked in the narrative to natural time both because Alex and Emil arrive at Cole's before sunrise on the day of the sweat and because Emil focuses on the sun once it has cleared the horizon. He acts as though the sun "invited him in for coffee" (160) after he has finished stretching the canvas over the arched saplings that form the skeleton of the sweat lodge. Those "arched saplings" (160) harken back to the third epigraph, which describes the "same night arched like a reed house," and thus suggest that the sweat lodge and the ceremony held within are connected to continuity and constancy, the renewal or rebirth that comes as a result of ceremony, and the cosmos and natural time. To accentuate the latter connection, the narrative strongly suggests that Emil considers the coffee Cole offers him a gift from the sun. To be invited in by the sun is to be invited into its realm, the realm of natural time, and to receive its gifts is to become aware of the value and goodness that can come from that realm. The narrative also indicates the amount of time, twenty minutes, between the moment Onatima tells Cole that it is necessary for him to take part in the ceremony and when they are in the sweat lodge with Emil and Abby. While inside, however, the narrative makes no reference to chronological time, thus accentuating the "othertimeliness" of the ceremony itself. The sweat is not governed or informed by the clock but by prayer and the structure of ritual.

Owens's narrative also links different conceptions of time with Cole's third attempt at a healing ceremony—the Native American Church service and its peyote ritual—and does so well before the ceremony takes place. Alex asks Cole if they can also use his house for the service, Cole agrees and asks if the service will be before or after the sweat ceremony, and the conversation turns to differing senses of time:

"Well, the sweat's this weekend, and Uncle Emmet probably won't be here for a while."

"Peyote's just as illegal at my house as yours, Alex."

"Technically, yes."

"Hell, why not? Just don't expect me to eat any cactus."

"That's great. Uncle Emmet might be here in a week or so."

"Indian time, right?"

"Yeah. Tomorrow, next month, next year."

As they passed the college fishpond, Alex pointed at a big spotted carp. "That guy wouldn't last long on a reservation." (97)

"Indian" time is different from non-Indian time—is, as we have been suggesting, biological rather than anthropological—and the narrative stresses that at the same time it articulates the connections between that "different" time, ceremony, and place. Reservations are, of course, a place where Natives can and do exist in and as a community. It is also, again as the narrative emphasizes with the reference to Cueloze Pueblo, the place where ceremonies are performed to ensure the continuance of the community—its "survivance," to use Vizenor's provocative term—and the integration into it of its individual members. Tellingly, the Native American Church service itself exists in the narrative with neither preamble nor reference to chronological time, as Owens's narrative moves Cole and the reader directly into the liminal time of the service (195).

It is within the liminal time and space of the service that Cole takes peyote, prays, and then has a vision that brings together past and present, California and Mississippi, the painted gambler, Attis, Uncle Luther, and himself. When it is his turn to pray, Cole remembers his silence in the sweat ceremony, fights back panic as he searches for the appropriate words, and offers the only ones that come to him—those of a Luiseño song: "'I had been looking far,' he whispered, so quietly that he was certain no one could hear, 'sending my spirit north, south, east, and west, but I could find nothing, no way of escape'" (197). Like the Luiseño singer, whose song Cole had offered to his class in its entirety early on in the narrative, Cole has been "trying to escape from death" (40), but the phrase is left out of the song when he offers it as prayer because the ceremony and the vision it produces will help him cease trying to escape from death and instead begin to see that death does not imprison one if one has the proper sense of time.

This will not be easy for Cole. Indeed, he must lose himself if he is to find himself. Once again, a recognition of the relationship between the scene and the epigraph is instructive. When Cole leaves the room and goes outside to vomit after *Nílchi bee íiniziinii*, the "in-standing wind soul" that is the "ghost" (198) of Venancio Asisara, appears at the door, he sees the bear's shadow silhouetted against the moon, while behind it "an unknown pattern of stars wheeled madly across the sky" (198). The stars, which had been merely "holes in the dark" (75) when he looked up at them at de los Jumanos, are now completely unfamiliar to him. This is precisely the opposite of the stars in the third epigraph, which are those of the Ohlone's birth in the "same sky" and the "same night." Having completely lost his bearings, then—having, like Venancio Asisara, "awakened" to a seemingly strange new world in which he thinks himself alone (7)—Cole feels a desperate need to reenter the house. He cannot do so, however, for the vision and what it has to show him about himself beckon.

In his vision, Cole feels himself chased by the great bear and thinks that it "was pursuing him through time but not space" (199). Upon entering a clearing in which there are both a half-dozen tradi-tional Ohlone huts and several men, women, and children, however, Cole realizes his error. The bear is not pursuing him through time because, as Luther had reminded Hoey much earlier in the narra-tive when discussing California and the death of Hoey's wife, Ida, "It's all one time" (85). This is evident by the traditional Ohlone settlement in which Cole finds himself. Moreover, if it is all one time, then there is no past. Therefore, death cannot produce the sort of loss Cole thinks it does. We return to the silence of the ellipsis in the narrative when Onatima gently cuts Cole off as she talks with him after the sweat ceremony. "I don't know . . ." (165), he says, trying to evade her and thus not have to think about what he feels he has lost.

Like Onatima, the vision will allow no evasion. Attis becomes the gambler as Cole plays the bone game in his vision because, like the gambler of his dreams, Attis haunts Cole. Early on we learn that "the strange Indian [Cole] lies in his house fearing the dreams Venancio sends" (7) because they deal with violence, death, and loss—that is, because they are all too easily connected to Attis. In the vision, Cole sees Attis about to enter the cabin in which they were born and knows that somewhere inside will be their mother. Try as he might to shout out his brother's name, Cole is unable to do so. Later in the vision his drowned brother beckons to him, but Cole is still unable to "form the shape of his brother's name" (201). This inability suggests Cole's desire to live, for in the Choctaw tradition the deceased's outside shadow will try to appease its loneliness by having someone living join it by saying its name.

However, Attis is home, thanks to Cole's act of retrieving the bones, an act Onatima reminds him of (165), and as such his hands reach out to grasp his brother, not to pull him into death, but to establish a connection that Cole will carry with him beyond the time and space of the vision and into a world he needs to know. This is made clear in the vision's conclusion, for after Venancio Asisara, the bear become man with the paws of a grizzly, strikes Cole to the ground, "it was Attis who reached toward him where he lay. His brother's hand closed on his, and he felt himself pulled from the earth with a force beyond any he had ever known" (202). Within the vision Uncle Luther also gives Cole the medicine pouch Attis made and Cole had thought lost, figuratively giving his nephew what he will literally find around his neck after the vision so that he might have the power he will need to face the painted gambler. By disabusing him of his disabling sense of time and the past, then, the vision gives Cole the knowledge of his brother's continuing positive presence in his life.

That vision also compels Cole to confront two questions that are themselves linked and which yoke together the sweat ceremony

with the Native American Church service. The questions also emphasize the importance of place to identity that we have been tracking
throughout Owens's narratives. On the morning of the sweat, Emil
Redbull asks Cole, "You know those woods?" (161). At that time
Cole can only respond that he has been too busy to get to know
them, but the question returns to him after his peyote vision leads
him to ask himself, "Where was home?" (204). Ruled by time and
his take on the past, Cole had avoided the woods of the mountains
around Santa Cruz, although prior to moving there "he'd never
lived anywhere before where he didn't know the terrain of his existence" (211), opting instead for the open spaces where "the sun and
the stars, even veiled in fog, were constant markers" (212). The peyote
vision, which takes place under an unfamiliar night sky, has revealed
all that is problematic with this assertion, has indicated how what
Cole takes to be markers are less than accurate because of his imprisonment by and in a particular sense of time, just as the narrative
does so here for the reader by telling us that the markers are constant when they are veiled in fog. Now, however, Cole, having made
sense of time and the past, is in a position to finish lifting the veil that
shrouds his sense of self by getting to know the physical landscape
so that he can then answer the question the vision leaves him with.

Home is associated with a specific sense of time as well as place,
and Owens accentuates this with the story Alex tells Abby as they
walk to a bus stop in order to get to Cole's home for his birthday
celebration. The story concerns the only other time Alex had acci-
dently drained dead his car battery. He had gone deep into the
heart of the Navajo reservation for a naming ceremony, left on his
car headlights, and been stranded with his younger brother Tony
because they were the last guests to try to leave. It was two days
before a relative showed up with a vehicle so they could get a jump
start. That was his last summer at home, he says, and then adds,
"Now I can't even imagine a time when two lost days could mean
nothing, when I hadn't looked at a calendar for weeks at a time. It
was really beautiful out there" (217). Over beers at the Catalyst, Alex
had told Cole, "I refuse to be deracinated" (46), but we see here

that he is threatened with a violent uprooting because of an adherence to Western, or anthropological, time. The memory triggers other memories of home, and Alex experiences "a sharp pang of homesickness" that leads him to say aloud, "I think I'll go home this summer. . . . I'll spend the whole summer there, up at the sheep camp with Tony. I miss being Navajo" (218). His announcement speaks volumes, for both Abby and the reader, because it indicates both that being separated too long from one's home leads to deracination of one's very identity, in Alex's case Navajo identity, and that returning to one's home is a return to biological time, seasons, and in the case of the Navajo, a life tuned to natural cycles.

The narrative marks of Cole's return to health are a sunrise and sunset in which neither clocks nor chronological time intrude. In the former instance, Luther awakens Cole for the sunrise the morning after Paul Kantner, one of the two serial killers who has terrorized Santa Cruz, is killed (225–27). In the latter, fittingly in the final chapter of *Bone Game* when he has returned to the home he has made for himself in the American Southwest, Cole, Onatima, and Abby sit together on the deck of his house and talk of home while "the red New Mexico sunset was stitched by a ragged line of forest" (241). The scene closes with the sunset in a fashion that returns the narrative to the chapter's beginning and highlights healing: "Below the mountains, a broad gust of wind had lifted a layer of mist from the treetops, sending it across the valley. Against the last light of sunset, the vapor looked like a cloud of yellow-orange pollen that spread until it covered everything they could see" (243).

Cole's exploration of the forest above his house both reinforces his decision to return home to New Mexico with his daughter and reveals the identity of one of the murderers, although he will not yet be able to recognize the latter, for as he looks into the window of Robert Malin's house he envisions the twisted bodies of the young woman and two toddlers who were to be his last sacrificial victims. Like Cole, Robert is situated in a liminal state throughout much of the novel. His first appearance in the narrative fixes him in a betwixt-and-between position, standing "with one foot inside the door" (16) of Cole's university office. Robert is also seen "balanced on a hanging bridge" (121) leading to his cabin and stopped "in the middle of a span" (170) above a ravine cutting through the mountains above the campus at Santa Cruz. Moreover, fearing that a catastrophic earthquake will occur if he does not offer thirteen human sacrifices, Robert thinks "I'm in the middle place" (44) as he lurks in the forest and plots where to find his victims.

Like Cole, Robert is visited in dreams by the painted gambler. Venancio Asisara recognizes that Robert hungers for dreams. It is that hunger that draws him to the mysticism of Edgar Cayce and the romanticized image of the Native American that he holds and cherishes. The difference between the two men, however, is that while Cole has a community to help him through his liminality and be there for him when he emerges from that betwixt-and-between state, Robert remains isolated and alone. From the one-room cabin described as "the cell of a scholarly monk" (213) that he built atop a stump in the middle of a stream to his lack of awareness of the effect he has on women and men, everything about Robert's life suggests that he is by himself and wishes to remain that way. Therefore, his intimate knowledge of the forests and mountains ringing Santa Cruz, the terrain of his existence, does not help him to have a healthy, balanced sense of place, home, and his relationship to the earth. Robert looks out the window throughout the Native American Church service, waiting for Venancio Asisara to make his appearance, and does not pray aloud when the rattle is passed to him because the ceremony and the community that is formed for and by it mean nothing to him. From first to last, he stays in the "middle place" of his own making and choosing, telling Abby just prior to raping her that "Native Americans know that the world is precariously balanced between good and evil" (238) and invoking Cole's reading of the importance of "sacrifice and agony" (237) for the modernists in order to justify what he has done and is about to do.

Cole "love[s] the painful sincerity of the modernists" (39) in plain sight as they struggled to use their art to find something they had lost. They lived a world at once "bereft" because of the loss and "haunted" by it (39). Their turn to art, and especially writing, as the medium for recovery is to be lauded, then, even as the texts they produce are to be read critically. For as we have seen, Owens knows that canonical American literature, including that produced by the modernists, all too often articulates a worldview that silences the Native in favor of the Indian. The memory of Onatima from twenty years past surfaces early in *Bone Game* and serves to remind Cole and the reader of the power of story to create a particular world that suits those in control: "For the first time in years, in his mind he saw an image of Onatima in Uncle Luther's cabin as she had been when he met her, pulling a paperback from the pocket of her apron. . . . 'That's how they make the world,' she had said that day, and for twenty years he'd tried to make his own world with words, like they did, always remembering Onatima" (19–20). As she did in *The Sharpest Sight*, Onatima stresses the importance of creating their own stories to stand against the stories that have been told about them. She tells Cole's daughter, "They would imprison us in their vision and their stories, and we can't let them do that. We have to have our own stories" (140).

Uncle Luther reiterates the point the morning following Paul Kantner's death when he and Cole are awake to see the sunrise. He goes so far as to suggest that writing is connected to Cole's health, first remarking that his nephew is cheerful this particular morning and then adding, "Which reminds me. How come you ain't wrote no more of them books? You used to write good stories" (226). A description of and commentary on the sunrise situated between Luther's questions and Cole's response accentuates the connection between natural time, healing, good health, and stories. More than Cole's good health is at issue, of course, for the good stories he writes help to heal others by standing against the stories that imprison created by the dominant culture. In effect, by "writing in the oral tradition," to invoke Kimberly Blaeser's provocative phrasing with regard to Vizenor's writing, Cole helps to ensure that a particular other worldview is passed on.

Louis Owens is no different from Cole McCurtain. He too needs to write. The epigraphs are instructive here as well, for from first to last Owens's writing is an exhumation, an unburying that is an uncovering of truths about Native identities and worldviews, particularly Choctaw, Ohlone, and Diné in *Bone Game*; about Americans and America; and about Native–non-Native relations in this country—past and present. The crucial difference, of course, is that Owens's act of exhumation is not sanctioned by the authorities. Given this, and given that writing and the novel are typically instruments of the authorities of the dominant culture, Owens and other Native American writers must come to terms with the medium in which they work in order to write within and against the dominant culture. We have seen how Owens uses trickster discourse in *Wolfsong* in order to position himself vis-à-vis the medium and then how in the best trickster spirit he invokes and takes apart canonical American literature in *The Sharpest Sight*. In *Bone Game*, more than in the earlier novels, liminality is emphasized. Indeed, just as the middle space of liminality serves to articulate the identity of Cole and others while being vital to Cole's search for healing, so too does the middle space serve to help Owens situate his own discourse on discovery in relationship to the person considered the master discoverer in the minds of the subjects of the dominant culture: Christopher Columbus.

Heading west to come to Cole's aid, Uncle Luther and Hoey remark while crossing the Rio Grande that the way people were driving on the short stretch of freeway leading up to the bridge indicates that everyone is "mad" or "nuts" (82). The conversation next turns to the Rio Grande itself, and how in Luther's opinion a river John Wayne made famous with the movie *Rio Grande* should have more water. Then, while still on the bridge, the figure of Christopher Columbus comes up via the person of Columbus Bailey as Luther tries to "think of the fish" (82) in the Rio Grande. He tells Hoey that Columbus Bailey, back home in Mississippi, quit fishing because he "started hearing the fish scream when he took 'em out of the water" (83). The throughline of the conversation that takes place in the betwixt-and-between space of the bridge leads from Christopher Columbus to John Wayne to madness or insanity, and then comes back to Columbus Bailey and Owens himself. As Owens has Jim Joseph make clear in *Wolfsong*, Christopher Columbus "discovers" and lays claim to both that which is not his and that which cannot be laid claim to in any Western sense of possession: "That's like when you need a new radio, so you go in the back window of your neighbor's house when he ain't home and discover his radio. Then you say, 'Oh, look at this wonderful radio I have discovered'" (81). The example is especially apt, both because it is with and in language that discovery and possession are manifested and because what is discovered is an instrument for the continual transmission of a particular ideology and worldview. That ideology and worldview, moreover, violate the proper relationship between neighbors, one that is necessary if people are to live together.

When Columbus discovers and declares his claim to the New World, then, he begins the perverse cycle of laying claim, of taking what is not one's to take. In Luther's reading of the popular culture icon John Wayne and the movie *Rio Grande*, at least, that cycle is tacitly celebrated when Wayne's character defeats the Spanish and claims the land and water. The acts constituting the cycle lead to madness, not in the Foucaultian sense (the mad people acting in complete accordance with the dictates and ideology of bourgeois culture), but at a deeper register. Against that tradition or pattern, begun by Christopher Columbus just as assuredly as Western notions of time "began" in the Americas with his discovery of the New World, Owens offers an alternative Columbus in the figure of Columbus Bailey, one sensitive to the natural world and thus one who operates differently in relation to it. While Christopher Columbus's act of discovery leads to madness, Columbus Bailey's leads to an understanding of the world that necessarily situates humans within rather than against and above; such an understanding is essential to good mental and physical health and the well-being of the planet and its inhabitants.

Columbus Bailey, the discoverer who starts Luther "thinking that maybe them fish been screaming like that all along and couldn't nobody hear 'em before" (83), is linked to Cole in the passage by virtue of the shortened version of the former's name that Luther and Hoey both use: "Col." If the street sign in Gallup for Coal Avenue is a sign that Luther recognizes is like Cole's name even though it is spelled differently (113–14), so is Col, like but not the same as Cole's name, a sign connected to the protagonist, especially given that early in the narrative Owens highlights the slipperiness of language and plays with pronunciation and meaning in order to reveal what Cole must discover. Awakened by the sixth night's dream, Cole talks to himself as he heads to the kitchen: "'*Shilombish* or *shilup*,' he said tentatively, as if afraid to put too much weight on any syllable. '*Shilup* or *shilombish*? Which is which? Which is witch? *Aholhpokunna*? My words flee like rabbits, Grandmother'" (9). His musings on the relationship between his dreams and the inside and outside shadows of the Choctaw deceased lead to language play, "which is witch," indicating that Cole will have to discover the relationship between witchery, the painted gambler, and the murders occurring in and around Santa Cruz if he is to put a stop to them and appease Venancio Asisara. The latter will necessitate that Cole put weight on each syllable as he clearly calls out to Venancio Asisara by name. Having seen the sign of Coal, Luther and Hoey will then discover the witches and witchery that are plaguing the Diné.

Owens's narrative in *Bone Game* necessitates that we speak of the liminality *of* the novel as well as the liminality *in* the novel. Beyond giving us the conversation on the bridge over the Rio Grande, which can be read as a metaphorization of the literary narrative insofar as both are situated between places and deal with discoveries, *Bone Game* highlights the liminal nature of its narrative with chapter 14. That chapter, which tellingly includes the story of Cole's trip to Pueblo de los Jumanos, opens with the phrase "Cusp of evening" (72) and adds to that a description of the point of land that helps to form Monterey Bay in order to accentuate the idea of a point in both time and space between other points. Nor is this any point, for although we can always isolate three points and declare that one is between the other two, the point in time and space being stressed in and with chapter 14 is one which is poised between, which is transitional. On the cusp, "the sun [is] caught in a red web on the sea's horizon" (72). Cole sits on the coastal spine and salutes "the dying sun" with his beer. Then the narrative, situated with the evening precisely on the cusp in order to highlight its liminal nature, proceeds over the course of the next four pages to give the reader the story of the disintegration of Cole's marriage and family, the relationship he has with a colleague's ex-wife, his three-month affair with Rita, and his trip to Pueblo de los Jumanos and the sacred middle space of the kiva before informing us that the sun "slips the spider's filaments and falls to the sea" (75). The middle place of the kiva, it bears repeating, is traditionally where ceremonies occur that articulate community in the process of healing and protecting individuals, cultures, and the earth.

The liminal nature of fiction that *Bone Game* highlights in and with its narrative, then, is what enables it to be, like the kiva, a positive, life-affirming middle place rather than a negative, life-denying one. It is this understanding to which Owens's novels move, and to which the reader moves, as the relationship between liminality, identity, and healing is accentuated, first in *Wolfsong* with Tom Joseph's immersion in the liminal phase of the Coast Salish vision quest, and then in *The Sharpest Sight* with Cole's position in the liminality of Choctaw ceremony as he prepares his brother's body for its return home. Onatima tells Abby that the desire of the dominant culture's subjects "to imprison us in their visions and their stories" is "a matter of power" (*Bone Game* 140). The conversation on the bridge that models the time and space of literary fictions even as it subverts and recasts a trope of the dominant culture helps us to see that it is thanks to its liminality that fiction can be a powerful tool against hegemony. Indeed, Luther says that he guesses Columbus Bailey "got that power [to hear fish scream] from his grampa" (83). Onatima receives from her grandmother the knowledge that the stories told by the dominant culture are about power and a will to power; Columbus Bailey receives from his grandfather the power to sense what has perhaps always been there; Cole receives from Onatima an awareness of how important it is "to make his own world with words" (20); and Owens understands and uses the power of fiction to write the stories, coming from a worldview different from that held by the majority of Americans, that critique the dominant culture and enable Natives and the world (and, I think, non-Natives) to be healed and protected.

The Catholic church at Pueblo de los Jumanos may have represented an attempt to kill and bury one sense of community and worldview by literally and figuratively erecting another over it, but that edifice has fallen, revealing a sacred middle place of Cueloze Pueblo in need of repair. The middle place that is *Bone Game* contributes to the repair of the sacred middle place and a restoration of its power by acknowledging the text's and Owens's connection to the Native American literary tradition and a community of Native American writers. Whereas in *The Sharpest Sight* Owens incorporates allusions to canonical American literature in order to reveal what is wanting and problematic in that canon even as he distances himself and his text from it, a process analogous to that which we have seen operating in and through the incorporation of Christopher Columbus in Luther and Hoey's conversation, in *Bone Game* Owens alludes to Native American literary texts and figures in order to articulate a connection to them and thus affirm an important community.

It is worth beginning with the obvious, the references to *Black Elk Speaks*, for it serves to indicate how the Native American literary texts themselves can be or become instruments of the aforementioned efforts to the contrary that Owens and others must recognize and combat. We all know the story by now: how John Neihardt "found" the Indian he was looking for in the figure of Black Elk, a figure that may be part of but was certainly not the sum of the Lakota man with the name Nicholas Black Elk. Cole teaches *Black Elk Speaks* to his students in an effort to "*free* Black Elk from the romantic visions of John Neihardt and the students" (35, emphasis added). What Neihardt created with *Black Elk Speaks* is yet another in the long line of romantic, doomed Indians. Cole's job is to first rescue Nicholas Black Elk from the "ethnostalgia" which makes him a tragic figure so that then he and the students together might find him "in all those words. All those fucking words" (43). When we link Cole's comment to what Rita says to him when she ends their affair—"You're in love with the past. You're fucking the past, Cole, not me" (74)—it becomes apparent that Neihardt's words are born of and bound up in a romance with the past. "Fucking" is the key word, for two reasons. First, the adjective shocks the reader, here and elsewhere in the narrative, giving him or her a jolt and wake-up call analogous to the shock Cole gives to his students to help free them from their romantic vision of Black Elk in particular and the Native American in general. Second, because the word is a "meaning-less" intensifier to the expression here, as the narrative highlights by offering the phrase "all those words" and then repeating it with the addition of "fucking," we see that the words that capture and imprison Black Elk are less than meaningful because they are not grounded in the full reality of Nicholas Black Elk. Owens's narra-tive will up the ante to include more than Black Elk and the words given us in *Black Elk Speaks* when Alex says, "Words have ceased to have meaning in the Western world" (118). Given the importance of words for the Diné, who recognize that the world was created with speech, his statement could not be more grave.

Once jolted into awareness by Owens's narrative, the reader can better appreciate the connections to works by N. Scott Momaday, Leslie Marmon Silko, and James Welch and the shared concerns that are invoked with and through them. It is fitting that Momaday's *The Way to Rainy Mountain* is alluded to when Cole looks up at the night sky from inside the kiva at Cueloze Pueblo because Momaday's text bears directly on Owens's narrative and his efforts to use the middle space of literary fiction to educate, enlighten, and produce change. Owens writes: "Beyond the swirling snow, the stars were holes in the dark, not relations in the sky, and he felt the immensity of his solitude" (75). In his introduction to *The Way to Rainy Mountain*, Momaday recounts the Kiowa story of seven sisters who go to a tree in an attempt to escape their brother after he has been transformed into a bear. The tree tells them to climb it, and as they ascend it rises higher into the air, to be scored all around by the bear and become what the Kiowa call Tsoai but is typically known as Devil's Tower in eastern Wyoming.[3] The escape transports the sisters into the sky, where they become the stars that form the Big Dipper. Momaday, who was told the story by his grandmother, writes: "From that moment, and as long as the legend lives, the Kiowas have kinsmen in the night sky" (*Rainy Mountain* 8). Not so for Cole, so the allusion serves to accentuate his isolation.

It is fitting that *Bone Game* refers to relations in the sky, for astral bodies are important in the worldviews of both the Pueblo peoples, into whose night sky Cole gazes, and the Chumash, whose night sky is looked up into by Venancio Asisara. For instance, in *The Names* Momaday writes of the "long blue mesa" that is "the rule of a solar calendar" (121) for the Jemez people. There, the sun's position in relation to points on the mesa helps the people know their relation to it, to the earth, and to the trajectory of their individual and common lives. Joe Sando of Jemez Pueblo notes that the Pueblo peoples, not just the Jemez, "studied the movement of the sun, the moon, clouds, the wind, and the timing of the vernal equinox" (24).

The Chumash, too, tracked the movement of celestial objects prior to and after contact with Europeans and told stories about beings in the night sky that the West recognizes as planets, the moon, stars, and constellations. According to Travis Hudson and Ernest Underhay, these bodies were also vital to the understanding and maintenance of relations: "The changing position and visibility of celestial objects were no doubt associated with their possible inter-actions with one another and with the cardinal directions" (144). Their interactions with the Chumash were recognized as well, at least insofar as Chumash astronomy and cosmology indicate that the people "must have regarded the entire universe as a complex net-work of interaction involving man and these beings, who caused all celestial phenomena and some natural (earthly) phenomena that could only be understood in causal terms" (141).

The subtle and minor revision of the passage from *The Way to Rainy Mountain*, then, serves to accentuate connections, stories, and how they are mutually invigorating and actualizing. The allusion also effectively stresses the importance of stories and storytelling, for the former help the Kiowa make sense of their world and their place in it and the latter ensures that the knowledge is passed on and the community therefore remains vibrant and vital. All of this has bearing on *Bone Game*, and not just for Cole and the Choctaw. As the Diné elder Robert Jim tells Hoey and Uncle Luther after they meet him on their journey west to help Cole, "We got sacred peaks in ever direction, and stories to tell us where we are. You know, them stories that tell us how to live here" (88). His phrasing is especially apt, for "ever" makes clear that the sacred geography of the Diné makes sense of and brings together time and space. That union is articulated in stories that enable the Diné to know the world, themselves, and how to live.

The meaning and importance for Momaday of the story of the seven sisters is also relevant to Owens and his narrative. Indeed, given that the kiva is a symbol of the middle space of the literary text, the allusion to *The Way to Rainy Mountain* indicates the community of Native American writers that come together in and through the middle space of the literary text, why that space is sacred, and how the texts can be used to heal and protect individuals and the world. Kimberly Blaeser points out that in the tale of the seven sisters, the fact that their brother becomes a bear and a tree sacrifices itself highlights the power of imagination even as it helps Momaday make sense of his relationship to his grandmother and their people. In Blaeser's words, the Kiowa "had imagined and, therefore, created compatriots who could follow them into their new life. Their action reflects Momaday's view about the power of imagination to create" ("Momaday's Work" 51), a view reflected in Momaday's statement, "We are what we imagine. Our very existence consists in our imagination of ourselves" ("Man Made of Words" 55).

Such vital acts of imagination are intimately connected with language, and from *Wolfsong* on Owens has made clear the problematic nature of the English language for Native Americans and the dangers inherent in its use. The intertextual connections between

Bone Game and *The Way to Rainy Mountain* indicate how Owens and other Native writers avoid being paralyzed by "the realization that words can say what they don't mean and mean what they don't say, that to an Indian every sentence in English may be a broken treaty" (*Bone Game* 43), by reminding author and reader of the particular nature of language.

In the eighth part of the section of *The Way to Rainy Mountain* entitled "The Setting Out," Momaday uses his "translation" of a traditional Kiowa story as a point of reference for a consideration of language itself. The story concerns the trouble twins raised by grandmother spider get into when they disobey her and throw their rings into the air. The twins fall into the cave of a giant and his wife while chasing the rings, and only by remembering what grandmother spider had told them and saying "the word *thain-mom* over and over to themselves" (*Rainy Mountain* 32) are they able to avoid being killed. Both commentaries on this story offered by Momaday, one "documentary" and the second "privately reminiscent," focus on the power of the word and bear quoting in full:

> A word has power in and of itself. It comes from nothing into sound and meaning; it gives origin to all things. By means of words can a man deal with the world on equal terms. And the word is sacred. A man's name is his own; he can keep it or give it away as he likes. Until recent times, the Kiowas would not speak the name of a dead man. To do so would have been disrespectful and dishonest. The dead take their names with them out of the world.

> *When Aho saw or heard or thought of something bad, she said the word* zei-dl-bei, *"frightful." It was the one word with which she confronted evil and the incomprehensible. I liked her to say it, for she screwed up her face in a wonderful look of displeasure and clicked her tongue. It was not an exclamation so much, I think, as it was a warding off, an exertion of language upon ignorance and disorder.* (*Rainy Mountain* 33)

There are multiple points of contact between the two commentaries and *Bone Game*: the emphasis on names, the relationships between a dead person and his or her name, the use of a Native word or phrase—*zei-dl-bei* and *Nítchi bee ííniziinii* (*Bone Game* 197)—to announce the presence of that which is frightful, the need to ward off evil with language because one recognizes that it cannot be destroyed, the power of language to create a world, the sacredness of language itself. We have seen that Onatima, Luther, and Cole know that language has the power to create a world; the narrative makes sure that the reader sees that this power of language, and an awareness of this power, is not specific to the Choctaw. We also see the connection stressed by Momaday between language and making the world in the Ohlone creation story, when Coyote "sang his song. Eagle and Hummingbird answered, and together those three made the people. That was the sacred time" (*Bone Game* 33). For the Diné, the world is created by thought, and spoken language is essential to creation because speech is thought's outer form. With regard to language, then, the intertextual connection between the two commentaries from *The Way to Rainy Mountain* and *Bone Game* leads the reader to a fundamental truth about fictions. The sacredness of words is what makes the middle space of fiction sacred. Therefore, the words of and in fictions are powerful because they can be "an exertion of language upon ignorance," whether it be ignorance concerning death, evil, Native American identities, or our relationship to and with the world.

The connection to *The Way to Rainy Mountain*, finally, also highlights the concerns with time and worldview that Momaday and Owens share. According to Blaeser, "Momaday, the reader/creator, comes to the view that racial memory, like blood, passes from one generation to the next and storytelling awakens the sleeping giant of racial memory until the past lives in the present" ("Momaday's Work" 50). With the act of imagination that is *The Way to Rainy Mountain*, then, Momaday reconfigures time into an eternal present so that he and his reader can transcend the historical in order that connections and community might be recognized and ongoing. So too for Owens and *Bone Game*. Indeed, as we have seen, it is this sense of time reimagined so as to transcend the historical that Owens offers in and with his text, a sense of time Cole and the readers of *Bone Game* need to recognize and embrace, for in doing so healing can take place and positive change can occur. It is no wonder, then, that Momaday and his words are alluded to elsewhere in *Bone Game* when Alex tells Cole, "We're going to bring back all those bow-and-arrow skills. Give that memory in the blood a wake-up call, so to speak" (81). Cole repeats the phrase "memory in the blood" in order that the reader not miss the use of Momaday's famous phrase, one he turns to early in the brief essay "Personal Reflections" to help make his argument regarding the essential differences between whites and Natives concerning time and worldview.[4]

In "Personal Reflections," Momaday focuses on natural time, sunrise and sunset, and words in order to show what he means by the phrase "memory in the blood." He writes of the sun-watcher in Rio Grande Pueblos, of which Cueloze Pueblo was one, "whose sacred task it is to observe, each day, the very point of the sun's emergence on the skyline" (157). For the sun-watcher and his people, the earth is the place from which the sun emerges at sunrise and to which it returns at sunset. The "words" of Koi-khan-hole's morning prayer to the sun that Momaday heard when he was young "made one of the sun and earth, one of himself and the boy who watched, one of the boy and generations to come" (158). What Alex proposes that is related to archery practice, then, is also what literary fictions can awaken and bring to the fore because it is by means of the words of fiction that Owens, Momaday, and other Native American writers can make a world that establishes connections and thus enables them and sensitive readers—Native and non-Native—to deal with the world on equal terms with the subjects of the dominant culture.

The connection established to Leslie Marmon Silko's *Ceremony* is more overt than that established to either Momaday's *The Way to Rainy Mountain* or "Personal Reflections." If the latter two texts help Owens to articulate the nature and role of language and literary fictions, on the one hand, and the concerns with time, language, and worldview his text shares with Momaday's, on the other, then with the references to Laguna Pueblo and Silko and the allusion to *Ceremony* Owens articulates a shared concern over evil and what witches and witchery attempt to accomplish. On their trip west, Hoey and Luther go past a sign for Laguna Pueblo, causing Luther to ask, "That's what they [the Native Americans who call Laguna home] call themselves?" and Hoey to reply, "It's a name the Spanish gave them" (*Bone Game* 81–82). Luther knows then that the Laguna, like the Choctaw, had "trouble" with the Spanish, and the narrative indicates that the trouble is related to acts of naming that are violations and acts of imprisonment.

Silko, like Owens, writes out of this imprisoning act; she uses the English language and the novel to offer an alternative sign identifying Laguna Pueblo, the Laguna people, and Native-white relations. There too she reveals and explores the witchery loose in the world, witchery that cannot be killed but can be warded off with language and story. Emo, a Native American who has succumbed to the witchery and is alive at the end of *Ceremony*, rumored to be in California, "appears" in *Bone Game* as one of the three witches Luther and Hoey come across, follow, and capture outside Gallup, New Mexico (126). The intertextual connection indicates that Owens shares with Silko, and other Native American writers, an awareness of and concern over the witchery that, in *Ceremony*, "almost ended the story according to its plan; Tayo had almost jammed the screwdriver into Emo's skull the way the witchery had wanted. . . . The white people would shake their heads, more proud than sad that it took a white man to survive in their world and that these Indians couldn't seem to make it" (*Ceremony* 253). In order to make it, Silko and Owens turn to fiction to offer a different story. In *Bone Game*, after Hoey and Luther have stopped the three witches from taking the kidnapped Navajo woman Katherine Begay to California, leaving them stranded but alive, Hoey says what Luther knows: "Remember what you always said about evil. . . . How you can't kill it, and it's the white man's way to try? That all we can do is be conscious of it" (154). And later, after Cole has his vision, Onatima cautions him, "No matter what else you do, you should know that you can't win over this dream. He's part of something too big. We all have to live with this thing" (209).

In both *Ceremony* and *Bone Game*—indeed, in Native American texts and life in general—it is, as Onatima says, "a matter of power. They would imprison us in their vision and their stories, and we can't let them do that" (140). The witches and the dominant culture want power because it lets them tell their story in their way. The dress Onatima wears when she goes out to explore the woods around Cole's rented house above Santa Cruz tells a different story. It was made for her long ago and helps her remember who she is and where she comes from. The dress contains many symbols, including that for the diamondback rattlesnake, a powerful being for the Choctaw. While acknowledging the snake's power, Onatima says that real power comes "from all of us—fullbloods and mixed-bloods, those who live together and those who live apart" (173–74). The references to works by Momaday and Silko in *Bone Game* suggest that what is true of the Choctaw is also true of the community of Native American writers. That community produces a body of texts of real power, texts that individually and collectively serve to articulate and affirm identity in the face of hundreds of years of efforts to the contrary.

The connection to James Welch's *The Death of Jim Loney* is more complicated and takes us to the text's humorous register. Owens alludes to Welch's second novel when Alex gives Cole the name Pretty Weasel as they play the parts of CNN field reporter and network anchor in the narrative, a reference to Myron Pretty Weasel, whom Jim Loney accidentally kills while they are hunting together and Jim mistakes him for a bear. *The Death of Jim Loney* and *Bone Game* have much in common. Beyond the central role played by a bear in each text, in both the protagonist is a mixedblood at least seemingly caught between worlds. Like Cole, Jim is haunted by dreams. Both men must come to terms with their dreams and their past if they are to move beyond a liminal state that is deadly to one that is liberating. The context of the allusion that establishes the connection between the two texts—namely, the appropriation by Alex and Cole of the global news network that helps people make connections with others and the world with its around-the-clock coverage—highlights the idea of a community of Native American writers whose texts connect people. There is a crucial difference, naturally, given that CNN is a part of the "techno-mediatic power" that communicates and reinforces the "politico-economic hege-mony" of the West (Derrida 53), while the texts produced by Native American writers like Momaday, Silko, Welch, and others speak against that culture.

At the same time, the reference to *The Death of Jim Loney* is a cautionary one insofar as it reminds the reader of the path Cole must not take. Jim Loney remains isolated throughout the novel, and Myron Pretty Weasel's attempt to reestablish a connection with his old friend leads to disaster. As Owens notes in his reading of *The Death of Jim Loney*, "In shooting Pretty Weasel, Loney symboli-cally kills the Indian potential in himself—that which could believe in the bear" (*Other Destinies* 153). In order to avoid killing the Native in himself, Cole must accept and embrace the community offered by his family and Alex.

For Owens and *Bone Game*, the way to avoid the plight of Jim Loney as revealed by Welch is to turn to humor. Owens crystallizes the need and the turn itself both in the scene just mentioned and in the Rio Grande bridge scene that speaks to the nature of fiction itself. In the former, Onatima remarks "What a horrifying thought" when Alex says, "Imagine what it would have been like if our ancestors had had CNN" (155). Cole chimes in on what the tribal news network would have covered, but he and Alex do not begin playing at it, and with it, until after Alex switches the station to another news channel, sees "soldiers in blue helmets . . . running for cover while black tribal people waved rifles" (155), and then returns to CNN. The image of the United Nations soldiers in armed conflict with African tribal people is pivotal. It reveals the truth that the UN cannot gloss over: not all nations are united, and the conflicts that boil up frequently do so along lines and issues that are intimately connected to ethnicity and the construction of Otherness. At the same time, the news report indicates that such conflicts will be resolved neither by the power of the authorities (the UN soldiers are running for cover, after all) nor by armed insurrection, for Alex switches the channel. The narrative, rather, supplements the image of the tribal people waving guns with Alex and Cole's playful appropriation of CNN for their own ends.

The ends are humorous. People turn to humor when confronted with a painful reality that must be faced. As Alex says, "humor's what gets Indians through the tough times" (190). With humor, the reality is made light of, pain is transformed into pleasure as we move from grimace to laughter, and that transformation enables us to survive in order that we might work to transform the reality that produced the pain in the first place. In the scene with Cole and Alex, the painful reality is that CNN—or any other news station, for that matter—has precious little interest in bringing the reality of Native American life to its viewers. There are "the usual heartbreaking pictures" offered on the anniversary of the Wounded Knee massacre of Lakota men, women, and children frozen where they fell by the deep cold that swept over the South Dakota plain after the slaughter; the television will also show Cole, and us, a "group of Indians [who] made the long Bigfoot Memorial Ride through a chill factor of forty below" (32). But like John Neihardt, who finishes with Black Elk's life at Wounded Knee, the media is for the most part content to capture and fix Native Americans as Indians situated firmly in the past, frozen there just as Bigfoot's people were. As Anishinaabe Jim Northrup writes in "brown and white peek":

> We have TV, that window to America
> we see you, you don't see us.
> I watch the news every night, whenever they show
> Indians it's always the same tired tub of walleye
> maybe some kind of bingo doings (104–5)

In the light of this reality, one can either despair or make the turn to humor, and Cole and Alex take the latter course.

So too does Louis Owens in the scene on the bridge over the Rio Grande. As we have seen, Owens introduces the John Wayne movie *Rio Grande* there in order to suggest the root of the madness that grips the subjects of the dominant culture. It is also there that Owens suggests that he, along with his characters, will turn to humor in the face of the painful reality valorized and validated by the movie. He gives Luther a joke: "You could walk across that river, Hoey, and you ain't tall" (82). However, the joke is not so much on Hoey, who does not even acknowledge it, as on John Wayne, a man of short stature who was built up through lifts in his boots and by being filmed riding and standing beside smallish horses in order to make movies that champion a way of life and a worldview that are similarly unnatural and achieved and perpetuated by deceit. The joke skewers the popular icon and the ideology of acquisition it embodies, bringing John Wayne down to size and it to light, and thus reveals the truth even as it transforms pain into pleasure.

The act of exhumation that is *Bone Game* depends on humor. Indeed, the emphasis on exhumation in the epigraph foreshadows a discussion between Alex and Cole on exhuming bodies which indicates how, with and in good humor, what has been buried is revealed. Alex tells Cole that he has applied to the National Science Foundation to fund his proposed "dig in the cemetery at the Old North Church in Boston" (180) by a team of Indian anthropologists. He says that his "basic argument is that it's imperative we Indians learn more about Puritan culture. Puritans had a significant impact on us" (180). The genesis of Alex's idea is "the remains of twelve thousand Native people in the Hearst Museum in Berkeley. . . . The bones of our relations" (180). That painful fact necessitates a turn to humor, and Alex's tongue is firmly in his cheek as he appropriates the language and argument of those in authority, past and present, in order to make fun of and turn the tables on them. Cole's smile in response to Alex's proposal indicates that he recognizes what Alex is doing, and Owens's inclusion of that smile is meant to help the reader make the turn to humor rather than irony. At the same time, Alex's humor reveals the truth that at least some of the scientists who exhumed the Native American remains would have had stay buried: their science was tainted by a racist agenda and they were in it for monetary as well as "scientific" gain. The Native anthropologists on Alex's team will "do cranial measurements to figure out how intelligent the Puritans were, compared to us, and test teeth and bone samples for dietary information" (180). That is, they will do exactly what was done by some of the white scientists in an effort to prove that those of western European ancestry were superior to the Indians. Alex exactly reverses what was held by the majority when he says "Puritans were a primitive but fascinating people" and "We can't allow their primitive superstitions to stand in the way of science" (180). He then reveals the economic motivation of the scientists by adding, "And here's the best part. Those graves are probably full of artifacts, buttons from Puritan clothes, whalebone corsets, dildos, things we can sell to collectors. And skeletons, of course" (180). Tacking on the skeletons after the list of valuables cuts right to the heart of the matter, and the heart of the humor, as does the phrase "of course," which members of the dominant culture would use to conscript their audience and which Alex uses to emphasize that the skeletons are ancillary to the real purpose behind the exhumation of Native American remains.

"Of course" is an attempt by subjects of the dominant culture to fix and limit, to close off discussion as a matter of course. With Alex, the embodiment of trickster in the text, Owens opens up the possibility of discussion and dialogue. This is crucial because the stakes are so high in *Bone Game*. Thanks to Alex, trickster, the sign of freedom, possibility, and chance, is squarely before characters and readers throughout the text, putting us off our mark, destabilizing fictional characters and audience alike in order that, once shaken from our comfortable positions, we might see and approach the world differently. There are both differences and similarities between Owens's use of the trickster in *Wolfsong* and in *Bone Game*. Whereas in *Wolfsong* the signifier of trickster is the other-than-human person of Raven, in *Bone Game* trickster "appears" in the figure of Alex Yazzie. This suggests the greater importance of humor as a survival strategy in the latter text, as Owens frequently turns to Alex in dialogue with Cole and others in order, as we have seen, to humorously bring to light and make light of the painful realities many Native Americans confront every day. Also, while Tom Joseph can attain and understand his identity and its connection with the wolf spirit *staka'yu* without completely understanding trickster, Cole needs to recognize and embrace trickster and what s/he represents.

Gerald Vizenor situates trickster within language and narrative discourse: "The trickster is a chance, a comic holotrope in a postmodern language game that uncovers the distinctions and ironies between narrative voices; a semiotic sign for 'social antagonism' and 'aesthetic activism' in postmodern criticism and the avant-garde, but not 'presence' or ideal cultural completion in narratives" ("Trickster Discourse" 192). Trickster is neither real nor a fictional character; rather, s/he is a sign that signifies not presence but possibility, the presence of possibility. Karl Luckert's depiction of the Diné trickster Coyote accords with Vizenor's more general formulation of the trickster: "There is no single label which can contain Coyote in a neat and controllable scholarly category. Coyote is too much for academic systems, too lively and too restless to submit to analytic scalpels" (7). Coyote, like the human mind, "roams the landscape . . . within the limits of all conceivable human possibilities" (8). As such, Coyote (and trickster in general) reveals the arbitrariness of boundaries even while crossing them. So it is that, as Vizenor writes, "In trickster narratives, the listeners and readers [can] imagine their liberation; the trickster is a sign and the world is 'deconstructed' in a discourse" ("Trickster Discourse" 194) so that healing can take place. That healing is intimately connected to community, for the trickster is "a communal signification that cannot be separated or understood in isolation" (Vizenor, "Trickster Discourse" 189).

The initial description of Alex Yazzie "with a quick, gap-toothed grin" remindful of a coyote (25) yokes him with the Diné trickster, and with grins and winks, cross-dressing and good humor, Alex works to free Cole and the reader. Near the beginning and end of the novel, Alex will strike the "dramatic profile of a warrior" (28) in order to give the crowd and television audience, respectively, what they expect and desire, "the Indian warrior come to rescue the white world from its nether self" (222). Alex, and Owens, will undercut the pose when he tells Cole that he learned the "disguise" of dressing as a woman in order to "capture" Paul Kantner "from the Jim Chee tribal investigator correspondence school" (223). The image of the warrior in profile is no more authentic and true to Diné reality than is the disguise learned from Tony Hillerman's detective and the world of his novels: both are images of the Indian created and perpetuated by the dominant culture in order to avoid facing not only the reasons behind the production of these Other images, but also the reality of Native-white relations in this country, past and present, and the survival and persistence of the Native despite the efforts of many to write, and screen, them off.

What Alex tells Cole is what Owens tells the reader: "You have to loosen up your imagination" (30), "keep all options open" (31), and "prefer infinitions to definitions" (46). One must do precisely those things if one is grasp the sign of trickster. Once the imagination is loosened, it becomes possible to imagine alternatives to the existing state of things and the status quo. It is no wonder, then, that Alex, a trickster through and through, tells Cole when they first meet, "Against the law is my middle name. Besides, whose law are we talking about?" (26).

Trickster stands against the law of authority and the dominant culture. Because s/he stands for possibility and embodies the range of human behavior, the sign of trickster must not always be foolish or humorous. Alex knows when to be serious. He says "This isn't a time to joke around" after Cole recounts his dreams of Venancio Asisara and Padre Quintana, lies about how he is feeling, and then says "And I know a little about ghost sickness. I read Silko and Hillerman. He is Navajo, isn't he?" (96). Likewise, Alex will be dead serious when he discusses the Native American Church service with Robert because the healing ceremony is no laughing matter. Finally, when Abby asks him if he is lonely, Alex will look at her for the first time without a "trace of laughter" and reply "I'm so lonesome

I could cry" (151). The allusion to the Hank Williams song that Myron Pretty Weasel listens to as he watches Jim Loney hustle to the liquor store reinforces the connection between *Bone Game* and *The Death of Jim Loney* and captures the complexity and multiplicity of the trickster. Like Pretty Weasel, Alex, and trickster, can be lonely. And like Pretty Weasel, Alex can reach out and attempt to make contact and connection with someone else. Pretty Weasel fails, of course, whereas Alex succeeds, helping Cole, realizing a deep love for Abby, and having at novel's end the promise of living with them in New Mexico.

It is one thing to contain a multitude of possibilities and embody the variety of human experience and identity. It is something else to succumb completely to one possibility and thereby close off all others. As the other sign of the trickster in the text, Coyote alerts us to this danger. Coyote appears and disappears before Hoey, Luther, and Robert Jim as they drive through Navajo country. When they drop Robert Jim off he tells them, "Watch out for that coyote back there. . . . Don't let him trick you" (91). The trick to watch out against is being defined and then consumed by appetite. The cause may be greed or despair, and that which is hungered for may be property or alcohol, but in either case the result is a deadly disrespect for self, others, and the natural world. Get too far along down that path and, like the person who "looked like a man with the head of a coyote" (110) glimpsed for just an instant by Hoey and Luther in a Gallup alley, you cannot be helped. Approached correctly, however, the trickster can, like the coyote who leaves the gift of a rabbit on Cole's New Mexico doorstep on the morning he leaves for California, give a gift of untold measure: freedom for and with the imagination.

"Against the law" can stand as more than Alex's middle name; it can also be the name for the middle space that is Owens's fictions, for in them he writes against the law of authority and the dominant culture in order that his readers might discover the truth about aspects of Native American life, contemporary America, and Native-white relations. The texts, therefore, become the embodiment of trickster, themselves "signs of social antagonism and aesthetic activism."

We would do well in closing, then, to remember Alex's act of burying the guard dog named Custer and his proposal to exhume the Puritans buried in the Old North Church cemetery. Yazzie and Owens need to bury Custer, the historical figure, and the will to power and domination of the Other he represents. This will not be easy, for rigor mortis has set in, the clock is ticking, and the bedrock is close to the surface (191). Still, with acts of ingenuity and imagination, and with instruments of the dominant culture such as chainsaws and the written word, Alex and Owens can get Custer buried so he may "rest in peace" (192).

The Winthrops are the only Puritans Alex specifically refers to when he describes his proposed dig to Cole. It was John Winthrop who in his sermon "A Model of Christian Charity" offered the words that came to serve as a justification for Manifest Destiny and the systematic attempt to annihilate Native American people and cultures: "For we must consider that we shall be as a city upon a hill. The eyes of all people are upon us, so that if we shall deal falsely with our God in this work we have undertaken, and so cause Him to withdraw His present help from us, we shall be made a story and a by-word through the world." Winthrop is thought by some to have composed and delivered his sermon mid-passage, on the ocean betwixt and between the Old World and the New, and now Owens uses the betwixt-and-between nature of fiction to reveal the connection between Winthrop and what has happened and is happening in America. There is neither charity nor the connections it signifies, only greed, then and now: "First they sail the Atlantic with bloody teeth, he thinks, the deaths of ten million in their invader's imagination, and then they pile their loot on little boats and let the wind drive them in circles upon the bay" (*Bone Game* 72). In the light of this truth, and to bring its buried ideological subtext to light, Alex turns to humor to unearth Winthrop, the rest of the Puritans, and what they represent, and Owens turns to trickster humor in his fiction in order to write against the law so that characters, author, and readers can be set free.

CHAPTER FOUR

NIGHTLAND AND THE NATION

Although differing from its three predecessors in terms of the tribal cultural grounding and setting, *Nightland* (1996) shares with the earlier works concerns with and over identity and representation. Those concerns are born of Owens's awareness that the dominant culture is uninterested in seeing beyond the stereotypes, conventions, and familiar stories of the Indian. The desire for the invented Indian predisposes the publishing industry to, in Owens's words, all too often simply look "for commodities that have obvious, pre-sold value, and as far as indigenous writing is concerned, the value is determined by what has sold before" (qtd. in Purdy 19). Given this, it is remarkable that *Nightland* was first published by a New York house, for while Owens appears to give the industry and the dominant culture what it wants—a novel in the mystery/thriller genre à la those by Tony Hillerman—he produces a narrative that highlights his concerns with and over the nation and its relationship to others in general and the Native in particular.

Owens's fourth novel is grounded in his Cherokee heritage. The protagonists, Will Striker and Billy Keene, are mixedblood Cherokee who live on adjacent ranches in New Mexico started by their parents in the 1930s. The fullblood Cherokee men and their Euroamerican wives were drawn away from the dust bowl that had become the nation in Oklahoma by the promise of available and affordable land.

Both sets of parents die in accidents as their sons approach adulthood, and the young men are left with the ranches. Near financial ruin at the novel's opening due to a drought that the text makes clear is connected to the massacre of a group of Apaches by the original Spanish possessors of the Meléndez land grant, Will and Billy see fall and then find what turns out to be a suitcase full of money that is connected to drug smuggling and double cross. The men also watch fall the body of Arturo Cruz, a young Pueblo whose uncle, Paco Ortega, has been bringing drugs into the United States, not in order to make a profit, but to return the gift of genocide that the dominant culture has given the first peoples of North America. The consequences of finding and attempting to keep the close to a million dollars that Billy proclaims is "a gift from the Great Spirit" (7) are intertwined with the characters' efforts to come to terms with issues of mixedblood identity in what Linda Helstern correctly notes is a "post-contact Indian country inhabited by a cultural mix of Anglos, mixedbloods, fullbloods, animals, and ghosts" (61). The movement of their parents from Oklahoma to land in New Mexico originally granted to a Spaniard, land "cursed" when a descendant of the Spanish patriarch massacres a group of Apache adults and children on it, crystallizes for the reader the text's concerns with displacement and death. Thus, whereas *Wolfsong*, for instance, explores the relationship between the idea of the vanishing Indian and the identity of the country and its subjects, *Nightland* highlights how displacement, often but not exclusively at the expense of the Native, produces a series of haunting images that transforms the idea and reality of home and the land.

If the postcolonial, postmodern moment is marked by displacements that reveal the in-betweenness of the contemporary moment, then the emphasis on displacement, both literal and figurative, in *Nightland* encourages us to see the "post-contact Indian country" as liminal. Such liminality resonates with Owens's refiguring of the frontier. As we have seen, with his literary criticism and theorizing, Owens works to shift our gaze away from the literal and metaphoric city as center that Winthrop anticipated in mid-journey to the New World. Tellingly, the place toward which Owens's eyes are turned, and to which he attempts to turn ours, shares with Winthrop's defining utterance a connection to the liminal or the betwixt and between. Whereas one of the Puritan founding fathers opted to divert attention from that other space and time, penning a sermon that moves resolutely to the image of a city on a hill on which he wants his listeners to focus, Owens labors to reveal and then embrace it by championing a reformulation of the trope of the frontier.

In keeping with Owens's emphasis on the frontier, *Nightland* opens on indeterminacy and ambiguity with both its first word and its first sentence: "It looked like a black buzzard creased against the western horizon and angling toward him" (1). Just as the ambiguous image before Billy Keene resolves with the twist of its body into that of a man plummeting earthward to be impaled on a juniper, so too does the narrative resolve the ambiguous, indeterminate images of the Native and the mixedblood. What is more, the fact that the body initially appears to Billy as if it is "almost suspended between sky and earth" (1) introduces the notions of a middle space and of being betwixt and between that, as we have seen in *Bone Game* and elsewhere, is indicative of the middle space of fiction. The first sentence of *Nightland* cautions us about the dangers of appearances and judging too quickly. The body's twist reveals it to Billy for what it is. Similarly, Owens twists his narrative such that the Native and the mixedblood might come into focus for the reader. Such twisting begins with the first sentence's introduction of the black buzzard and its emphasis on the West. The Cherokee origin stories tell us that Buzzard is instrumental to the creation of the earth. After Waterbeetle dived deep beneath the water's surface, reached bottom, and brought back up the mud that then grew and spread to become the earth, Buzzard was sent by the animals in *Gǎlûñ'lǎtǐ* to make things ready for them. Buzzard grew tired as he flew over the soft earth, and by the time he reached Cherokee country his "wings began to flap and strike the ground" (Mooney 239), creating the valleys and mountains that constitute the homeland of the Cherokee. West is the direction of the Cherokee Nightland, the place where the dead journey and where danger comes from. With Buzzard and the West, then, the narrative lets the reader know that the story already forming is nothing less than one that speaks to the nature of the earth, its inhabitants, and that which threatens both.

Given that *Nightland* also wants to bring into focus the nation, its setting in New Mexico owes at least as much to the contested nature of that space as to the fact that Owens taught for years at the University of New Mexico and resided outside Albuquerque. Unwilling or unable to see the possibilities and promise of a frontier space where Native, Mexican, and Euroamerican peoples and cultures came together, politicians and opinion-shaping power brokers retarded New Mexico's statehood by focusing on what was seen to be the problem of a nonhomogeneous population. In 1848 Senator James D. Westcott voiced his opposition to statehood for both New Mexico and California on the grounds that the nation would be "compelled to receive not merely the white citizens of California and New Mexico, but the peons, negroes, and Indians of all sorts, the wild tribe of Comanches, the bug-and-lizard-eating 'Diggers,' and other half-monkey savages in those countries, as *equal citizens of the United States* (qtd. in Horsman 276, emphasis in the original). In that same year, Daniel Webster called the people of New Mexico "infinitely less elevated in mind and condition than the people of the Sandwich Islands" (qtd. in Horsman 276). Prior to the Mexican-American War, Russell Sage proclaimed that "there are not people on the continent of America, whether civilized or uncivilized, with one or two exceptions, more miserable in condition or despicable in morals than the *mongrel race inhabiting New Mexico*" (qtd. in Horsman 212, emphasis added). James Gordon Bennett, editor of the *New York Herald*, wrote in 1846 that the "the idea of amalgamation has been always abhorrent to the Anglo-Saxon race on this continent" and, most tellingly, used language reminiscent of that offered to explain and explain away the Indian on the continent when he said that the "imbecile inhabitants" of Mexico were "as sure to melt away at the approach of Anglo-Saxon energy and enterprise as snow before a southern sun" (qtd. in Hietala 155).

Of course, the voices of Bennett, Sage, and the others simply joined a nationwide discourse on miscegenation that had existed long before the new country's expansionist impulse had brought it to war with Mexico. The mixedblood was a subject of discussion, debate, and concern from the early days of settlement in the New World.[1] With regard to *Nightland* and its critique of the nation that evolved from that settlement, it bears remarking that roughly twenty years prior to the comments from Sage, Webster, and Westcott the accomplishments and hybridity of the Cherokee people in Georgia had proven to be unsettling for the state and the republic. Even as the Cherokee had worked to formalize a government, legal and judicial apparatuses, and laws in writing in order to protect themselves and their land from the United States, the People and the Nation articulated that which was most threatening to Georgia and the country. Congressman Wilson Lumpkin, who would be governor of Georgia during the height of the debate regarding the identity and status of the Cherokee in relation to the state and the nation, asserted that the Cherokee, especially the "mixed breeds and white bloods, had advanced in all the various arts of civilization to an extent that rendered it altogether impracticable to enforce the Laws of the United States passed by Congress for regulating intercourse with Indian Tribes within the United States, and for governing and restraining such tribes" (qtd. in Wald 27). Priscilla Wald stresses that Justice William Johnson's consenting opinion in *Cherokee Nation v. The State of Georgia* (1831) also lights upon what he saw as a troubling heterogeneity. Indeed, as Wald points out, with the word *kraal* Johnson transforms the Cherokee, and all other Native peoples, either into inhabitants of a country other than America or into livestock in an effort to avoid having to confront the perceived threat the Cherokee posed for the nation. In short, as Wald states, "The Cherokee Nation's becoming like but not of the United States political entity, mirroring without acceding to its conditions, seemed to jeopardize the terms of a United States national identity. And the threat of Cherokee nationalism was literally embodied by the 'mixedbloods,' who represented the mixing of bloods referred to by

Jefferson, but who did not fully accede to the terms of assimilation that the President had delineated, who had, that is, remained
Cherokees" (27).

Following Homi Bhabha's work on mimicry in a colonial context,
Wald recognizes that in opting to produce a written constitution and
laws, on the one hand, and to foreground agrarian practices even
prior to the creation of that constitution, on the other, the Cherokee
were mimicking without allowing the mimicked to rest easy. For
it does not necessarily follow that looking like and acting like lead
to becoming and being the same as, contra the case of Tom Joseph
and his Uncle Jim in *Wolfsong*, and the resemblance the Cherokee
gave back to the subjects and the nation was distressing precisely
because it was imitation rather than identification. The fact that the
Cherokee maintained their symbolic structure while adopting elements of the Euroamerican political system and writing is indicative
of their unwillingness to do more than mimic the dominant culture
(Champagne 92–93). The resemblance was revealed to be only that
when it came to the issue of property, especially land, and its relation to natural rights. The Cherokee Constitution stipulated that land
was "the common property of the nation." Thus, Wald notes, the
document "showed how a recognizable code of laws could grow out
of a combination of tribal and (contingent) individual ownership" (31).

The relationship between land and Cherokee identity is stressed
in *Nightland* when Grampa Siquani refers to the Trail of Tears and
the Cherokee rolls while talking with his grandson Billy Keene in
order to suggest the danger he is in as a result of finding the money:
"The government people said they had to count us and give us
numbers. If we didn't let them give us numbers, then we didn't get
none of our land. All them half-breeds was the first to get numbers,
but a whole lot of the old-timers stayed back in the hills and never
got numbers at all. That meant they couldn't be real Indians no
more. Some of them decided to become invisible then" (60). The play
is on "real Indian," of course. Without a number, a Cherokee cannot
be a real Indian. For the government and the nation, as FBI agent
Lee Scott reminds us in *The Sharpest Sight*, being an Indian means

being identified in a fashion that renders you manageable; more to the point here, being a real Indian means being individuated in order that you might eventually be assimilated.

Unwilling to look at the Cherokee, both as a people and as a culture, the state of Georgia fought to have them removed. Facing the very real possibility that the conflict between the Cherokee and Georgia, between the Cherokee and the federal government, and between the federal government and Georgia would rend the Union and sound the death knell of the fledgling nation, those who championed the Cherokee's cause in *Samuel A. Worcester v. The State of Georgia* (1832) backed down, President Andrew Jackson and the state of Georgia had their way, and the Cherokee were forced onto the road that would become the Trail of Tears.

That road threatened the Cherokee's sense of identity, because for the People and the Nation identity is tied to and comes from the land and community. The same holds true for the Pueblo peoples of New Mexico. The individual Pueblos traditionally hold land in common. Both prior to and following contact with the Spanish, land was vested to each particular Pueblo and was distributed in a fashion that helped to ensure an equal distribution of wealth among community members (Ortiz 4). The Pueblo system of land tenure was adopted by a large portion of the Spanish settlers, their descendants, and the Mexican settlers. Consequently, at the time the Cherokee problem was being debated and decided, to the detriment of the People, the Pueblos of New Mexico held land collectively and distributed it among community members with an eye for the good of the whole; Hispanics had a "community land tenure system" as well, characterized by a combination of "private agricultural landholding, encumbered by various collective constraints, and communal pasturage and woodlands with individual rights of usufruct" (Van Ness and Van Ness 8).

Nearly one hundred years later, New Mexico remained a contact zone or frontier, but one in which the United States had a stake and participated as a major player. A 1921 bill introduced in Congress by Senator Holm Bursum of New Mexico sought to capitalize on the heterogeneity and concomitant ambiguity of the state, especially with regard to land. The Bursum bill, as revised and returned to Congress in 1922, would have had the ambiguous nature of entitlements serve the interests of the dominant culture by forcing the Pueblo Indians of the state to prove their title to lands they held that were in many cases connected to grants made by the governments of Spain and, later, Mexico (G. Taylor 11). The expensive legal procedure necessary would have prohibited many of the Pueblos from validating their claims in the eyes of the state and the nation. Non-Native settlers on Pueblo lands, on the other hand, would receive title if they could prove "continuous possession, with color of title, before or after 1848" and could claim title with proof of continuous possession, sans color of title, from 29 June 1900 (Philp, *Collier's Crusade* 32).

That the Bursum bill failed to win passage is a testimony to the efforts of activists for Native rights, including the artists, writers, and aesthetes who had come to New Mexico and lived in Taos, Santa Fe, and elsewhere. Nevertheless, the issue of land and water rights for all the people of New Mexico remained to be resolved. When the parents of Will Striker and Billy Keene left the Nation in Oklahoma to find arable land in the 1930s, the New Deal Rio Grande land project was working to obtain land for the state's Native and Mexican American populations at a time when the confluence of modern influences, traditional practices, economic realities, and the actions of the nation and its subjects created, in the words of one historian, "a complex and changing setting" characterized by ambiguity and exploitation (Dinwoodie 292).

Rising from the beginning of the narrative as surely as its satellite dishes rise from the high plains of San Agustin in the contact zone that is New Mexico, the Very Large Array helps to bring the concerns of *Nightland* into focus. Created by an Act of Congress in 1972 and completed in 1981, the array is a radio telescope comprised of twenty-seven 230-ton dish antennas linked together to produce the resolution of an antenna twenty-two miles in diameter. Connected by railroad tracks and linked by computers, the antennas can be set in configurations ranging from one kilometer to thirty-six kilometers of maximum separation. This makes the array, which is used to explore and map celestial space, one of the most powerful radio telescopes in the world.

The Very Large Array's relation to the federal government helps connect Owens's fourth novel to *The Sharpest Sight*. *Nightland* makes clear that the array is an instrument of the federal government and that "the feds" (148) are as interested as the state officials in the helicopter that crashed near it after blowing up in midair. Created and supported by the government, the array looks to the stars, but both the array's website and the on-site facilities for visitors indicate that its technology could be directed earthward: the former lets us know that the array can see an object the size of a golf ball one hundred miles away; the latter includes a whisper gallery where dual model satellite dishes are set up and configured such that a person can hear another whispering from thirty feet away.

It is precisely the array's perceived ability to act as an instrument of surveillance that drug runner and hit man Duane Scales remarks upon as he and his boss, Paco Ortega, drive past it on their way to recover the money Billy and Will have found. Duane's hyperbole and predilection for conspiracy theories notwithstanding, his comment that he bets "they got those things aimed straight at Indian country. See if you redskins are about to go on the fucking warpath again" (230) helps us understand the movement of the array when we first see it. The twenty-seven dishes start to turn in unison toward Billy after the body of Arturo Cruz has been impaled on the juniper and the suitcase full of money has smashed into the middle of a bush juniper nearby. What the nation wants to keep its eye on—symbolically, at least—is the Native, mixedbloods and fullbloods, that disturbs the dominant culture either by mimicking it or by refusing to strike that pose.

Growing up, Billy had thought that "if I was half white I could just choose what I wanted to be" (160). Grampa Siquani makes light of Billy's thinking when he asks his nephew "which half you think it is" (61) and speculates on the best and worst possible splits. The conversation turns serious and then ceases when Grampa responds to Billy's remark that he thinks the split is right down the middle by saying, "That's a shame, Grandson, because that way a man's just fighting with himself all the time" (62). Uncomfortable with the implications of Grampa's statement, Billy will try to avoid it by thinking in either species or national terms. He tells Will that now "most of the time I think to hell with all that Indian stuff. I mean we're just human beings and here we are like everybody else" (159). When asked if he can prove he is a "real Indian," a question that repeats the phrase Grampa uses to articulate the federal government's confirmation of identity upon the Georgia Cherokee in the 1830s, Billy tells Mescalero Apache Odessa Whitehawk that he does not have any official papers and adds, "I guess I'll just have to be American" (117). The response of the woman who becomes Billy's lover in order to get her hands on the drug money whose theft she had masterminded tells Billy what the rotation of the satellite dishes reveals to us: Odessa replies tersely, "Don't count on that" (117).

The third appearance of the array in the narrative, sandwiched between the dishes' turn toward Billy and Duane's commentary on the device's use, serves to reveal the lie of the nation. In a dream, Will sees the impaled body of Arturo Cruz move and his eyes search for him while, "On the plain below, the white faces of the Array had turned in swift unison, each one a pale eye, and with their turning a vast sky of sharp-pointed stars had begun to tumble out of control" (65). Revealed as the white faces of the nation, the instrument of exploration, identification, and control that is the Very Large Array does nothing less than bring about disorder and destruction.[2]

It is fitting that this revelation comes in a dream, for it is the hidden or buried truth that the nation would rather not be seen and that its subjects would rather not see. Paco Ortega asks Mouse Meléndez, descendent of one of the original Spanish soldiers with Don Juan de Oñate, if the American dream is "to commit every kind of filthy thing it takes to get ahead and then pretend it never happened" (259). Paco recognizes the willful amnesia of not just

America, but the modern nation. Such amnesia (what Bhabha terms "forgetting to remember") is possible because of the synchronic, ahistoricizing time of the nation and nationalist discourse. Mouse's pronouncements of his Spanish ancestry speak beyond his awareness to articulate the refashioning of time that enables one to forget. When compelled to establish his national ancestry, Mouse says, "'Not Mexican, *pendejo*, Spanish. My family come up here,' he looked at Odessa, 'in the eighteenth century with Oñate'" (127). He is off by two centuries, and he reveals the mistake when he tells Paco, "I'm Spanish. . . . My family came up here with Oñate in the sixteenth century" (258). Mouse's use of the present tense in the first instance reveals the ways in which a claim to national and nationalist identity can constitute an emptying of time. Eighteenth century or sixteenth century: it makes no difference if in tracing your roots you are bound and determined to forget to remember the historic particulars of your origin in, in this case, the brutalities and atrocities of colonialism. It is precisely those particulars that Paco calls to Mouse's attention.

The fact that Paco's question to Mouse is met with silence speaks volumes. If America is predicated on acts of forgetting that constitute nothing less than repression, then it is Owens's task throughout his writings to bring the buried to light. Paco's journey from Jemez Pueblo to the lands around Magdalena takes him and the reader from the site of one atrocity to another. Jemez was where a 1694 massacre saw the Spanish kill more than 80 people and capture an additional 360 as part of their efforts to retake the territory they had been forced from by the Pueblo Revolt of 1680. Mouse's great-great-grandfather slaughtered between 20 and 30 Apache, including children, whom he found roasting one of his steers. In addition, en route to the grant land, Paco, Duane, and the reader pass by Acoma, site of the 1599 massacre of 800 Acoma. The survivors were charged, pled guilty under advice of Spanish legal counsel, and sentenced: able-bodied men had their right foot cut off; other men, women, and children were enslaved.

Both the Jemez and the Acoma were displaced as a consequence of the atrocities committed by the Spanish. Each overcame it, however: the Jemez moved downstream and reestablished their community in the same river canyon; most of the enslaved Acoma escaped and returned to their mesa in 1601. Thus, both peoples haunt the nation by being that strangeness that is irremovable. On the one hand, the historical fact of the displacement of the Jemez and Acoma serves to remind the nation and its subjects of the ground upon which the former is built. On the other hand, the return of both peoples to or near their original homes indicates the shakiness of that ground. Anxiety carries the day, for if the Acoma and the Jemez can be displaced, and violently so, than so too can the Americans. Moreover, the return of the Acoma and Jemez speaks to the nation's deepest fear: that the People will come back. That fear is articulated in *Wolfsong* by the Lakota pipe carrier Aaron Medicine and in *The Sharpest Sight* by FBI agent Lee Scott. It is the fear that motivates the continued return to, surveillance of, and attempts to conjure away the Indian.

Even as the Very Large Array is directed outward and skyward, then, it directs us to the two major concerns of *Nightland*: the nation and that which is buried. Will's dream indicates that the latter includes not just painful and troubling national history, but personal history and essential elements of the Cherokee worldview as well. At first glance, Will's dream and its precipitating event seem straightforward enough. His ruined television remains in the living room as a reminder of both when and why he shot it with his 30-06 rifle. When Will returns home with his share of the money and sees the set with its shattered picture tube, he briefly thinks of the country he wants no part of before letting the thought go (38). The nation and his relation to it return that night in his dream. The wish of the latent dream-content corresponds to that of the manifest dream-content insofar as we take it to be the desire to make plain the affects of the array and, via the mechanism of condensation, what it represents on people, place, and the nation. For Will, those affects do not come into focus until Arturo Cruz tumbles earthward and ends up impaled betwixt and between sky and earth. At the same time, Will's interpretation of the dream's meaning upon waking correctly focuses attention on the roles played by the dead and things properly and improperly buried.

However, the mechanism of displacement operates on the latent dream-content to transform the portion of the nightmare that jolts Will awake. After realizing that the stars, the body of Arturo Cruz, the helicopter that had materialized out of the rainstorm to attack them as they left with the briefcase of money, and the array are all connected, Will wants to say that "it wasn't his fault, but he felt a wire tighten and was hurled suddenly against the light breaking through his bedroom window" (65). The censor is in full display here, as the wires that connect the array with everything else prohibit Will from speaking. The desire to speak is the indistinct element of the dream that most directly speaks to the latent dream-content.

The core of the dream-thought or latent dream-content is to speak and, in speaking, to recognize and accept responsibility not just for one's self and actions, but for the world. Early in life Will had recognized the relationship between utterance and the world, believing that "the Cherokee world was made of spoken words . . . made again and again when his father or Billy's grampa told the stories" (34). The world spoken into being is our responsibility and must be cared for, as Will repeatedly reminded his children while telling them portions of the Cherokee origin story. The Cherokee recognize that the world is an island that is kept from disappearing into the sea on which it floats by four ropes, one on each of its corners, connected to the vault of the sky. Will tells his daughter and son that "it's up to strong human beings like Holly and Si Striker to think good thoughts and keep those ropes in good shape" (70) in order to ensure the survival of the earth and the order of the universe.

If we join the array in looking heavenward, we are in a position to see how the order of the universe as understood by the Cherokee is fundamental to *Nightland* and its characters. Midway through the narrative, Billy and Odessa go through a box of old photos that Billy had avoided looking at until now, not wanting to be reminded of what he had lost or to think about where he came from. All that changes with Odessa's arrival and his love for her. After talking about family and identity, Billy opens the trailer door and looks toward the eastern horizon while "overhead, the stars of Orion showed in the dark, gray-streaked sky as the hunter wheeled slowly westward" (143). The constellation and its position are striking examples of the syncretism that Margaret Dwyer sees operating in *The Sharpest Sight*. That is, read as a figure from classical Greek mythology, Orion's entrance into the text as the hunter whose death is directly connected to his desire foreshadows Billy's fate at Odessa's hands. At the same time, the figure can be seen to allude, ironically, to Odessa, as she hunts first Billy and then Will. Moreover, the constellation's movement westward, toward the Nightland, tells the reader knowledgeable of Cherokee cosmology and stories that Billy's efforts to focus eastward, toward Sunland and the place "good things come from" (59), will not bear fruit. More importantly, though, as is the case with Buzzard and the West invoked in the novel's opening sentence, the constellation's presence in the text subtly directs us to fundamental elements of the Cherokee worldview.

Orion hunts the Pleiades. That group of stars figures in the Cherokee origin stories. They tell of seven boys who enjoy playing *gatayû'stï*, a game in which players attempt to strike a rolling stone in the shape of a wheel with a thrown stick that has been tapered at both ends (Mooney 258), instead of doing their work in the corn-fields. Scolded by their mothers, the boys dance and pray to the spirits to help them. As a result of their actions and words, six of the seven boys ascend to the sky and become *Ani'tsutsä*, The Boys, or what the West calls the Pleiades. The seventh boy is grabbed and yanked down by his mother with the aid of a *gatayû'stï* stick; she pulls so hard, though, that he is driven into the ground and covered by the earth. The people grieve for the lost boys, and the mother whose son is underground cries at the spot where her child disappeared. Over time the tears soak the ground, a shoot appears, and a pine tree grows from it to maturity. Tree and *Ani'tsutsä* have the same nature.

Like the Kiowa story of the seven sisters and their brother that N. Scott Momaday recounts in *The Way to Rainy Mountain* to help articulate the Kiowa cosmos, the Cherokee story of The Boys and the pine tree lets the people know that they have kin in and with the stars. Moreover, that connection draws the underearth, earth, and heavens together. The story is also about respect and reciprocity, as the boys are reminded by their mothers of the importance of tending to the cornfields. They should do this out of respect for Selu, the Corn Mother, whose story, as Marilou Awiakta tells us, "is a timeless and reliable compass to right relationships with Mother Earth, with the human family and with oneself" (16). By including Orion in the night sky, then, Owens subtly and doubly brings into presence both the story of the Pleiades from a Cherokee perspective and the importance of connections, respect, and reciprocity for the people.

Billy misses Orion, and thus The Boys, when he looks eastward to Sunland. Indeed, earlier, after he first meets Odessa in town and looks up at the night sky, he sees only that the "stars were bright, forming vaguely familiar patterns across the moonless arc" (109). The fact that the stars are only vaguely familiar indicates the degree of separation between self and world that Billy suffers. In this regard he is akin to Cole McCurtain when the latter in *Bone Game* fails to recognize the stars above him. The emphasis in *Nightland* on what is less than familiar and thus at least potentially troubling can be read as emblematic of *Nightland* as a whole.

Nightland presents us with more than instances of the vaguely familiar, however. After pulling up to his home with his share of the money he and Billy have found, Will "reached into the pickup and shut off the headlights, jerking the duffel out before he kicked the door closed. With the rifle in one hand and the duffel bag in the other, he turned toward the house and abruptly stopped. Without the illumination of the pickup lights, the home he'd been born and grown up in seemed suddenly distant and strange, a dark stone set down in the night" (30–31). Freud's thoughts on the *heimlich* and the *unheimlich*, the canny and the uncanny, help illuminate the scene. Will pulls up short here, as that which had been *heimlich*— had been long familiar, comfortable, and belonging to the house and the family—becomes in an instant "suddenly distant and strange." The home is linked to Heidegger and modernity, as well. In Anthony Vidler's words, the "coincidence of the sensibility of exile, intellectual and existential, with the forced nomadism and lived homelessness of the Depression only reinforced the growing feeling that modern man was, essentially and fundamentally, rootless: 'Homelessness is coming to be the destiny of the world,' wrote Heidegger in his celebrated 'Letter on Humanism' in 1947" (8). Certainly Will's parents, and Billy's, were forced into a nomadism by the depression, having left the "ovens of hell they called the Nation, or Indian Territory, or Oklahoma, the home of red people" (*Nightland* 51) in the 1930s. However, their journey west brought them, ultimately, to the adobe house in New Mexico that they repaired and made their home. Why, then, does Will suddenly fail to recognize his home? Freud recognized, first through case studies and then by an examination of language, that *heimlich* can mean its opposite, *unheimlich*. In Freud's examination of linguistic usage, this point is driven home with the penultimate example of the first sense of the word—"intimate, friendlily comfortable":

> "Heimlich"? . . . What do you understand by "heimlich"? "Well, . . . they are like a buried spring or a dried-up pond. One cannot walk over it without always having the feeling that water might come up there again." "Oh, we call it 'unheimlich'; you call it 'heimlich.' Well, what makes you think that there is something secret and untrustworthy about this family?" (222, 223)

Far from intimate and friendly, *heimlich* can also mean "concealed" or pertain to the act of concealing; to keep secret and thus from view or knowledge. Thus, *unheimlich* "is in some way or other a sub-species of *heimlich*" (226). The canny becomes the uncanny when something that has either been repressed or surmounted suddenly comes to light. That is, in Freud's words, "the uncanny proceeds from something familiar which has been repressed," the "un" being the "token" or marker of repression (247, 245).

Freud held that the long familiar but repressed were infantile complexes and the long familiar but surmounted were associated with what he considered a "primitive" view of the universe as animistic. Although humankind had "developed" beyond this early state of being, Freud thought that residues of the thinking that marked the state remained in an individual's psyche. In particular, Freud held that "there is scarcely any other matter, however, upon which our thoughts and feelings have changed so little since the very earliest times, and in which discarded forms have been so completely preserved under a thin disguise, as our relation to death" (242).

The connections between Freud's essay and *Nightland* are themselves uncanny. As is the case with E. T. A. Hoffmann's short story "The Sand-Man" as Freud reads it—the reader joining the protagonist, Nathaniel, in looking at the uncanny through a pair of spyglasses—*Nightland* is the device or instrument whereby the uncanny is brought to light. At the same time, if Coppelius the lawyer and Coppola the optician represent, as Freud holds, one side of the father-image for Nathaniel, then *Nightland* reveals what the paternalism of the nation, rooted in the law, attempts to conceal regarding the objectification of the Native and the ideology that drives it. Moreover, just as Freud's text turns on the particular language with which to talk about family, water that is underground, and that which is buried, revealing the ambiguous nature of the word and in the process serving as an entrance to the relationship between the uncanny and repression, so too does Owens's novel turn on the language he uses to reveal the importance of the same things to his characters, their stories, and ultimately the reader. In the former, it is one's understanding of and perspective on *heimlich* that determines the reading or misreading of the sentence "*The Zecks . . . are all 'heimlich.'*" In the latter, it is one's understanding of and perspective on home, especially as it relates to kin and kinship, that determines the reading or misreading of *Nightland*.

Will Striker is brought up short outside his house because his home has gone from the first sense of the canny to the second. It is only after he forces himself to approach the house, enter it, and think about the life he has lived and lives there that he is able to put his finger on what has precipitated the change. Looking at the duffel bag, he realizes that the money threatens to change every-thing and that the body of the dead man in the tree is indicative of what threatens to dictate everything after the change. Will sees "in his mind . . . the body out there, poised in a kind of isolation he had never even imagined" (45). The emphasis on the lack of connection between that body and everything else indicates that connections are being concealed from Will as he looks at his home in the passage we have been plumbing. The way that house typically appears on a moonless night accentuates the relationship between home and connections, for on such nights the house "became an upthrust of the earth itself" (31). The narrative suggests that this image does not typically give Will pause. Thus, the realization that home and earth are intimately connected—indeed, that they are inseparable and that one must act accordingly—is what Will is in danger of losing, thanks to the money.

Money and the earth, property and the land, the nation and the Nation: the spirit deer that leads Billy Keene to the spot where he can see the falling body and suitcase leads us to the spot from which we begin to see how the former threatens the latter.[3] That spot, like the wilderness area in *Wolfsong*, is fundamental to the nation's idea of itself. When convincing Will to take the money, Billy reminds him that "we're way the hell and gone out here in the middle of the Cibola National Forest" (8). Although seemingly "way the hell and gone," the two men are really at the center of things for the West and the nation. Comprising 141 million acres of land in the eleven western states, including much of the high country produc-ing the yearly snowpack essential to water levels in the West, the national forests are literally and figuratively "the spine of the American West" (Wilkinson 118). The effects of these areas and the management decisions made by the Forest Service are so wide ranging that, in the words of western legal scholar and historian Charles Wilkinson, "However you articulate it, the national forests are on any short list of ingredients that make the American West a distinctive region" (118). It is small wonder, then, that when Will asks Billy to "think what Grampa Siquani would say about this, and about that body down there" (8), his friend responds, "Grampa lives in a different world, Will" (9). Different, indeed.

While the wilderness area in *Wolfsong* serves to indicate how the nation attempts to turn to nostalgia in an effort to counter what is most disturbing about its origin, that it is born of displacement, the National Forest system invoked in *Nightland* helps to reveal the nation's justification for the displacement. The world that Billy and Will are quite literally positioned in as *Nightland* opens is characterized by the nation's sense of its relationship to land as phrased and practiced by Gifford Pinchot. The father of American forestry and the Forest Service, Pinchot became head of the Division of Forestry the year after the 1897 Organic Act ensured an increasingly active federal presence with regard to the nation's standing timber reserves. The wealthy Pinchot had studied forestry in Europe but argued in 1900 for the creation of the Yale School of Forestry on the grounds that what was needed were "American foresters trained by Americans in American ways for the work ahead in American forests" (qtd. in Langston 109). The work ahead was to transform the nation's forests into what amounted to efficient factories. For Pinchot and his followers, this meant thinking that "to grow trees as a crop is forestry" (*Breaking New Ground* 31). The concept of sustained-yield forestry directed the Forest Service's efforts, both during and after Pinchot's fourteen-year tenure as its head, and it was ultimately based on Pinchot's belief that "the first duty of the human race is to control the earth it lives upon" (*Fight for Conservation* 45).

The Enlightenment basis of Pinchot's conservationist thinking—namely, control being exerted in order to improve nature—was yoked to the democratic idea of the nation. Indeed, Pinchot made clear that conservation dealt with much more than natural resources of timber, water, soil, and minerals. He had championed the 1907 name change of federal timberlands from reservations to national forests in order to replace the idea of reserving resources with that of conserving them in the best interests of the nation and its people.

Thus, in Pinchot's words: "Conservation means the greatest good to the greatest number for the longest time. One of its greatest contributions is just this, that it has added to the worn and well-known phrase, 'the greatest good to the greatest number,' the additional words 'for the longest time,' thus recognizing that this nation of ours must be made to endure as the best possible home for all its people" (*Fight for Conservation* 48).

Pinchot recognized that America was shaped, finally, by the right to property guaranteed its citizens by the Fourteenth Amendment. That right, however, could lead to dire consequences for the nation if individual greed carried the day. Thus the idea of property and its relationship to home compelled Pinchot to act in the best interests of the nation. He did not want to replace the centrality of property, though. Rather, his appeal for conservation is based on the recognition of the nation's best interests in order that it will prosper and that individual rights might thereby be maintained. He rounds out his argument with nothing short of an appeal to patriotism that is at once a call to action and a phrasing of anxiety:

> The application of common sense to any problem for the nation's good will lead directly to national efficiency wherever applied. In other words, and that is the burden of the message, we are coming to see the logical and inevitable outcome that these principles, which arose in forestry and have their bloom in the conservation of natural resources, will have their fruit in the increase and promotion of national efficiency along other lines of national life.
>
> The outgrowth of conservation, the inevitable result, is national efficiency. In the great commercial struggle between nations which is eventually to determine the welfare of all, national efficiency will be the deciding factor. So from every point of view conservation is a good thing for the American people. (*Fight for Conservation* 50)

The idea of the greatest good for the greatest number for the longest time that drives Pinchot's conservation will drive the nation, indeed must drive the nation if it is to compete against other nations. Without it, the unstated fear is, America will be lost. And with it will go individual freedom and the right to own property. What was implicit in 1910 was explicit in 1947 when, on the heels of America's ascension to a recognized position of world power and leadership, Pinchot wrote that "nationally, the outgrowth and result of Conservation is efficiency. In the old world that is passing, in the new world that is coming, national efficiency has been and will be a controlling factor in national safety and welfare" (*Breaking New Ground* 505).

The problem, of course, is in thinking that the earth is a resource that can and must be controlled for the good of the nation and its citizens. Pinchot might well have imagined that his "other words" championing conservation and the nation would counter the short-sighted policies and practices he and his followers were combating. However, insofar as those words still imagined land as property and economic well-being as the goal, his words were not "other" at all. In fact, in the first two decades of the twentieth century, con-servationist thinking led to the destruction of old-growth forests, deemed inefficient and thus economically inviable, so that a managed forest might take its place. What the narrative terms the "body tree" upon which Arturo Cruz was impaled is described as "old wood" and "ancient cedar" (*Nightland* 2). As such, the tree is both a reminder of the old-growth forest and what it represents and the trace of the anthropocentric, capitalist ideology, infused with arrogance and control, that can only see such stands in economic terms. In making economics and economic efficiency paramount, the Forest Service and the nation destroy the connections and intricate relationships that characterize a forest at equilibrium. Pinchot was more correct than perhaps he knew when he remarked that the principles of control, commodification, and economic efficiency would extend well beyond the Forest Service; they would permeate the nation and national life, creating a home that is, finally, no home at all.

Fittingly, Pinchot figures in the territorial history of New Mexico at a crucial moment for the territory, the Forest Service, and the nation. In 1907, territorial governor Herbert Hagerman was involved in a transaction concerning public lands that had begun prior to his assuming the governorship in 1906. Hagerman completed the transaction between the government and the Pennsylvania Development Company in what can best be characterized as suspect fashion. The particulars of the transaction, done while the commissioner of public lands was absent from the territorial capital on government business, were especially damning given that abuses in the disposition of public lands were widespread in the territory and it was thought that Hagerman was appointed to put a halt to the illegal practices.

In April 1907, President Theodore Roosevelt requested Hagerman's resignation. The governor complied, but he also sent a telegram to Pinchot asking him to bring to Roosevelt's attention that hundreds of telegrams had been sent to the president testifying to Hagerman's good character, applauding his work as governor, and protesting the call for resignation. Pinchot showed the telegram to Roosevelt, compelling the president to write to Hagerman and spell out in no uncertain terms the basis for his decision. Hagerman's reply makes it clear that a desire for reinstatement was not what motivated him to enlist Pinchot's help. Rather, Hagerman felt that the "material prosperity" of the territory was threatened (qtd. in Twitchell 2: 558 n) by the president's action.

Pinchot's role as go-between for Hagerman and the president stemmed from his friendship with Roosevelt. Together, the two men had orchestrated the massive increase in public land set aside as forest reservations in the West.[4] As we have seen, in shaping the West, Pinchot and Roosevelt were helping to shape the nation. Pinchot's presence in Hagerman's case and the future of territorial New Mexico tellingly accentuates the role his vision of land and land use had in the formation of the state and the country. Indeed, he continually reminded Roosevelt to keep a close eye on the territory in order to try and curtail the loss of public lands (Lamar 18). Pinchot may well have had his own agents in the territory working to expose fraud and misuse. In determining what public land should be set aside as forest reserves and in uncovering the fraudulent transfer of public lands, Pinchot was following his conservation philosophy that placed the best interests of the nation first. Regarding the national forests, which would include 12 percent of New Mexico's land by the time statehood was granted, Pinchot made clear that they were for the individual "home builder first of all" (qtd. in Wilkinson 128).

However, the land is "nobody's home," to borrow Arnold Weinstein's felicitous phrase, if it is viewed only in economic and national terms. *Nightland* makes clear that home turns to unhomely when connections are severed and an awareness of them is lost or repressed. The world as understood by both the Pueblo and the Cherokee, after all, is marked by connections between people, between people and place, between people and things both animate and inanimate, and between those things and place. Arturo tells Siquani that when he was falling he "saw the earth then, the way the eagle sees, and I could tell everything was part of everything else, you know, everything in balance like the old people always said" (250). It is telling that Arturo sees the way an eagle does, for Eagle is the Jemez men's society associated with war and defense. What must be defended is the balance and interconnectedness of the earth and its creatures. One fights those who would destroy it, for they threaten home. Arturo sees this, too, as he falls, for he has a vision of home as he plummets earthward. The picture that comes to him situates his family's home and his Pueblo community in relation to both the river and careful stewardship of the land and water.

The Cherokee recognize that if fundamental connections, beginning with those between men and women, are maintained, then the People, all others, and the world will remain in balance. Awiakta stresses that the balance of relationships necessitates "taking and giving back with respect" (25). Thus, losing an awareness of connections and the importance of reciprocity leads both to a loss of harmony in the world and to a loss of self. This is why Will sees himself reflected in the mirror as something "heavy and dark, a block of shadow rather than a man" (35). The lack of a "true, right specular image" (Derrida 156) here also reinforces that the commodification of land, which is nothing short of a commodification of home, transforms Will, and us, into something unrecognizable. To his credit, however, Will recognizes the danger symbolized by Arturo's body impaled on the juniper spire, its terrifying isolation, and through his dream later that night he recognizes what he must do in order to keep connections from being lost.

If the house is *heimlich* for Will in the sense that something is being concealed from him, it can very well be *unheimlich* for the reader. What has been long hidden but has now come to light is the recognition of connections between all things. That recognition has been repressed by the dominant culture, and the agent of that repression has been money and its accumulation.[5] Just as Will has to recognize the importance of connections, particularly as they relate to things that are buried, so too must the reader recognize connections. For both, recognition is rooted in traditional Pueblo and Cherokee practices and stories.

Pueblo ceremonies are essential to the maintenance of the land and the people's relationship to it and each other. Thus, the Pueblo have ceremonies to send the dead on their journey in order that the deceased might bring the rain to the people. In *Nightland*, Arturo's burial both brings the long, hard rain that soaks the earth after a lengthy drought and helps to free the water held beneath the earth by the massacred Apaches. It puts Arturo on the path home to his people as well. While Siquani is digging the shallow grave beside the spring, Arturo tells him he was "crazy for a long time" (250) because he had ceased making a pattern of his life that was grounded in home and traditional cultural practices. Indeed, Arturo had become so immersed in the white way that when Siquani asked "Ain't you got someplace to go?" after first calling him away from the body tree, the young man replies with "Who knows?" (91). Now the white sheet containing his corporeal remains is tied in a shape remindful of the clouds overhead, and as Arturo recognizes the similarity he also recognizes that, as a spirit, he is making the pattern that will make and keep him sane. Revising Foucault here, the narrative makes clear that one is crazy when one crosses the border or boundary of traditional Pueblo culture.

There are border crossings here, however, ones that acknowledge and make use of the frontier space where Pueblo and Cherokee cultural practices come together, for Siquani adds Cherokee medicine to Arturo's burial in the shroud that resembles a rain cloud. Siquani also sends Arturo on his way with a prayer grounded in Cherokee culture. In chanting "The Red Raven is with you, Arturo. . . . Your path is toward the Sunland. The Red Man walks with you" (252), Siquani lets Arturo know that Thunder, the great helpmate of the People, travels with him eastward to the place from which all good things come. What is more, as one of the versions of "Thunder and the Uk'ten'" collected by Jack and Anna Kilpatrick (53–56) makes clear, Thunder's presence reminds the audience, in this case the reader, of the connection between realms and people, the importance of reciprocity, and the fact that if it were not for Thunder humans would not be living today.

Just as the yoking of Pueblo and Cherokee power helps Arturo and the people, so too does the yoking of the interment rite and Cherokee purification ritual help the earth and all its inhabitants. Siquani begins preparations for the *amó:hi atsó:sdi* ("Going to the Water") rite well before he digs Arturo's grave. He burns the wood of a pine struck by lightning (174) prior to setting out to cut down the body tree and offers the smoke of remade tobacco and green cedar to each of the four directions and to the juniper once there. Both acts highlight the importance of transformation to Cherokee purification rituals. Burning the lightning-struck wood, moreover, is important "in purification rituals involving dealings with a supernatural being such as a *skili* (a colloquial term for a witch)" (A. E. Kilpatrick 53). The witch here is Odessa, to be sure, but the *amó:hi atsó:sdi* is also meant to protect the people and the land from the greed and ideology that make Odessa a "brown-skinned Yankee" (302). In keeping with tradition, Siquani practices the rite near flowing water, albeit just a trickle from the spring because the Apache "dead have the water" (51), and times it to coincide with sunrise. He sings, however, in both Cherokee and English, yoking the two languages just as he has yoked Pueblo and Cherokee traditions in order to create a powerful instrument for healing. Siquani knows, after all, that like Betonie in *Ceremony*, who is not afraid to make changes to the traditional healing ceremonies, at times "a person's got to try new things" (*Nightland* 223) if the rite is to be successful, the witchery to be warded off, and the sickness cured.

The frontier space created when Pueblo tradition and world-view, Cherokee tradition and worldview, Cherokee language, and English are brought together by Siquani, and Owens, remakes time and space as well. As a result, Siquani is able to dance and then run down a red path to the Trail of Tears. He follows *A`wi' Usdi'*, the deer tribe's chief (Mooney 263), to a hilltop from which he sees a line of the People so long he can make out "neither beginning nor end" (253). Siquani descends from the hill to walk among his people and share their suffering. He then hears "a sound from long before" (253) which he recognizes is that of dancing bones. The bones dance after the floodwater that covered the world recedes. The sole sur-vivors of the flood, a Cherokee man and his family, hear the sound of the bones dancing after they come ashore.

Linda Helstern has pointed out the importance to *Nightland* of what she terms the "archetypal Cherokee survival story" (75), for like the Cherokee man, Will will survive. In conflating the Trail of Tears and the deluge and its aftermath, moreover, Owens's narrative stresses that the People always have survived and will continue to do so. That survival is predicated on listening and seeing well, inter-pretation, sacrifice, and reciprocity. The man's dog warns him of the coming deluge, offers him a sign that what he says is the truth, and tells him that he must do something in order that he and his family will be saved. Most importantly, survival is predicated on story and storytelling themselves, for it is in the act of telling that survival is articulated. The audience is brought together with that way of seeing, thinking, and being in and with the world that ensures survival. Siquani suggests the importance of both this particular story and stories and storytelling in general when, while talking with Arturo about witches, witchery, and the story that is unfolding before their eyes, he says "Here's a story, Grandson" (134) and then tells Arturo of the survivors of the flood and the dancing bones.

Will Striker and Louis Owens both know that stories are a place where the self can be either found or lost. Thanks to the Cherokee stories he heard while a boy, Will learned the stories that would help him know how to act in the world. At the same time, "when he'd read books, [he'd] lost himself" (35) in them. If the books are those of the dominant culture, then Will ran the risk of having lost himself in the worst sense, for the world of those texts either elides the Native, on the one hand, or presents him or her as the Indian, on the other, while all too often presenting a will to power and mastery on the part of Euroamericans. The allusion in *Nightland* to Fitzgerald's *The Great Gatsby*, coupled with the revision of that allusion, indicates the cost and consequence of that will to power and control.

Painted on the side of a two-story building in Socorro, New Mexico, that Billy and Odessa drive by on their night out on the town is an owl, "eyes fixed on the street and its curving wings seeming ready to enfold everything into itself" (172). Owens plays with the Owl Cigar advertisement on the side of the Knights of Pythias Hall building on Manzanares Street in Socorro here in order to resolve the image and bring what it represents into focus. Reminiscent of the eyes of Doctor T. J. Eckleburg and in fact painted on the side of a building that houses an eye doctor's office, the owl, faded by years of exposure to wind and weather, oversees the wasteland that is Socorro. The advertisement dates from Victorian times, when Socorro was booming thanks to mining nearby and advances in smelting. The ad, then, is both a product of Socorro's late-nineteenth-century heyday and a reminder that that period was predicated and built upon resource extraction at the expense of the environment.

In *The Great Gatsby*, the eyes of the advertisement indicate that what surveys the wasteland is, finally, simply the ideology that created and perpetuates it in the first place. Owens revises the Owl Cigar advertisement in Socorro to emphasize the owl, its eyes, and its threatening posture. By doing so, the narrative both establishes an intertextual connection to *The Great Gatsby* and emphasizes that the bird connected with witchery and evil or disastrous tidings for the Cherokee looks down upon that which is its prey. The image, therefore, emphasizes how the witchery that, to echo *Ceremony*, produces the whites and their worldview leads to death and destruction. What is stressed, then, is nothing less than the fact that Socorro's boom times come at the expense of the world, and all its inhabitants. Siquani tells Arturo, "Us Cherokees believe a human being's power is in his eyes and his thinking" (250), and it is the power to see well—that is, seeing coupled with thinking that recognizes and is built upon the importance of reciprocity and maintaining balance—that enables one to recognize the witchery and keep it at bay.

Countering the written stories in which one might lose oneself, then, stories like *Gatsby*, are written stories in which one might find oneself. In *Nightland*, one such particular story alluded to is James Welch's *Winter in the Blood*. Like old Bird in Welch's novel, Will's mare Jezebel passes gas, and Will responds "You trying to tell me something profound, old girl?" (75). Recognizing the allusion, we know that the answer is yes. In *Winter in the Blood*, Bird's expulsion of gas carries with it the truth that Yellow Calf is Teresa's father and the narrator's grandfather. That truth brings the personal and the historical together for narrator and reader, establishes the correct kinship lines, and goes a long way toward helping the earth recover from being—as Yellow Calf has told the narrator more than once and as Uncle Luther remarks in *The Sharpest Sight*—"cockeyed" (*Winter in the Blood* 68). The narrator of *Winter in the Blood*, who like Will Striker has suffered an injured knee that never healed properly, also tells us that his stepfather, Lame Bull, his mother, Teresa, and everyone else has been "taken for a ride" by and because of greed. Indeed, as he and Bird struggle to free the cow from the mud he thinks of America as "This greedy stupid country" (169).

The bad knees of both the nameless narrator of *Winter in the Blood* and Will Striker are remindful of Wounded Knee. The fact that those injuries still torment both men suggests that the country has not yet healed from its Wounded Knee. In order for healing to occur, stories like Welch's and Owens's are necessary. Throughout *Nightland*, then, as throughout his other novels, Owens stresses the importance of oral and written stories. Odessa and Will share an understanding when it comes to stories, both non-Native and Native. Odessa knows that up until now the dominant culture's stories have been told and Euroamericans have been doing the telling. Further, she recognizes that "stories were what Indians had, and the story was born anew with every telling" (208); therefore the story can be changed. Even as a boy Will had recognized the dynamic nature of Cherokee stories when he listened to his father or Grampa Siquani tell of A`wi̇' Usdi', of Buzzard and Raven, of Kana'ti and Selu, of the Thunder boys, of many others, and of the world as a whole; he believes that "the Cherokee world was made of spoken words, told into being with living breath" (34). The white world, on the other hand, had been formed a long time ago and captured in written words.

Will grasps what Lyotard characterizes as the essential nature of traditional stories when, as a boy, "to his young mind, it was as if the Indian world was always new, made again and again when his father or Billy's grampa told the stories" (34). When an adult, moreover, he both hears "his father's voice in his own" (70) and names his children when telling them the Cherokee origin stories: "It's up to strong human beings like Holly and Si Striker to think good thoughts and keep those ropes in good shape" (70). That is, Will both recognizes how the oral basis of traditional Cherokee culture necessitates the creation of the world and worldview with each telling and how those tellings privilege the pole of reference and the addressee rather than, as in the West, the pole of addressor. This is why Will names his daughter and son in the story and hears his father's voice in, not behind, his own.

Odessa, on the other hand, hears finally only her voice, cares to tell only her story, and tells that story to the addressee only because she intends to kill him. Owens is doing much more than appropriating one of the conventions of both the thriller genre and melodramatic fiction when he has Odessa stand over her victims and announce her plans. Far from being simply a plot mechanism to bring strands of the novel together and clarify motive, the stories Odessa tells to first Billy and then Will reveal her awareness and denial of the addressee pole. That denial explains why Odessa invokes her home and ancestors only to deny her connection to both when she tells her story to Will. She says "This land was the home of my ancestors" (301) to rationalize murdering Billy and preparing to murder Will, but she plans to leave her homeland and go to South America, where she will "be a rich, brown-skinned Yankee in the middle of all those poor Indians" (302). Cutting herself off from the land, from kin and kinship structures, and from stories, Odessa could not be more correct when she names and identifies herself as a Yankee.

Contra Odessa, Grampa Siquani recognizes that stories forge connections between place and people. He also recognizes that, as he tells Arturo, "So much has been forgot. Cherokee people like that boy [Billy] don't remember where they came from or how to talk right. The stories tell them of those sacred places, but they only see those places in the stories. And they stop listening" (132). Odessa is more correct than she knows when she tells Billy, "Maybe you don't know your grandfather as well as you think you do" (143), for if Billy had known Grampa better he would not have stopped listening to the stories of the People. He would also have been in a better position to see and understand the importance of "try[ing] new things" (223) within the context of Cherokee culture and worldview. Trying new things is trickster's signature, of course, and Grampa Siquani's words and deeds serve to remind us of how trickster and trickster discourse can help heal self, others, and the world. Once again, then, Odessa is more correct than she knows, this time when she suggests that Siquani is a trickster (143).

Siquani knows both that Billy has stopped listening and that as a consequence his grandson will die. He also knows that Billy is not alone in having turned a deaf ear to the stories and what they teach. Owens's narrative makes clear that for at least some of the People the process of ceasing to listen to traditional stories began in the eighteenth century when they started listening to the Euroamericans and the ideology of "the greedy stupid country" that underpins their discourse. Twice we read that the whites paid the Cherokee to kill "all the deer" (132, 225). Balance was destroyed once the wholesale killing began, and both the traditional seasonal round and the spiritual practices of the People were casualties as well (Dunaway 462–63). And so, according to the stories Grampa Siquani tells, A`wǐ' Usdi' led the surviving deer deep into the mountains and far away from the Cherokee after the People failed to heed his request to stop. Through Siquani's stories, moreover, Owens makes clear that killing the deer for the whites was the beginning of a sequence that led to enslavement, the loss of land, and finally the long march west with death to the Darkening land (132, 225–26).

Siquani's emphasis on homeland and correct discourse echoes that of the Cherokee storyteller Siquanid', who serves as the character's model.[6] Siquanid' was one of the sources for the stories Jack and Anna Kilpatrick collected in *Friends of Thunder: Folktales of the Eastern Cherokee*. More than is true of at least some of the others who told stories to the Kilpatricks, Siquanid's reliance on formulaic openings and closings and repetition throughout the body of the stories grounds his tellings in the oral tradition. Siquanid' begins many of his stories either with "we will tell" or "we shall talk." He begins others by telling his audience that the story was told to him. In the latter instances, the stories tacitly remark upon the importance of either elders or kinship structure (as he lets his audience know that his father or grandfather has told him the stories) to the transmission of stories. Both stratagems serve to situate him in an oral community. He closes most of his stories with "That's all I know" or some variation of the same. In between, his use of repetition helps to situate stories and audience in relation to place and each other. In one story he repeats the location of the dam so that his audience will know where the voices of the spirits known as the Little People were heard. In another both specific locations and topography are reiterated. Thus, the way in which Siquanid' tells stories is a compelling example of "how to talk right" (*Nightland* 132).

It bears repeating that Owens and his fellow Native American writers need to follow Siquani's lead and "try new things" (223) in order to talk right with writing. One of Siquanid's stories in *Friends of Thunder* enables Owens to both create an intertextual connection with his character Siquani and to have a model of how to talk right on the page. The Kilpatricks entitle one of the two love charms they collected from Siquanid' "The Little Person and the Hunter." The story tells us of a young man who hears a voice singing while he is out hunting squirrels. He searches for the source of the voice and eventually discovers a Little Person who teaches him the song. With it, the hunter will be able to charm any woman who is indifferent to him. He brings the charm back to his people and after that time adults would teach subsequent generations the song and its magic. Eventually, however, the magic is lost, either because the people forgot it or because the Little People took it back.

The first thing we note when we read the transcription is that Siquanid' appears to replace the traditional opening framing device with the Euroamerican "Once upon a time" (92). In effect, what we have is a hybrid text, one that incorporates elements from both Cherokee and Euroamerican traditional tales. Siquanid' does not abandon the traditional Cherokee frame, however, so much as he revises it while remaining true to what it communicates to the audience: that is, at the end of the story, after telling his audience what happened to the hunter and subsequent generations of Cherokee, Siquanid' says, "My father told me that. Tsali Usgasit' was my father" (93). Here, then, Siquanid' accentuates, in a new fashion, the importance of family, kinship structures, and the pole of the addressee.

All this is vitally important for Owens, for Siquanid's seeming deviation from the traditional form while remaining true to the principles that govern it suggests a storytelling strategy that Owens can adopt as well. It could well be that Siquanid' opened "The Little Person and the Hunter" as he did because he knew he was addressing a Euroamerican audience. If so, then he is doing nothing less than offering that audience something that is familiar to them in order that they might be in a position to hear and learn from what follows. So too for Owens, who offers the audience of *Nightland* the familiarity of the thriller in order that they might learn much more than they could possibly imagine about themselves and the world prior to opening the cover of the book. One need only look at the blurbs printed with the Signet paperback edition to see just how familiar the novel was to its reviewers.[7] And even if Siquanid' was not taking his Euroamerican audience into consideration with his fairy-tale opening, nevertheless his decision to communicate the traditional in a new and different way is commensurate with Owens's decision to do the same. Both storytellers break from tradition while remaining traditional.

As is true of the form of "The Little Person and the Hunter," the content of Siquanid's story speaks to and through Owens's novel. The charming song the Little Person teaches the hunter serves to help combat the separation and isolation that, as the Kilpatricks indicate in *Walk in Your Soul: Love Incantations of the Oklahoma Cherokee*, can lead to the profound loneliness the Cherokee call *uhí:so?dí*. Like the Little Person, Grampa Siquani offers to teach a charming song. When Will goes to Billy's ranch the day after finding the money and talks to Grampa Siquani, the first question the latter asks is "Are you here to learn the wisdom of the elders, some Cherokee love medicine maybe to get that wild wife of yours back?" (68). Siquani knows that a man can get into trouble when he is alone and that being alone can bring upon *uhí:so?dí*; therefore to pique Will's interest he sings just a bit of a song that will charm Jace back and Will and Jace back together. What is more, by yoking Will and Kana'ti, Grampa Siquani's narrative makes clear that Will's isolation is neither unique to him nor that only the individual suffers as a consequence. Alone and bored, Kana'ti took to killing too much game, thus threatening the balance of the world. Created to ensure that Kana'ti has a partner, Selu also ensures both that the earth and its creatures are protected and that the People pay homage to and respect their mother.

Reunion with Jace is not easily accomplished, however, in no small measure because Will has shut himself off from his wife and, to some extent, the world. While his mother had "giv[en] in to loneliness only enough to wall herself in with books" (34), Will, like Cole McCurtain in *Bone Game*, has walled himself off from his personal past. That act began when he moved out of the bedroom he had shared with Jace the day she said she was leaving to take a job in Albuquerque. At once aware both that he is acting out of sorrow and self-pity and that he is unable to do otherwise, Will turns his back on his wife, his marriage, and the room where he was born and his second child was conceived. That is, he turns his back on the site that reminds him of his personal and familial past, present, and future. In doing so, he graphically upsets the balance between genders that is part of the Cherokee philosophy of harmony (Awiakta 23). Small wonder, then, that when Will opened the door to the bedroom for the first time in he knew not how long and looked around, "he felt like a man who'd gone back to the country of his birth from long exile and found the familiar world shrunken and strange" (36).

Because Will has not completely walled himself off from his cultural past and heritage, however, he is able to survive his long exile from Jace and his family. Indeed, the narrative's references and allusions to Kana'ti and Selu and the stories about the Corn Mother foreshadow Will's survival and reunion with his partner. Will nurtures seven stalks of corn through the dry, hot summer, suffers with a half-grin the sheriff's joke about the size of the crop, and tells Nate that he "just grew enough so the earth wouldn't forget" (147). The fact that Will carries water by the bucketful in order to keep the plants alive while the rest of the smallest garden he had ever planted withers away in the drought indicates that he has not forgotten the importance of paying homage and respect to Selu. She, in turn, will reciprocate with both corn and balance in order that the earth and its inhabitants might live harmoniously.

Most significantly, the seven stalks Will tends harken to the story of when Kana'ti and Selu's son and the Wild Boy gave seven grains of corn to strangers who had come a great distance because of the stories they had heard about the grain. Those seven grains become seven stalks overnight, each with one full ear, after the strangers do as they are told, plant the seeds in the evening, and watch the plants grow throughout the night. The story, then, is about the importance of sharing and returning the gift, about keeping one's eyes open, and about the power of stories to bring people together so that they and the earth might benefit. Grampa Siquani breaks into a wide grin when Will tells him that the corn is ripe and that they will have seven ears for dinner that night because he hears the traditional story echoing in the last words Will speaks in the novel. With those words, Owens makes clear that Will, the People, and the earth will survive.

ENDGAME

"We don't play games" (*Dark River* 156), Steve Stroud tells Jake Nashoba when they meet on tribal land hard upon a bank of the Dark River. For Stroud and his partner Phuong Nguyen, the paramilitary courses they offer have become a business, a way to make money and live comfortably rather than, as originally intended, a way to train like-minded individuals for an uprising against the United States government. Nevertheless, Stroud is serious here, for he wants to convince his Vietnam War buddy, and everyone else within earshot, that they are not fooling around in the Dark's canyon. He says what he does in order to satisfy his customers' desire "to be Rambo or that muscle-bound cartoon in the movie *Predator*, saving Western civilization from alien invasion. They wanted to live the warrior life they'd missed as clerks in Nam or, even more often, had only seen in movies" (113). Stroud strives for a certain verisimilitude—in ordnance, equipment, activities, and chain of command—for the same reason. He recognizes that his trainees want to take his "as if" with the utmost seriousness; it may be a game, but they do not want to be playing at it.

Like Stroud, Owens constructs an "as if," his fiction, and it is one that he would have us take seriously. Bent on revealing and replacing the Indian with the Native, on interrogating the nation and its narrative, and on disclosing the relationship between the Indian and the nation, on the one hand, and the relationship between both and canonical American literature, the discipline and practice of history, and ideas about the land, on the other, the five novels constitute nothing less than a long-overdue and necessary "taking apart" of the constructions that do violence to the people and the earth. As such, the texts from *Wolfsong* onward join with those produced by other Native American writers, "taking a part" in the enterprise of educating an audience in order that all might benefit.

Stroud's game turns deadly serious when Lee Jensen takes control of it and has the men hunt Jake Nashoba. Jensen gets "the excitement of a real combat mission" by creating what in a "business-like voice" he terms a "virtual reality war, except the reality bleeds" (188, 182–83). In short, his postmodern game, complete with rules that he takes pains to spell out to both Nashoba and the men who will hunt him, reiterates what Owens's other novels stress as well: that simulations can do real harm. By invoking *Chato's Land* as an example of the sort of clichéd story Jensen does not want to have be repeated, moreover, the narrative makes clear that simulations of the Indian do violence to and harm the Native.

The narrative yokes Jensen, language games, and death prior to the deadly game he creates and orchestrates. Tellingly, this occurs when the dead body of Jessie is brought back to camp. Jensen is quick to correct Tom Peters when the man makes an error in pronoun case while trying to explain how it happened that Henry shot Jessie. Jensen must correct "Henry and me just happened along when he was playing wolf" with "Henry and I" (118–19) because it will not do to have a white man in the position of object. That location is reserved for the dead Indian.

The Indian keeps being brought back in order to be killed in what we should think of as acts of compulsory repetition. Death and anxiety are linked on an individual level, because the latter is "the mood whereby we tell ourselves that our present desire is an inadequate response to the reality of our death. The reason that consciousness feels threatened by anxiety is that anxiety is that immediacy of self-consciousness which reveals how we stand with respect to the fact of death" (Davis 137). Anxiety also tells us not to stand, but to act (Davis 131). Such acts, when writ large at the levels of the nation and the dominant culture, only serve to keep the possibility of anxiety in play. That is, if we follow Bhabha's recognition of the gap between the event or idea that grounds a culture and nation and the everyday material practices of its people we see both how a recognition of the gap can foster anxiety that produces the need to make a narrative or enunciation to bridge or close the gap and how anxiety remains nevertheless. Now, though, the anxiety is over the possibility that we have simply enunciated, and thus instantiated, an incommensurability.

Dark River's narrative makes clear that Jensen's position is that of the dominant culture with his invocation of Sheridan's "The only good Indian is a dead Indian" just prior to correcting Peters. When Jensen's voice empties into the ellipsis after he looks down at Jessie's body and says "Dead as hell, too. The only good one . . ." (118) and then emerges from it to offer a grammar lesson, the narrative does nothing less than emphasize both how widespread and well-known Sheridan's statement is, and therefore how unnecessary it is for it to be completed in order to be heard and understood, and how it is thanks to the language games of the dominant culture that the white man is awarded the subject position and that from that position he tells a story that transforms the Native American into an Other object that is best dead.

Games become unjust, Lyotard holds, when they are motivated by and owe their efficacy to the fear of death. Here death includes all that interrupts the social bond, whether it be, for instance, "imprisonment, unemployment, repression, hunger" (*Just Gaming* 99), or literal death itself. Jensen's game, then, is unjust, for it uses the terror of death in order to make its rules regulate all other games, and all others in the process. Thus, he tells everyone that he was speaking metaphorically when he said that those who are expecting the same old Hollywood plot "might as well pack up" (183) and go home. No one is allowed to leave. That violence and death drive Jensen and his game is made clear by his preferred ending to the game. He tells Shorty Luke, Jessie, Alison, and the others still alive, "I vote for total annihilation, bad guy victorious, and all that" (283). Jensen pictures a particular apocalyptic end, one that has the Indian as its stock character, in order that, after "kill[ing] everybody, finishing with a dramatic speech to the helpless ranger and a bullet between the eyes," he can be seen "walking away through all this beautiful nature" (283). The dramatic speech before an intended victim is remindful of Odessa Whitehawk's in *Nightland*, of course. Here we recognize that Jensen's story, his game, culminates with a landscape emptied of its native inhabitants in order that it can be taken by the dominant culture. This is a story that has been told and repeated all too often.

  Dark River will not tolerate such an ending. More significantly, the novel, like *Wolfsong*, will not tolerate a simplistic reading of the end. The sign of the dominant culture's desire to close the book on the Native once and for all is writ large immediately beneath the final sentence of *Wolfsong*: END. As we have seen, Owens employs the trickster and trickster discourse throughout that text so that we might see END for what it is when finally we reach it: the sign of closure and completion that signifies a will to power and mastery that must be resisted. The END of *Wolfsong* is ironic, for there must be no end either to Tom Joseph's ceremonial flight to freedom or to the creation of texts that articulate identity while resisting closure. What is true of *Wolfsong* holds for Owens's other novels, including *Dark River*.[1] Thus, Jensen is shot by tribal chairman Xavier Two-Bears, only to have the blood and the wound disappear because such an ending would be too predictable. The audience can see it coming from the moment they see Two-Bears emerging from behind a tent, toilet paper in hand. Other endings are dismissed because they are either too postmodern or too noir, are not in keeping with tradition and traditional behavior, or will not be found suitable by the Black Mountain matriarch, Mrs. Edwards. Far from being too clever, this playing with the end accentuates how the indeterminacy of the text, conceived of as a frontier in Owens's sense of that term, allows for, even demands, the opening up of possibility. With that opening comes the possibility of change. It is thanks to that opening, on the one hand, and the refusal to close it, on the other, that one is able, finally, to know and find one's way home.

After all, "change is traditional, too" (*Dark River* 213), as Shorty Luke reminds his friend Avrum Goldberg. As evidence, Shorty asks the anthropologist to "look at those old pictures of the warriors" (213) and see proud people holding guns and dressed in clothes made of cotton. The people are not wearing the costumes that take the place of "real clothes, ceremonial vestments, or the languages of clothes and fashions" (Vizenor, *Fugitive Poses* 159) in so many nineteenth- and early-twentieth-century photographs of the Indian. These, then, are not photographs of a subject transformed into an object and fixed at a moment in time that is irrecoverably past. Rather, the photographs and their subjects speak to the capacity for adaptation and change that counters the dominant culture's desire to bury the Native. Viewed in this light, one different from that cast by either the patrol car spotlight Mundo Morales shines at the opening of *The Sharpest Sight* or the flashlight Jake Nashoba switches on at the opening of *Dark River*, we recognize the ways in which these photos avoid the spirit capture that is threatened by the camera while capturing the spirit of the People.[2]

With Vizenor, Owens recognizes that "photographs are never worth the absence of narratives because languages are imagination and photographs are [all too often] the simulations of culture and closure" (*Fugitive Poses* 157). With the presence of narratives, however, and with the presence of Native peoples in those narratives, we can then see both the dominant culture's desire captured in the figure of the Indian, image and text, and the traces of the Native that elude that capture. This is what Billy Keene sees when he looks at photographs of his parents in *Nightland*, for instance. He shows the photos to Odessa Whitehawk both so that she might know where he came from and, perhaps, so that he might know the same. For that to happen, he must flesh out the pictures, telling the story of the "scandal" of his mother's marriage to a Cherokee in order that she, he, and we can see her and him. In doing so, we see how the story of Billy's father and mother is part of the story of appropriation, manipulation, and the desire for land that leads to the creation of the Indian. The story Billy tells resolves the picture for Odessa and for us, just as the knowledge of the story resolves the picture for Billy as "he looked again at the picture she held at an angle to his vision" (*Nightland* 139). That angle returns us forcefully to anamorphosis, and reminds us that it is with and in story told with and in a Native perspective, in this case Cherokee, that we can see clearly and counter the death's head that dictates the image of the Indian perpetuated by the dominant culture.

Such other narratives, Owens's texts make clear, offer more than a different ending to the sort of game Jensen plays in *Dark River* and the terror that it contains; they put a different sort of game in play. The nature of that different game is articulated in *Dark River* by the game that counters Lee Jensen's deadly one: basketball. Six feet, five inches tall and over two hundred pounds when in high school, Jake Nashoba has the size and athletic ability that should have drawn him to football. He refused to play that sport, however, because the lines' banging into each other, regathering themselves, and then hurtling into each other again was too much like a white man's war. Basketball, on the other hand, reminded him of his readings about the plains tribes' practice of counting coup. He and his high school teammates "flew like a raiding party into enemy territory and [they], invariably, fed the ball to him so he could bring his coup stick down on the enemy, and then they'd explode whooping toward the other end, their own camp, and punish each transgression" (110). The emphasis is not on conquering, nor on headlong and headstrong bashing; one explodes back to one's camp, not into the enemy's, and with a whoop announces a successful raid.

Counting coup and the cries that announced it were declarations of honor for the plains peoples, according to Allan Ryan. The act of reaching one's enemy on his territory, touching but not killing him, and returning to your own homeland was also, Ryan recognizes, "tribal teasing on a grand scale" (24, n. 17). It is a trickster act, done in good humor. Plains Cree artist Gerald McMaster captures this with his painting *Counting Coup*. A plains male, complete with war bonnet, and a U.S. calvary officer stand side by side, faces predictably in profile to the audience, above a caption that reads "All Plains Indian tribes shared certain types of coup, yet each held its own views as to special ones." The Native counts coup with the pistol he points and shoots at the officer. Rather than a bullet, however, the gun "fires" the word "BANG" written on white. The delivery is dead-pan, but that is part of the coup. The Native offers himself as what the white man wants to see, a noble and silent warrior in profile, and uses one of the dominant culture's instruments of domination, a gun, in order to count coup on the white man, the government, and the dominant culture with yet another of its instruments of domination: writing. Such a trickster act, done in all good humor, turns the tables on the dominant culture and its subjects while highlighting their misrepresentations and misunderstanding.

Jake Nashoba's game of counting coup depends on humor and is humorous. It also depends on leaving things open, as Jessie reveals when he says that Jake "never finish[es] a game" (22). The same, as we have seen, is true of Owens's acts of counting coup with and in his novels. It is fitting, then, that Owens's acts of good humor begin with a text informed by and infused with the Coast Salish culture and worldview and "conclude" with a text that is grounded in the Western Apache culture and worldview,[3] for both the Coast Salish and the Western Apache turned and turn to humor in response to contact with the dominant culture and the threat it poses. For the Coast Salish, this meant "the most traditional of native tales and native mythic figures being used to respond to particular historical situations" (Holden 274). These "new" stories have a "'weighted humor'. . . meant to expose the folly of this new [Euroamerican] 'power' in Salish culture" (Holden 272). Similarly, the Western Apache tell jokes in which the joker imitates "the whiteman" in order to make clear what the Western Apache "regard as conspic-uous inadequacies in the social behavior of Anglo-Americans" (Basso, *Portraits* 57). Such behavior, predicated on what is seen by the Western Apache as the Euroamericans' "powerful need . . . to be regarded as separate and distinct from other people" (54), is harmful to all. It is small wonder, then, that the Western Apache end joking portrayals of "the whiteman" with some variant of *indaa'* *dogoyą́ą́da* (white men are stupid).

The white man's stupidity is captured, at least in part, by Jessie's comment to Lee Jensen after he is shot by Xavier Two-Bears: "'Don't make any facile jokes,' Jessie said. 'Violent scenes shouldn't be tempered with wit or jokes, or they lose their force, right, Uncle Luke?'" (281). Jessie's question is itself a joke, one that Shorty is in on thanks to his years as a Hollywood extra, and we would do well to be in on it as well. Such an ending, which denies humor, is, as Shorty says, "too predictable" (282) and must be avoided. Indeed, as we have seen throughout Owens's fiction, it is with trickster humor, not superficial but fluent and easy, that the stupidity and ignorance of the dominant culture can be articulated and overcome. Such ignorance is not confined to whites, as Onatima tells Luther in *The Sharpest Sight*.[4]

The humorous turn in response to stupidity and damning definitions of the Indian is captured in the joke about the Lone Ranger and Tonto that Owens includes in *Dark River*: "The way the joke went on the res was that the Lone Ranger called his sidekick 'Tonto,' which meant 'stupid' in Spanish, and the Indian called his boss 'El Que No Sabe,' meaning basically, 'he who doesn't know shit'" (17). The joke is on the dominant culture here, for believing that the Native is stupid means that they do not "know shit." The vulgar word for excrement, moreover, serves to remind us that, as was the case in *Wolfsong*, the dominant culture does not know what it can only conceive of as the remainder or excess that is from its perspective poisonous—the Native. Sadly, such a perspective will not enable the subjects of the dominant culture to see that what must be purged if they are to survive is the worldview that denies connections, privileges mastery, and creates Others.

Like the warriors in the photographs that Shorty Luke reminds Avrum Goldberg of, then, Owens meshes the traditional and the Euroamerican in order to count coup on ignorance. It is fitting, finally, that Owens begins writing novels in order to take apart and take a part when the willful ignorance of the dominant culture enabled its subjects in Washington State to hold that "Indians posed a danger to the fish . . . [and] that the Indian treaty right, as affirmed by *U.S. v. Washington*, presented a danger to the fishing economy of the Northwest" (Cohen 16). The Boldt decision enabled Washington State residents to blame the Indians and thus avoid having to face what Fay Cohen recognized as the "long-standing problem of too many fisherman chasing too few fish" (16). The situation in Washington State from and out of which Owens begins writing his fictions indicates that we must move beyond ignorance, then, not just in order to reimagine the nation in order that its being and becoming might be brought into harmony, but because the fate of the world is at stake.

Situating the beginning of the contemporary Native activist movement in 1964, the same year Chadwick Allen cites as the beginning of the American Indian Renaissance, places the fish-ins in Washington State at the center of the birth of the political and literary movements. Stephen Cornell recognizes the fishing rights march on the Washington State capitol in 1964 as a key early example of "sub- or supratribal groups taking politics into their own hands or taking their concerns directly to Congress, the states, the courts, and the public" (194–95). Robert Warrior also acknowledges the importance of the fish-ins, because of both the role played by the National Indian Youth Council (NIYC) and the fact that "by defying state law in full view of media and law enforcement personnel, these Natives were among those initiating a new way of bringing their political struggles to the attention of the United States and the world" (26). The fish-ins showcased what Warrior labels a "new, adversarial style" (27) on the part of Native activists. That style would be adopted by other nations and groups, most notably the American Indian Movement (AIM), and serve as a hallmark of what Paul Chaat Smith and Warrior call "the most remarkable period of activism carried out by Indians in the twentieth century" (269).

The remarkable period came to an end after Wounded Knee, "disintegrating under the weight of its own internal contradictions and divisions, and a relentless legal assault by federal and state governments" (Smith and Warrior 269). Consider the invasion and occupation of Alcatraz Island from November 1969 to June 1971 by Natives united under the title Indians for All Tribes. Adam Fortunate Eagle, an organizer and supporter of the occupation, notes that the goals of many of the occupation's Native supporters on the mainland differed from the goals of those on the island. What he saw as "a serious split between the people on the island and the people on the mainland" was signaled at a press conference early on where signs announced that "Indians on Alcatraz will rule Alcatraz" (109). Smith and Warrior note the same dividing line, with at least some of those weathering the hardships of life on the island holding that their presence on Alcatraz confirmed upon them the right to speak for and make decisions concerning Indians for All Tribes. Smith and Warrior also write of the lack of organization and coherence that was apparent to Hank Adams and Browning Pipestem, both veterans of the NIYC's efforts with the fish-ins in Washington State six years earlier, when they visited Alcatraz in January 1970. Equally apparent at that time to the student activists who had participated in the takeover and occupation was that "the heady days of idealism had given way to criminality, petty infighting, and vicious rumormongering" (Smith and Warrior 67).

AIM was not immune from disorganization either. Warrior and Smith note that "confusion, missed cues, bungled orders, and ineptitude" (157) characterized the movement's 1972 occupation of the Bureau of Indian Affairs building in Washington, DC. The pressures within AIM threatening its efficacy and existence were matched by external pressures in the form of the federal government's "campaign to discredit and cripple" (Cornell 202) it and other radical Native organizations. Lengthy and costly court cases, harassment, and the divisive work of federal agents having infiltrated AIM increasingly hamstrung the movement. Indeed, in the words of one AIM leader, speaking in 1978, "We've been so busy in court fighting these indictments we've had neither the time nor the money to do much of anything" (qtd. in Cornell 203).

Vizenor has long held that in addition to the ideological divisions that surfaced nearly immediately, AIM was undercut by the seduction of the Indian constructed by the dominant culture. He writes that from the early days of the movement the "poses of tribal radicals seem to mimic the romantic pictorial images in old photographs taken by Edward Curtis for a white audience. The radicals never seem to smile. . . . [T]he new radicals frown, even grimace at cameras, and claim the atrocities endured by all tribal cultures in first person pronouns" (*People* 130). While AIM leaders decried assimilation as, in Russell Means's words, part of the government's "genocidal policies against Indian people," policies that forced Natives to "become facsimiles of the white man" (qtd. in Vizenor, *People* 126), in Vizenor's view they did not recognize how their poses constituted a humorless mimicry of a construct that signifies, finally, only Othering and absence.

Nevertheless, Smith and Warrior and Vizenor acknowledge the attraction of AIM. In *Like a Hurricane*, the former write that "AIM still commanded the respect of many Indian people" (272) even after Wounded Knee. They also record Vine Deloria's experience of participating along with AIM members in a two-day meeting on a reservation in South Dakota in June 1973. According to Deloria, a critic of AIM, "As I listened to Russell Means I continually looked around the room to see the faces of the people as he spoke. Almost every face shone with a new pride. . . . Old men sat entranced and nodded ever so slightly at the different points Russell discussed" (qtd. in Smith and Warrior 273). For Vizenor, attending an AIM meeting just prior to Wounded Knee made him aware of the "spiritual warmth" produced as members worked together. Rather than "rais[ing] my rifle to that airplane over the village in the morning," however, Vizenor opted for a literary activism: "Instead, my pen was raised to terminal creeds. . . . I listened to the voices, the racial politics, the ironies, the lies, and tried to turn the sound of drums in my heart into a dream song, into literature" (*Interior Landscapes* 235).

In 1976, then, as Owens drafts *Wolfsong* in a Forest Service bunkhouse in Washington State, there is both a backlash against the

Natives and the gains won thanks in part to the fish-in protests of the 1960s and a recognition that the militant, extrainstitutional actions of groups like AIM were only somewhat effective in producing meaningful and lasting change. The close of Smith and Warrior's *Like a Hurricane* suggests that a significant difference between the NIYC and AIM was the intellectualism of the former. They quote at length Jerry Wilkinson's 1989 critique of AIM, in which the executive director of the NIYC contrasts AIM's "terribly anti-intellectual" nature with the NIYC's intellectualism. Smith and Warrior write that Wilkinson specifically refers to the letters in NIYC files from Clyde Warrior, Herb Blatchford, and Mel Thom in which the direction and future of the organization was debated (276).[5]

In and with writing, then, an activism can be articulated and sustained, one that perhaps, like AIM, can produce a sense of pride and community, nods of agreement on the part of Natives across generations and nations, and understanding on the part of non-Natives. While the radicalism of the students who burned the Bank of America building in Santa Barbara is doomed to fail in its effort to bring about change, as Owens recounts in *The Sharpest Sight*, perhaps the literary activism of Louis Owens—grounded in the intellectualism of movements like the NIYC, the intellectualism articulated by Gerald Vizenor, and the wisdom of trickster—can succeed. That success, moreover, shares with the activist movement a "supratribal character," to use Stephen Cornell's phrase (207), insofar as Owens's novels articulate a community of Native writers from a number of tribal cultures, writers whose texts supplement and call for the revision of the nation's national narrative and its construction of home and Others.

In *Nightland*, Grampa Siquani divines for water in order that the parents of Billy Keene and of Will Striker might know where to make a home in the arid landscape of the American Southwest. Later he practices the *amó:hi atsv:sdi* ("Going to the Water") rite in order that the land be healed and what had become unhomely will become homely again. Hidden water that needs to be found is central, too, to Owens's father, who, we learn in the memoir "Water

Witch," divined for water in central California. The water never failed to be where his willow wand told him it would be. Owens and his older brother Gene would go with him at times, and "Water Witch" recounts how they would follow behind their father while "he would walk, steps measured as if the earth demanded measure" (*Mixedblood Messages* 184). Those measured steps keeping Owens's father in touch with the earth and the water he sought beneath its surface are the antithesis of the measured steps, literal and figurative, that the mapmakers take when they step off the land as property. The image of the elder Owens and his sons together, moreover, brings together family and familial connections, memory, water, and the idea of the need to search for something vital that is hidden from view and not easily accessible.

What holds for Grampa Siquani and for Hoey Louis Owens holds for Louis Owens as well. The younger Owens also takes measured steps in and with his fictions in order that he might find and reveal what has been and is still today largely hidden from our sight. And in those fictions water plays a key role, as we have seen. It reveals, reminds, and reinforces for characters and readers the vital importance of kinship structures and connection, of cycles and return, and of medicine and healing. Small wonder, then, that as Vizenor has recognized and Owens freely acknowledges, "Well, you know water has always been an obsession. I guess I'm really obsessed with it" (qtd. in Purdy 14).

If the Native and proper relations to and with the land are what have been buried by the dominant culture, then buried water and the buried truth about it are what Owens's fictions work to have readers see and learn. This truth has a cultural connection, as we have seen, for the Cherokee recognize the healing power of water. Indeed, Owens has said that he thinks that the powerful medicine connected with water is "why we've survived this long. Water's really important" (qtd. in Purdy 14). Beginning with *Wolfsong*, then, Owens's trickster activism, both more appropriate and more effective than the activism of the "bunch of dumb amateurs" (*Dark River* 120) who burned the Santa Barbara branch of the Bank of America, constitutes powerful medicine that is directed at bringing about the fundamental changes in seeing the Native and the world that are necessary if the People are to be allowed to have a home, on the one hand, and to have that home, the earth, be habitable, on the other.

NOTES

INTRODUCTION

1. As is true of place-names and stories, power has a particular cultural valence for the Western Apache. Power is "an invisible but potent attribute of any class of objects which is said to possess it" (Basso, "Western Apache Witchcraft" 30). Power is connected to *godiyo'*, or holiness, but the objects in any particular class are not themselves holy; power is. Mrs. Edwards should not be feared as a witch, for she uses her power to help cure the surviving twin of his illness.

2. The scholarship on representations of the Indian in print, photographs, and film is, of course, voluminous. Useful places to begin include Robert Berkhofer, Jr., *The White Man's Indian: The History of an Idea from Columbus to the Present* (1978); S. Elizabeth Bird, ed., *Dressing in Feathers: The Construction of the Indian in American Popular Culture* (1996); Susan Scheckel, *The Insistence of the Indian: Race and Nationalism in Nineteenth-Century American Culture* (1998); Philip J. Deloria, *Playing Indian* (1998); Christopher Lyman, *The Vanishing Race and Other Illusions: Photographs by Edward S. Curtis* (1982); Alfred L. Bush and Lee Clark Mitchell, eds., *The Photograph and the American Indian* (1994); Tim Johnson, ed., *Spirit Capture: Photographs from the National Museum of the American Indian* (1998); and Richard W. Hill, Sr., "Developed Identities: Seeing the Stereotypes and Beyond," in Tim Johnson, ed., *Spirit Capture: Photographs from the National Museum of the American Indian* (1998).

3. Naming the Western Apache band Black Mountain, then, is an example of the act of disclosure that Wolfgang Iser, following Hans Vaihinger, sees as fundamental to literary fictions. One wonders, too, if this particular

act of naming also discloses Owens's awareness, and subtle critique, of the tendency to see ethnicity and race in terms of and in the terms of black and white. We will have more to say on the significance of acts of naming that blur the distinctions between the real, the imaginary, and the fictional in relation to *Wolfsong* (see chapter 1).

4. Iser's work on the identity of the literary text and the nature of fictions is an outgrowth of his earlier explorations of reader-response and reception. See, for instance, *Prospecting: From Reader-Response to Literary Anthropology* (1989), *The Fictive and the Imaginary: Charting Literary Anthropology* (1993), and "Fictionalizing: The Anthropological Dimension of Literary Fictions" (1990). Iser's reader-response theory has garnered the attention of scholars focusing on Native American literatures, of course: see, for instance, Kimberly Blaeser, "*The Way to Rainy Mountain:* Momaday's Work in Motion" (1989); and James Ruppert, *Mediation in Contemporary Native American Fiction* (1995).

CHAPTER 1

1. Authority and surveillance are closely linked, as we will have occasion to see in more detail when we examine *The Sharpest Sight*. See Vizenor, *Fugitive Poses* (1998); John Tagg, *The Burden of Representation* (1988); and, on the relationship between photography and anthropology, Christopher Pinney, "The Parallel Histories of Anthropology and Photography," in Elizabeth Edwards, ed., *Anthropology and Photography: 1860–1920* (1992); and Melissa Banta and Curtis Hinsley, *From Site to Sight: Anthropology, Photography, and the Power of Imagery* (1986).

2. As Linda Helstern has pointed out to me, one can also read the attempt to smile in the light of the stereotype of the emotionless Indian. Doing so, Tom's attempt signifies Owens's effort throughout his fiction to move beyond the stereotype of the stoic, unfeeling Indian, even as Tom's failure signals both his difference and his inability, at this time, to turn to humor. The failed smile that means one thing in relation to Tom and something else in relation to Owens, then, functions in this regard like Raven in the text, as we shall see.

3. In order to see the Native American we must remain open to anxiety, refusing to short-circuit our efforts by escaping into nostalgia. Just as the absence of anxiety in analysis indicates that the process is at an impasse and the patient's defenses are all in place (Davis 269), so too does an absence of anxiety in the presence of the Native American indicate that the reader is too at home with and in him- or herself. Anxiety alerts us to a danger and is an "attempt to make that danger appear vague enough [blurred

enough] that one will have no choice but to flee" (Davis 268). This is an option we must not take. Rather, Bhabha clearly articulates the importance of staying in the unsettling, dislocating state when he writes that anxiety "constitutes a transition where strangeness and contradiction cannot be negated and must be continually negotiated and worked through" rather than run from ("Irremovable Strangeness" 35).

4. Ethnographers, folklorists, and anthropologists have collected the raven tales of many tribes of the Pacific Northwest. Among the most valuable collections are from John Reed Swanton, *Haida Texts and Myths* (1905) and *Tlingit Myths and Texts* (1909), and Franz Boas, *Tsimshian Mythology* (1916). The tales indicate that Raven is both creator and trickster; rarely, however, does he act solely with altruistic motives. Peter Goodchild brings together raven tales from many different tribes and peoples in *Raven Tales: Traditional Stories of Native Peoples* (1991). The touchstones for scholars examining the figure of the trickster in the Native American oral tradition remain Paul Radin, *The Trickster: A Study in American Indian Mythology* (1956); and Barbara Babcock, "'A Tolerated Margin of Mess': The Trickster and His Tales Reconsidered" (1975). One should also see Babcock, "Arrange Me into Disorder: Fragments and Reflections on Ritual Clowning," in John J. MacAloon, ed., *Rite, Drama, Festival, Spectacle: Rehearsals toward a Theory of Cultural Performance* (1984). More recent work on the trickster, in addition to that by Vizenor already cited, includes William Hynes and William Doty, eds., *Mythical Trickster Figures: Contours, Contexts, and Criticisms* (1993); Jeanne Rosier Smith, *Writing Tricksters: Mythic Gambols in American Ethnic Literature* (1997); and Allan Ryan, *The Trickster Shift: Humour and Irony in Contemporary Native Art* (1999).

5. Traditionally, the wolf spirit conferred the power of hunting prowess upon its recipient. This is the case with *staka'yu* and Jim Joseph. More must be made of the connection, however, for the wolf spirit can also confer war powers (Elmendorf 287). Knowing this, one can see Jim Joseph using his power when he becomes a warrior defending the wilderness. It is precisely this element of the wolf spirit that Tom will hear, respond to, and follow when he blows up the mining camp water tower.

6. The relationship between identity and dreams, stories, and traditions is at the center of Owens's next novel, *The Sharpest Sight* (see chapter 2).

7. We can compare Tom's weak grin just prior to reaching the summit of Dakobed with two earlier, failed attempts to grin or smile: the first is in the Peterbilt cab with Amel Barstow; the second is when he attempts to make a joke in response to Karen Brant's statement that he looks "like an Indian" (63) when they first meet after his return home from California.

Tom's ability to see the humor and to use humor to undo the sign "Indian" in the final instance is indicative of both his growth and the narrative's emphasis on humor as a survival strategy and critical tool.

8. See, for instance, Stewart Bird, Dan Georgakas, and Deborah Shaffer, eds., *Solidarity Forever: An Oral History of the IWW* (1985), 99–123; and Robert Tyler, *Rebel of the Woods: The I.W.W. in the Pacific Northwest* (1967), 65–76, 92–99, passim.

9. Susan Bernardin, personal correspondence.

CHAPTER 2

1. Even a cursory glance at texts by Native American writers indicates that Owens's emphasis on mixedblood identity in his fiction and criticism is shared by many of his contemporaries: N. Scott Momaday, James Welch, Leslie Marmon Silko, Linda Hogan, Betty Louise Bell, Kimberly Blaeser, Michael Dorris, Louise Erdrich, Heid Erdrich, Wendy Rose, Gordon Henry, Jr., and Gerald Vizenor all concern themselves to lesser or greater extent with the figure of the mixedblood—or crossblood, to use Vizenor's term. Blaeser's voice is instructive here; she writes that while "most mixedbloods in Native American literature (read marginal characters) have desired and sought this resolution of ambiguous identity that results from movement to one side of the border or the other (usually back to a tribal center). . . . Vizenor's mixedblood characters (read tricksters) seldom seek or desire resolution for their ambiguous or marginal state. Rather they celebrate that state, create from it new mixedbood identities, and exist in and are depicted in the comic mode" (*Vizenor* 158).

2. Vizenor has pointed out in his fiction and criticism the dangers of tragedy as a category within which to fix Native Americans, their "history," and their "plight." See, for instance, *The Trickster of Liberty* (1988) and "A Postmodern Introduction" (1993).

3. The Chumash artifacts that function as medicine for Cole also indicate a transnational concern on Owens's part. We will see below, especially in chapter 3, how that concern manifests itself in the articulation of a community of Native writers from a number of different nations. Owens's interest in what I am calling the transnational is fitting given his own mixedblood identity—Choctaw-Cherokee-Cajun-Irish—and his desire to write about a number of different Native nations.

4. The narrative emphasizes the horrifying nature of the violation and yokes Jessard Deal and Dan Nemi by having the former bring up a "piggy-wig" in a wood and grunt as he tears at Diana's clothes.

5. In this regard Owens's fiction is akin to the work of critics and theorists laboring to show how a literature can function to perpetuate the

ideologies and worldview of those in power. For instance, in looking at Kipling's children's literature, Satya P. Mohanty focuses on "the extent to which children's fiction might function . . . to fashion the imperial self from within, simultaneously shaping and articulating desires, patterning images of self and world not only in terms of value, but of possibility and necessity as well" (330–31).

6. Owens's phrasing echoes Vizenor's *The People Named the Chippewa* (1984), a text concerned with identity and how being "named" the Chippewa (the U.S. government's designation for the Anishinaabe) is an act of fixing that is emblematic of a larger pattern of misidentification.

CHAPTER 3

1. My approach to *Bone Game* shares much with Rochelle Venuto's compelling reading of the novel. While several of our points of contact and departure are similar, in what follows I stress Owens's critique of discovery and history, the importance of liminality both in and of the text, and the community of Native writers that *Bone Game* works to articulate.

2. Tellingly, it is by taking the emphasis away from "utterly" and focusing on its root, "utter," as verb rather than adjective, that Owens and other Native writers counter the totalizing efforts of the dominant culture by grounding their texts in an oral tradition.

3. I am indebted to Susan Bernardin for pointing out to me that the dominant culture's demonizing name for the sacred geophysical site is a striking example of the "fucking words" (*Bone Game* 43) Cole and Owens labor to reveal and supplement. As such, the name Devil's Tower is part of the tradition of demonizing the landscape of North America that begins with the first published accounts of the New World.

4. Momaday's trope of memory in the blood or blood memory has been both celebrated and criticized by scholars. For a useful and provocative summation of the trope as it is used by Momaday, its principal detractor's position regarding it, and Vizenor's trickster turn on both, see Allen, "Blood (and) Memory."

CHAPTER 4

1. That discourse was multivocal. For instance, while, as Dana Nelson points out, William Byrd's public *History of the Dividing Line betwixt Virginia and North Carolina* (1728–30) articulates the danger to Euroamericans of intermarriage and procreation with Natives, Thomas Jefferson's writings early in the next century indicate that he accepted Native/Euroamerican amalgamation. Jefferson held quite a different position with regard to

blacks and Euroamericans, of course. No matter the ethnicity of the feared Other, however, that fear had, and has, its roots in white male anxiety regarding sexuality. For instance, Ronald Takaki quotes a 1691 law passed by the Virginia Assembly prohibiting the "`abominable mixture and spurious issue' of interracial unions and . . . provid[ing] for the banishment of white violators" (*A Different Mirror* 67). The assembly "took special aim at white women," Takaki adds, in the form of fines and the promise of lengthy servitude for their "spurious issue" in an effort to control the threat posed by interethnic union. Useful places to begin an examination of the role miscegenation plays in the discourse of the land and the nation include Dana D. Nelson, *The Word in Black and White: Reading "Race" in American Literature, 1638–1867* (1992); Leonard Dinnerstein, Roger Nichols, and David Reimers, *Natives and Strangers: A Multicultural History of Americans* (1996); Frank Shuffelton, *A Mixed Race: Ethnicity in Early America* (1993); and Takaki, *A Different Mirror* (1993), *Iron Cages* (1990), and, as editor, *From Different Shores* (2nd ed., 1994).

   2. One should recognize, too, that the array's presence is connected to the novel's concern with land and the nation insofar as astronomy is linked to the creation of the imaginary grid that is used to map the earth's surface. The transit circle telescope at the Royal Observatory in Greenwich was used to fix 0 degrees longitude. From there, all other lines of longitude are measured. The imaginary grid is defined astrally in order to be precise, and once the grid was fixed in place, land "becomes a precisely measurable entity, divisible into parcels which may be located exactly on a map" (Van Ness and Van Ness 8). The planet's surface can be precisely measured, plotted, and fixed on a map without regard or recourse to landmarks. There is, then, no need to consider, much less heed, a storied landscape and sacred geography. The modern system of reckoning, intimately connected to the science and practice of astronomy, is "an absolute essential to Anglo-American land tenure and economics [because] this system permits both the resources and the products of a parcel or plot of land, as well as the land itself, to be brought into the national and international market" (Van Ness and Van Ness 8). Land, that is, becomes property.

   3. The connection between Buzzard and *Nightland* grows increasingly rich when we recognize the significance of the context in which the former is introduced in the latter's opening scene. In order that we might not miss that context, the narrative has Billy twice remind Will that they are hunting deer. A traditional Cherokee story tells of a buzzard who helps a man having no success on a deer hunt by changing places with him so that the Cherokee can fly high enough to see the deer beyond the ridge he is on (Mooney

294). Human becomes buzzard, buzzard becomes human, and in so doing the story emphasizes the possibility and importance of transformation for the People. The story also stresses sight and perspective, both of which are critical to *Nightland*, as we shall see, and indeed to each of Owens's novels.

4. Such dramatic increase came to a halt one month prior to Roosevelt's request for Hagerman's resignation because of legislation attached to an appropriations bill that forced the president to relinquish the power to withdraw land in six western states after March 4, 1907. Unable easily to withdraw public land by executive order, it makes sense that the federal government would increase its efforts to combat fraud and misuse of public lands. Regarding national forests, the West, and the Nation, see, in addition to works already cited, Paul Hirt, *A Conspiracy of Optimism: Management of the National Forests since World War Two* (1994), and William Robbins, *American Forestry: A History of National, State, and Private Cooperation* (1985).

5. It bears remembering that Winthrop composed and delivered "A Model of Christian Charity" in an attempt to counter the tendency to be greedy that he recognized would undermine the Puritans' attempt to create a model community in the New World.

6. Owens revealed the connection between Siquani and Siquanid' in a telephone interview with Linda Helstern.

7. *Winter in the Blood* benefits from a certain familiarity as well. In the case of Welch's novel, though, what is familiar, and thus comforting, to reviewers and readers is the text's amenability to a straightforward psychoanalytic reading that roots the narrator's dis-ease in both his troubling relationship with his mother and his inability to confront and come to terms with his role in his brother's death.

ENDGAME

1. Thus Venancio Asisara looks down on the town and the bay at the end of *Bone Game* both to remind us that there is no end to the battle against evil, for it cannot be destroyed, and that attempting to achieve final closure and completion is to be avoided. Imagining that the book is closed on Asisara and on evil is a mistake, for as Rochelle Venuto notes, "Venancio's continued presence . . . demonstrates that evil, which will always exist, must be acknowledged in order to maintain the world's balance" (39).

2. Tim Johnson turns around the typical notion that Native peoples were leery of being photographed for fear that their spirits would be captured by the camera, sees the photographs in the collection of the

National Museum of the American Indian from another perspective, and recognizes that the images capture "the 'spirit' or will of Indian peoples to continue to be who they are as they adjust to their changing realities" (24).

3. Here too we need to be wary of conclusions, and jumping to them, for Owens is at this writing working on another novel, one that focuses on Onatima and Luther.

4. It bears remarking here that just as Onatima is a voice of reason and representative of a strong female presence in Owens's fictions, *Dark River* includes the matriarch Mrs. Edwards, a new tribal leader in Tali, and a young woman leading at the end of the text in Alison. That these women are in positions of leadership is indicative, I think, of both the key role women play in Owens's fictions and, more importantly, the key role Native women and a Native-centered feminism can play in restoring proper relations between humankind and the earth.

5. This is not to say that Native activism and protest cannot be successful, mind you. For an example of one success, see Rick Whaley, with Walter Bresette, *Walleye Warriors* (1994). Winona LaDuke chronicles a number of Natives' efforts in *All Our Relations: Native Struggles for Land and Life* (1999).

WORKS CITED

Allen, Chadwick. "Blood (and) Memory." *American Literature* 71.1 (1999): 93–116.

Amoss, Pamela. *Coast Salish Spirit Dancing.* Seattle: U of Washington P, 1978.

Awiakta, Marilou. *Selu: Seeking the Corn Mother's Wisdom.* Golden, CO: Fulcrum, 1993.

Babcock, Barbara. "Arrange Me into Disorder: Fragments and Reflections on Ritual Clowning." *Rite, Drama, Festival, Spectacle: Rehearsals toward a Theory of Cultural Performance.* Ed. John J. MacAloon. Philadelphia: Institute for the Study of Human Issues, 1984. 102–28.

———. "'A Tolerated Margin of Mess': The Trickster and His Tales Reconsidered." *Journal of the Folklore Institute* 9 (1975): 147–86.

Banta, Melissa, and Curtis Hinsley. *From Site to Sight: Anthropology, Photography, and the Power of Imagery.* Cambridge, MA: Peabody Museum P, 1986.

Barthes, Roland. *Camera Lucida.* Trans. Richard Howard. New York: Hill, 1981.

Basso, Keith. *Portraits of "The Whiteman": Linguistic Play and Cultural Symbols among the Western Apache.* Cambridge: Cambridge UP, 1979.

———. "'Speaking with Names': Language and Landscape among Western Apache." *Rereading Cultural Anthropology.* Ed. George Marcus. Durham: Duke UP, 1992. 220–51.

———. "Western Apache Witchcraft." *Anthropological Papers of the University of Arizona* 15. Tucson: U of Arizona P, 1969. 1–75.

Berkhofer, Robert, Jr. *The White Man's Indian: The History of an Idea from Columbus to the Present.* New York: Vintage, 1978.

Bernardin, Susan. "Wilderness Conditions: Ranging for Place and Identity in Louis Owens' *Wolfsong.*" *Studies in American Indian Literatures* 10.2 (1998): 79–93.

Bevis, William. "Native American Novels: Homing In." *Recovering the Word: Essays on Native American Literature.* Ed. Brian Swann and Arnold Krupat. Berkeley: U of California P, 1987. 580–620.

Bhabha, Homi K. *The Location of Culture.* London: Routledge, 1994.

———. "On the Irremovable Strangeness of Being Different." *PMLA* 113 (1998): 34–39.

Bird, S. Elizabeth, ed. *Dressing in Feathers: The Construction of the Indian in American Popular Culture.* Boulder, CO: Westview, 1996.

Bird, Stewart, Dan Georgakas, and Deborah Shaffer, eds. *Solidarity Forever: An Oral History of the IWW.* Chicago: Lakeview, 1985.

Blaeser, Kimberly. *Gerald Vizenor: Writing in the Oral Tradition.* Norman: U of Oklahoma P, 1996.

———. "Like 'Reeds through the Ribs of a Basket': Native Women Weaving Stories." *Other Sisterhoods: Literary Theory and U.S. Women of Color.* Ed. Sandra Kumanoto Stanley. Champaign: U of Illinois P, 1998. 265–76.

———. "*The Way to Rainy Mountain:* Momaday's Work in Motion." *Narrative Chance: Postmodern Discourse on Native American Indian Literatures.* Ed. Gerald Vizenor. Norman: U of Oklahoma P, 1993 (originally published by the U of New Mexico P, 1989). 39–54.

Boas, Franz. *Tsimshian Mythology.* 1916. New York: Johnson Reprint, 1970.

Bryson, Norman. "The Gaze in the Expanded Field." *Vision and Visuality.* Ed. Hal Foster. Seattle: Bay, 1988. 86–108.

Bush, Alfred L., and Lee Clark Mitchell, eds. *The Photograph and the American Indian.* Princeton: Princeton UP, 1994.

Cadava, Eduardo. "The Whisper of Gazes: Walter Benjamin in the Image of Franz Kafka." *Genre* 29.1–2 (1996): 261–86.

Champagne, Duane. "Symbolic Structure and Political Change in Cherokee Society." *Journal of Cherokee Studies* 7 (Fall 1983): 87–96.

Clark, Norman. *Mill Town.* Seattle: U of Washington P, 1970.

Cohen, Fay. *Treaties on Trial: The Continuing Controversy over Northwest Indian Fishing Rights.* Seattle: U of Washington P, 1986.

Collins, June McCormick. *Valley of the Spirits: The Upper Skagit Indians of Western Washington.* Seattle: U of Washington P, 1974.

Cornell, Stephen. *The Return of the Native: American Indian Political Resurgence.* New York: Oxford UP, 1988.

Cushman, H. B. *History of the Choctaw, Chickasaw, and Natchez Indians.* Ed. Angie Debo. New York: Russell, 1962.

Davis, Walter A. *Inwardness and Existence*. Madison: U of Wisconsin P, 1989.

Deloria, Philip J. *Playing Indian*. New Haven: Yale UP, 1998.

Derrida, Jacques. *Specters of Marx: The State of the Debt, the Work of Mourning, and the New International*. Trans. Peggy Kamuf. London: Routledge, 1994.

Dinnerstein, Leonard, Roger Nichols, and David Reimers, eds. *Natives and Strangers: A Multicultural History of Americans*. New York: Oxford UP, 1996.

Dinwoodie, David. "Indians, Hispanos, and Land Reform: A New Deal Struggle in New Mexico." *Western Historical Quarterly* 17 (July 1986): 291–323.

Dunaway, Wilma. "Incorporation as an Interactive Process: Cherokee Resistance to Expansion of the Capitalist World-System, 1560–1763." *Sociological Inquiry* 66.4 (1996): 455–70.

Dwyer, Margaret. "The Syncretic Impulse: Louis Owens' Use of Auto-biography, Ethnology, and Blended Mythologies in *The Sharpest Sight*." *Studies in American Indian Literatures* 10.2 (1998): 43–60.

Eagle, Adam Fortunate. *Alcatraz! Alcatraz! The Indian Occupation of 1969–1971*. Berkeley: Heyday, 1992.

Edwards, Jonathan. *Puritan Sage: Collected Writings of Jonathan Edwards*. Ed. Vergilius Ferm. New York: Library Publishers, 1953.

Elmendorf, William. "Coast Salish Concepts of Power: Verbal and Functional Categories." *The Tsimshian and Their Neighbors of the North Pacific Coast*. Ed. Jay Miller and Carol M. Eastman. Seattle: U of Washington P, 1984. 281–91.

Freud, Sigmund. "The Uncanny." *The Standard Edition of the Complete Psychological Works of Sigmund Freud*, vol. 17. Trans. and ed. James Strachey. London: Hogarth, 1955. 217–48.

Galloway, Patricia. *Choctaw Genesis, 1500–1700*. Lincoln: U of Nebraska P, 1995.

Gasché, Rudolphe. *The Tain of the Mirror: Derrida and the Philosophy of Reflection*. Cambridge: Harvard UP, 1986.

Goodchild, Peter. *Raven Tales: Traditional Stories of Native Peoples*. Chicago: Chicago Review P, 1991.

Goodwin, Grenville. *Myths and Tales of the White Mountain Apache*. New York: American Folklore Society, 1939.

Grant, Campbell. "Chumash Introduction." *California*. Vol. 8 of *Handbook of North American Indians*. Ed. Robert Heizer. Washington, DC: Smithsonian Institution, 1978. 505–8.

Green-Lewis, Jennifer. "Picturing England: On Photography, Landscape, and the End(s) of Imperial Culture." *Genre* 29.1–2 (1996): 33–62.

Helstern, Linda Lizut. "*Nightland* and the Mythic West." *Studies in American Indian Literatures* 10.2 (1998): 61–78.

Hietala, Thomas. *Manifest Design: Anxious Aggrandizement in Late Jacksonian America.* Ithaca, NY: Cornell UP, 1985.

Hill, Richard W., Jr. "Developed Identities: Seeing the Stereotypes and Beyond." *Spirit Capture: Photographs from the National Museum of the American Indian.* Ed. Tim Johnson. Washington, DC: Smithsonian Institution, 1998. 139–60.

Hirt, Paul. *A Conspiracy of Optimism: Management of the National Forests since World War Two.* Lincoln: U of Nebraska P, 1994.

Holden, Madronna. "'Making All the Crooked Ways Straight': The Satirical Portrait of Whites in Coast Salish Folklore." *Journal of American Folklore* 89 (1976): 271–93.

Horsman, Reginald. *Race and Manifest Destiny: The Origins of Racial Anglo-Saxonism.* Cambridge: Harvard UP, 1987.

Hudson, Travis, and Ernest Underhay. *Crystals in the Sky: An Intellectual Odyssey Involving Chumash Astronomy, Cosmology, and Rock Art.* Ballen Press Anthropological Papers no. 10. Socorro, NM: Ballena, 1978.

Hynes, William, and William Doty, eds. *Mythical Trickster Figures: Contours, Contexts, and Criticisms.* Tuscaloosa: U of Alabama P, 1993.

Iser, Wolfgang. "Fictionalizing: The Anthropological Dimension of Literary Fictions." *New Literary History* 21.4 (1990): 939–56.

———. *The Fictive and the Imaginary: Charting Literary Anthropology.* Baltimore: Johns Hopkins UP, 1993.

———. *Prospecting: From Reader-Response to Literary Anthropology.* Baltimore: Johns Hopkins UP, 1989.

Johnson, Tim, ed. *Spirit Capture: Photographs from the National Museum of the American Indian.* Washington, DC: Smithsonian Institution, 1998.

Kidwell, Clara Sue. *Choctaws and Missionaries in Mississippi, 1818–1918.* Norman: U of Oklahoma P, 1995.

Kilpatrick, Alan Edwin. "'Going to the Water': A Structural Analysis of Cherokee Purification Rituals." *American Indian Culture and Research Journal* 15.4 (1991): 49–58.

Kilpatrick, Jack F., and Anna G. Kilpatrick. *Friends of Thunder: Folktales of the Oklahoma Cherokee.* Norman: U of Oklahoma P, 1964, 1995.

———. *Walk in Your Soul: Love Incantations of the Oklahoma Cherokees.* Dallas: Southern Methodist UP, 1965.

Lacan, Jacques. *The Four Fundamental Concepts of Psycho-Analysis.* Trans. Alan Sheridan. New York: Norton, 1978, 1981.

LaDuke, Winona. *All Our Relations: Native Struggles for Land and Life.* Cambridge, MA: South End, 1999.

Lamar, Howard Roberts. *The Far Southwest, 1846–1912: A Territorial History.* New Haven: Yale UP, 1966.

Langston, Nancy. *Forest Dreams, Forest Nightmares: The Paradox of Old Growth in the Inland West.* Seattle: U of Washington P, 1995.

Luckert, Karl. "Coyote in Navajo and Hopi Tales." *Navajo Coyote Tales: The Curly Tó Aheedlíinii Version.* By Berard Haile. Ed. Karl Luckert. Lincoln: U of Nebraska P, 1984. 3–19.

Lyman, Christopher. *The Vanishing Race and Other Illusions: Photographs of Indians by Edward S. Curtis.* Washington, DC: Smithsonian Institution, 1982.

Lyotard, Jean François. *The Inhuman.* Trans. Geoffrey Bennington and Rachel Bowlby. Stanford: Stanford UP, 1991.

Lyotard, Jean François, and Jean-Loup Thébaud. *Just Gaming.* Trans. Wlad Godzich. Minneapolis: U of Minnesota P, 1985.

Martin, Calvin, ed. *The American Indian and the Problem of History.* New York: Oxford UP, 1987.

Martin, Charles. "Curious Glance: Apocalypse and Photography." *Genre* 29.1–2 (1996): 243–60.

Mohanty, Satya P. "Drawing the Color Line: Kipling and the Culture of Colonial Rule." *The Bounds of Race: Perspectives on Hegemony and Resistance.* Ed. Dominick LaCapra. Ithaca, NY: Cornell UP, 1991. 311–43.

Momaday, N. Scott. "Man Made of Words." *Indian Voices: The First Convocation of American Indian Scholars.* San Francisco: Indian Historian P, 1970. 49–84.

———. *The Names.* Tucson: U of Arizona P, 1976.

———. "Native American Attitudes to the Environment." *Seeing with a Native Eye: Essays on Native American Religion.* Ed. Walter Holden Capps. New York: Harper, 1976. 79–85.

———. "Personal Reflections." *The American Indian and the Problem of History.* Ed. Calvin Martin. New York: Oxford UP, 1987. 156–61.

———. *The Way to Rainy Mountain.* Albuquerque: U of New Mexico P, 1969.

Mooney, James. *Myths of the Cherokee.* New York: Dover, 1995.

Nelson, Dana D. *The Word in Black and White: Reading "Race" in American Literature, 1638–1867.* New York: Oxford UP, 1992.

Northrup, Jim. *Walking the Rez Road.* Stillwater, MN: Voyageur, 1993.

Ortiz, Roxanne Dunbar. *Roots of Resistance: Land Tenure in New Mexico, 1680–1980.* Los Angeles: Chicano Studies Research Center Publications, University of California, Los Angeles, 1980.

Owens, Louis. *Bone Game*. Norman: U of Oklahoma P, 1994.

———. *Dark River*. Norman: U of Oklahoma P, 1999.

———. *Mixedblood Messages: Literature, Film, Family, Place*. Norman: U of Oklahoma P, 1998.

———. *Nightland*. New York: Signet, 1996.

———. *Other Destinies: Understanding the American Indian Novel*. Norman: U of Oklahoma P, 1992.

———. *The Sharpest Sight*. Norman: U of Oklahoma P, 1992.

———. "The Song Is Very Short: Native American Literature and Literary Theory." *Weber Studies* 12.3 (1995): 51–62.

———. *Wolfsong*. Albuquerque: West End, 1991.

Philp, Kenneth. *John Collier's Crusade for Indian Reform, 1920–1954*. Tucson: U of Arizona P, 1977.

Pinchot, Gifford. *Breaking New Ground*. New York: Harcourt, Brace, 1947.

———. *The Fight for Conservation*. New York: Doubleday, 1910.

Pinney, Christopher. "The Parallel Histories of Anthropology and Photography." *Anthropology and Photography: 1860–1920*. Ed. Elizabeth Edwards. New Haven: Yale UP, 1992. 74–95.

Purdy, John. "Clear Waters: A Conversation with Louis Owens." *Studies in American Indian Literatures* 10.2 (1998): 6–22.

Radin, Paul. *The Trickster: A Study in American Indian Mythology*. New York: Schocken, 1956.

Ridge, John Rollin. *The Life and Adventures of Joaquin Murieta*. Norman: U of Oklahoma P, 1955.

Robbins, William G. *American Forestry: A History of National, State, and Private Cooperation*. Lincoln: U of Nebraska P, 1985.

Rohner, Ronald P, ed. *The Ethnography of Franz Boas*. Trans. Hedy Parker. Chicago: U of Chicago P, 1969.

Rosaldo, Renato. *Culture and Truth: The Remaking of Social Analysis*. Boston: Beacon, 1993.

Ruppert, James. *Mediation in Contemporary Native American Fiction*. Norman: U of Oklahoma P, 1995.

Ryan, Allan. *The Trickster Shift: Humour and Irony in Contemporary Native Art*. Vancouver: UBC P, 1999.

Sampson, Martin. *Indians of Skagit County*. Mount Vernon, WA: Skagit County Historical Society, 1972.

Sando, Joe. *Pueblo Nations: Eight Centuries of Pueblo Indian History*. Santa Fe: Clear Light, 1992.

Scheckel, Susan. *The Insistence of the Indian: Race and Nationalism in Nineteenth-Century American Culture*. Princeton: Princeton UP, 1998.

Schweninger, Lee. "Landscape and Cultural Identity in Louis Owens's *Wolfsong.*" *Studies in American Indian Literatures* 10.2 (1998): 94–110.

Shuffelton, Frank, ed. *A Mixed Race: Ethnicity in Early America.* New York: Oxford UP, 1993.

Silko, Leslie Marmon. *Ceremony.* New York: Penguin Books, 1977.

Smith, Jeanne Rosier. *Writing Tricksters: Mythic Gambols in American Ethnic Literature.* Berkeley: U of California P, 1997.

Smith, Paul Chaat, and Robert Warrior. *Like a Hurricane: The Indian Movement from Alcatraz to Wounded Knee.* New York: New Press, 1996.

Swanton, John Reed. *Haida Texts and Myths.* Bureau of American Ethnology, Bulletin 29. Washington, DC: Smithsonian Institution, 1905.

———. *Tlingit Myths and Texts.* Bureau of American Ethnology, Bulletin 39. Washington, DC: Smithsonian Institution, 1909.

Tagg, John. *The Burden of Representation.* Amherst: U of Massachusetts P, 1988.

Takaki, Ronald. *A Different Mirror: A History of Multicultural America.* Boston: Little, Brown, 1993.

———, ed. *From Different Shores: Perspectives on Race and Ethnicity in America.* 2nd ed. New York: Oxford UP, 1994.

———. *Iron Cages: Race and Culture in Nineteenth-Century America.* New York: Oxford UP, 1990.

Taylor, Charles. *Multiculturalism and "The Politics of Recognition."* Princeton: Princeton UP, 1992.

Taylor, Graham. *The New Deal and American Indian Tribalism.* Lincoln: U of Nebraska P, 1980.

Turner, Dolby Bevan. *When the Rains Came and Other Legends of the Salish People.* Victoria, BC: Orca, 1992.

Turner, Victor. *Dramas, Fields, and Metaphors.* Ithaca, NY: Cornell UP, 1974.

———. "Social Dramas and Stories about Them." *On Narrative.* Ed. W. J. T. Mitchell. Chicago: U of Chicago P, 1981. 137–64.

Twitchell, Ralph Emerson. *Leading Facts of New Mexican History.* 2 vols. Cedar Rapids, IA: Torch, 1912.

Tyler, Robert. *Rebels of the Woods: The I.W.W. in the Pacific Northwest.* Eugene: U of Oregon Books, 1967.

Van Gennep, Arnold. *The Rites of Passage.* Trans. Monika Vizedom and Gabrielle Caffe. Chicago: U of Chicago P, 1960.

Van Ness, John R., and Christine M. Van Ness. Introduction. *Journal of the West* 19.3 (1980) [a special issue devoted to Spanish land grants in New Mexico]: 1–11.

Venable, William Henry. *A School History of the United States.* Cincinnati: Van Antwerp, Bragg, 1872.

Venuto, Rochelle. "*Bone Game*'s Terminal Plots and Healing Stories." *Studies in American Indian Literatures* 10.2 (1998): 23–42.

Vidler, Anthony. *The Architectural Uncanny.* Cambridge: MIT P, 1994.

Vizenor, Gerald. *Crossbloods.* Minneapolis: U of Minnesota P, 1976, 1990.

———. *Fugitive Poses: Native American Indian Scenes of Absence and Presence.* Lincoln: U of Nebraska P, 1998.

———. *Interior Landscapes.* Minneapolis: U of Minnesota P, 1990.

———. *The People Named the Chippewa.* Minneapolis: U of Minnesota P, 1984.

———. "A Postmodern Introduction." *Narrative Chance: Postmodern Discourse on Native American Indian Literatures.* Norman: U of Oklahoma P, 1993. 3–16.

———. "Trickster Discourse: Comic Holotropes and Language Games." *Narrative Chance: Postmodern Discourse on Native American Indian Literatures.* Norman: U of Oklahoma P, 1993. 187–211.

———. *The Trickster of Liberty.* Minneapolis: U of Minnesota P, 1988.

Wagner, Roy. *The Invention of Culture.* Chicago: U of Chicago P, 1981.

Wald, Priscilla. *Constituting Americans: Cultural Anxiety and Narrative Form.* Durham: Duke UP, 1995.

Warrior, Robert. *Tribal Secrets: Recovering American Indian Intellectual Traditions.* Minneapolis: U of Minnesota P, 1995.

Welch, James. *The Death of Jim Loney.* New York: Penguin, 1979.

———. *Winter in the Blood.* New York: Penguin, 1974.

Whaley, Rick, with Walter Bresette. *Walleye Warriors: An Effective Alliance against Racism and for the Earth.* Philadelphia: New Society, 1994.

Wilkinson, Charles F. *Crossing the Next Meridian: Land, Water, and the Future of the West.* Washington, DC: Island Press, 1992.

INDEX